The Land
of
Decoration

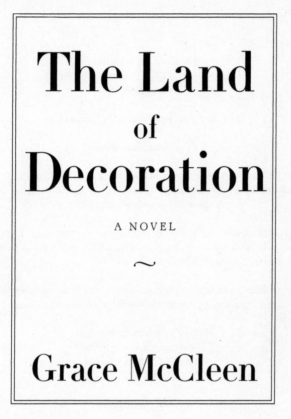

The Land

of

Decoration

A NOVEL

~

Grace McCleen

HARPERCOLLINS PUBLISHERS LTD

Published by HarperCollins Publishers Ltd

First Canadian edition

HarperCollins books may be purchased for educational, business, or sales
promotional use through our Special Markets Department.

HarperCollins Publishers Ltd
2 Bloor Street East, 20th Floor
Toronto, Ontario, Canada
M4W 1A8

www.harpercollins.ca

Library and Archives Canada Cataloguing in Publication
information is available upon request

ISBN 9781443408486

Designed by Meryl Sussman Levavi

Printed and bound in the United States
RRD 9 8 7 6 5 4 3 2 1

To the angel

This is what the Sovereign Lord said to me: "In the day that I chose the nation of Israel I also lifted my hand in an oath to their seed, to make myself known to them in the land of captivity. Yes, I lifted my hand in an oath and I said: 'I am the Lord, your God.' In that day I swore to them I would bring them forth from the land of captivity to a land that I searched out for them, a land flowing with milk and honey; it was the decoration of all the lands."

EZEKIEL 20:5–6

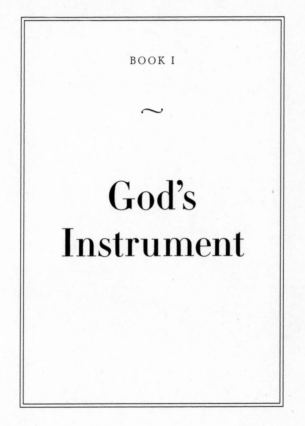

BOOK I

~

God's Instrument

The Empty Room

IN THE BEGINNING there was an empty room, a little bit of space, a little bit of light, a little bit of time.

I said: "I am going to make fields," and I made them from place mats, carpet, brown corduroy, and felt. Then I made rivers from crêpe paper, plastic wrap, and shiny tinfoil, and mountains from papier mâché and bark. And I looked at the fields and I looked at the rivers and I looked at the mountains and I saw they were good.

I said: "Now for some light," and I made a sun from a wire metal cage strung with beads that hung down from above, I made a sliver of moon and luminous stars, and at the edge of the world I made a sea from a mirror, reflecting the sky and the boats and the birds and the land (where it touched). And I looked at the sun and I looked at the moon and I looked at the sea and I saw they were good.

I said: "What about homes?" And I made one from a ball of dry grass and one from a hollow tree stump and one from a barrel that toffees came in and I gave it a fishing line and sail and made space for a blanket and toothbrush and cup, and a stove, and put a gull high on the mast (which was really a broom handle) and launched it out on the sea (which was really a mirror).

I made houses from chocolate-dip-cookie cartons: the plastic scoop where the chocolate was, that was the bedroom, and the round room below, where the cookies had been, that was the living room. I made houses from a matchbox and a bird's nest and a pea pod and a shell. And I looked at the houses and saw they were good.

I said: "Now we need animals," and I made paper birds and wool rabbits and felt cats and dogs. I made furry bears, striped leopards, and fire-breathing, scale-crusted dragons. I made glittering fish and cockleshell crabs and birds on very thin wires.

Last I said: "We need people," and I modeled faces and hands, lips, teeth, and tongues. I dressed them and wigged them and breathed into their lungs.

And I looked at the people and I looked at the animals and I looked at the land. And I saw they were good.

The Ground from the Air

IF YOU LOOK at the earth from the ground, it seems very big. Stand in a playground and bend down and put your face to the ground as if you were looking for something small, and it seems bigger still. There are miles of concrete going outward and miles of sky going upward and miles of nothing going nowhere in between. Boys playing football are giants, the ball is a planet, girls skipping are trees uprooting themselves, and with each turn of the rope the ground trembles. But if you look down from the sky, the boys and the girls and the ball and the rope seem smaller than flies.

I watch the boys and girls. I know their names but I don't speak to them. When they notice me, I look away. I pick up a candy wrapper next to my shoe. I will make it into flowers or a rainbow or maybe a crown. I put the wrapper inside a bag and walk on.

Through the concrete, weeds are growing. At the corners of buildings they are pushing through, whittling their way to the light. I wiggle some loose and settle them with soil in a tiny tin cup that held chocolate and a tube that held sweets. They will be planted again and then they will be oaks and pampas and beeches and palms. I pick up a shoelace lying in a puddle. "This will be a hose," I say. "Or a stream. Or a python. Or maybe a creeper." And I am happy because in just a few hours I will be back in my room making things.

Then suddenly I am falling; the ground rushes up to meet me, and gravel is biting my knees. A boy is standing over me. He is tall. He has a thick neck. He has blue eyes and freckles and white skin and a nose like a pig. He has yellow hair and pale lashes and a cowlick. Though I don't think anyone would want to lick him, not even cows, who lick their own noses. Two boys are with him. One takes the bag I am holding. He tips it up and wrappers and laces and can tops blow away.

The yellow-haired boy pulls me up. He says: "What shall we do with her?"

"Hang her on the railings."

"Pull down her pants."

But the boy with yellow hair smiles. He says: "Have you ever seen the inside of a toilet, freak?"

A bell rings and, all across the playground, groups of children run to line up at the double doors. The yellow-haired boy says: "Shit." To me he says: "Wait till Monday," pushes me backward, and runs off with the others.

When they are a little way off he turns round. He has a sleepy look in his eyes, as if he is dreaming and enjoying the dream. He draws his finger across his throat, then takes off laughing.

I close my eyes and lean against the dustbins. When I open my eyes I pick the gravel out of my knees and spit on them. I hold them hard at the edges to make them stop stinging. Then I begin walking back to the school building. I am sad because I will not be able to make flowers or a stream or an oak tree after all. But what is worse is that, on Monday, Neil Lewis will put my head down the toilet, and if I die who will make *me* again?

The bell has stopped ringing now and the playground is empty. The sky is lowering. It looks like rain. Then from nowhere a gust of wind rises. It whips my hair and balloons my coat and carries me forward. And tumbling and flapping and fluttering around me go wrappers and papers and laces and tops.

Holding My Breath

MY NAME IS Judith McPherson. I am ten years old. On Monday a miracle happened. That is what I'm going to call it. And I did it all. It was because of what Neil Lewis said about putting my head down the toilet. It was because I was frightened. But it was also because I had faith.

It all began on Friday night. Father and I were eating lamb and bitter greens in the kitchen. Lamb and bitter greens are Necessary Things. Our lives are full of Necessary Things because we are living in the Last Days, but Necessary Things are often difficult, like preaching. Preaching is necessary because Armageddon is near, but most people don't want to be preached to and sometimes they shout at us.

Lamb represents the firstborns God killed in Egypt and Christ, who died for mankind. Bitter greens reminded the Israelites of the bitterness of slavery and how good it was to be in the Promised Land. Father says they are full of iron. But I like to think of lambs in a field, not on my plate, and when I try to swallow bitter greens, my throat closes up. I was having more trouble eating than usual that Friday night on account of what Neil Lewis said. After a while I gave up and put down my fork. I said: "What's dying like?"

Father had his overalls on from the factory. The kitchen light made hollows around his eyes. He said: "What?"

"What's dying like?"

"What sort of question is that?"

"I just wondered."

His face was dark. "Eat up."

I loaded my fork with bitter greens and closed my eyes. I would have held my nose but Father would have seen. I counted, then swallowed. After a while I said: "How long could someone survive if their head was held underwater?"

"What?"

"How long could someone survive underwater?" I said. "I mean, I expect they'd last longer if they were used to it. At least until someone found them. But if it was their first time. If the person holding them down wanted them to die—which they would—I mean, if their head was held down."

Father said: "What *are* you talking about?"

I looked down. "How long could someone survive underwater?"

He said: "I have no idea!"

I swallowed the rest of the bitter greens without chewing; then Father took away the plates and got the Bibles out.

We read the Bible every day and then we ponder what we have read. Reading the Bible and pondering are also Necessary Things. Pondering is necessary because it is the only way we can find out what we think about God. But God's ways are unsearchable. This means you could ponder forever and still not know what to think. When I try to ponder, my mind slips to other things, like how I make a swimming pool and steps from an embroidery loop for the model world in my room or how many pear drops I can buy with my pocket money or how much more pondering there is still left to do. But afterward we always talk about what we have pondered, so there's no way you can pretend you have been pondering when you haven't.

It was getting dark outside the window. I could hear boys riding their bikes in the back lane. They were going up a ramp, and every time they came down it the board clanked. I looked at Father. I could tell by the way his eyebrows jutted that I must pay attention. I could tell by the way his glasses glittered that he must not be interrupted. I looked down, took a deep breath, and held it.

"In the ninth year, in the tenth month, on the tenth day, the voice of the Lord came to me: 'Son of man, remember this date, this very day, because the king of Babylon has laid siege to Jerusalem.' . . ."

At twenty-five seconds the room began to pulse and my breath escaped in little puffs. I waited a minute, then took another.

A dog barked. A dustbin lid clattered. Seconds dripped from the clock on the mantelpiece. At twenty-five seconds the room began to pulse again and I had to let my breath out again. I must have done it quite suddenly, because Father looked up and said: "Are you all right?"

I opened my eyes wide and nodded.

"Are you following?"

I nodded again and opened my eyes even wider. He looked at me from under his eyebrows, then began to read again.

" 'Now your impurity is badness. Because I tried to save you but you would not be saved, and you will not be saved again until my wrath against you has subsided. I the Lord have spoken.' "

I waited two whole minutes, then I took another breath.

I held it. And held it.

I said: "I am going to do this. I am *not* going to drown."

I hung on to the arms of the chair. I pushed my feet into the floor. I pressed my bottom to the seat. I got to twenty-four seconds when Father said: "What are you doing?"

"Pondering!" I said, and my breath came out in a rush.

A vein in Father's temple flickered. "You're very red."

"It's hard work," I said.

"This isn't a game."

"I know."

"Are you following?"

"Yes!"

Father blew a little air out of his nose, then began to read again.

I waited three whole minutes. Then I took another breath.

I filled each bit of my body with air: my stomach, my lungs, my arms, and my legs. My chest hurt. My head pounded. My legs jumped up and down.

I didn't notice that Father had stopped reading. I didn't see him looking at me till he said: "*What's going on?*"

"I don't feel well."

He put down his Bible. "Let's get something straight. I am not reading this for your entertainment. I am not reading this for the benefit of my health. I'm reading this because it will save your life. *So, sit up, stop fidgeting, and start paying attention!*"

"OK," I said.

He waited a minute, then began to read again. " '*The time has come. I will not hold back; I will not have compassion, nor will I relent. You will be judged according to your actions,' declares the Sovereign Lord.*"

I tried to follow, but all I could think about was the toilet bowl, all I could hear was the cistern flushing, all I could feel were hands pushing me down.

"*Then the people asked me, 'Tell us, what do these things have to do with us?' And I said to them, 'The voice of the Lord came to me, saying: "Say to the house of Israel, Judith!"' "*

Father read it just like that, without stopping and without looking up.

"What?" My heart snagged on my cardigan.

"Carry on reading please."

"Oh."

I looked, but the page teemed with ants. I turned and my face got hot. I turned back and my face got hotter.

Father closed his Bible. He said: "Go to your room."

"I can do it!" I said.

"No, you obviously have better things to do."

"I was listening!"

Father said: "Judith."

I stood up.

My head felt very hot, as if there were too many things going on in it. It was jumbled too, as if someone had shaken it up. I went to the door. I put my hand on the handle and I said: "It's not fair."

Father looked up. "What was that?"

"Nothing."

His eyes glittered. "It better be."

What Is Dying Like?

THERE IS A world in my room. It is made from things no one else wanted and it is made with things that were my mother's, that she left to me, and it has taken most of my life to make.

The world stretches from the second floorboard by the door to the radiator underneath the window. There are mountains by the wall, where the room is darkest, and great cliffs and caves. There are rivers running down from the mountains to hills and pastures, and here is where there are the first houses. Then there is the valley and the fields and the town, and after the town there are some more farms and then there is the beach and the beach road and a forest of pine trees and a bay and a pier, and finally, right by the radiator under the window, there is the sea, with a few rocks and a light-house and some boats and sea creatures. Strung from the ceiling on short strings there are planets and stars, from longer strings there is the sun and the moon, and from the longest strings of all, clouds, airplanes, and the light shade is a paper hot-air balloon.

The world is called the Land of Decoration. In the Book of Eze-kiel it says God swore to bring the Israelites out of captivity to a wonderful country. It was flowing with milk and honey. It lacked nothing, it was a miracle, a paradise. It was so different from every-thing around it that it stood out like a jewel and was called "the decoration of all the lands." When I close the door of my room, the walls fold back and there are planets and rainbows and suns. The floor rolls up and there are fields and roads at my feet and hundreds of small people. If I stretch out my hand I can touch the top of a mountain, if I blow I can ripple the sea. I lift my head and look right into the sun. I feel happy when I go into my room. But that Friday night, I didn't notice any of those things.

I closed the door and leaned against it. I wondered if I should go back down and tell Father why I had been holding my breath. But if I did he would only say: "Have you told the teacher?" and I would say: "Yes," and Mr. Davies had said: "No one is going to put anyone's head down the toilet," and Father would say: "Well, then." But I knew that Neil would just the same. And I wondered why Father never believed me.

I sat down on the floor. A wood louse was crawling out from underneath my knees, flicking its antennae and strumming its feet. It looked like a tiny armadillo. I watched it climb the sand dunes in the Land of Decoration and wondered if it would ever find its way out again. We did an experiment with wood lice in school. We built a plasticine maze and counted the number of times they turned left or right. They nearly always turned left. This is because they cannot think for themselves. I wondered if this meant the wood louse would come out eventually or would just keep going round in circles until it died in a little crusty ball.

Darkness was closing the valley up like a book between black covers. It was sifting down over the broken-backed streets, over roofs, and over aerials, back lanes, shops, dustbins and streetlights, the railway, and great chimneys of the factory. Soon the darkness would blot out the lights. For a while they would glow all the more brightly, but eventually they, too, would be eaten up. If you looked into the sky, you would see their glow for a little while. Then nothing. I wondered what it would be like to die. Was it like going to sleep or like waking up? Was there no more time? Or did time go on forever?

Perhaps everything I thought was real would turn out not to

have been and everything that wasn't real was. I don't know why but I looked for the wood louse. It suddenly seemed very important to find it, but I couldn't, even though only a few seconds ago it had been there, and there was not enough air in the room and it was like someone had struck a match and it was burning up all the oxygen.

I sat back against the wall and my heart began to beat hard. Something was coming toward me, unfurling like a cloud low down on the horizon. The cloud gathered. It filled my mouth and my eyes and there was roaring and things happening very quickly and all at the same time, and then I was sitting back against the wall and sweat was running down from underneath my hair and I felt stranger than I had ever felt in my life.

And if I had to say how I felt, I would say like a box that had been turned upside down. And the box was surprised by just how empty it was.

Why I Will Not Live Very Long

I DO NOT expect to live long in this world. This is not because I have an illness or someone is going to kill me (though Neil Lewis might). It is because very soon God will bring Armageddon.

At Armageddon there will be rock faces yawning and buildings buckling and roads splitting. The sea will rise and there will be thunder and lightning and earthquakes and balls of fire rolling down streets. The sun will be dark and the moon won't give its light. Trees will be uprooted and mountains flattened and houses will crumble to the ground. The stars will be hurled down and the heavens broken and the planets toppled. The stars will be torn down and the sea will crack with a sound like a plate and the air will be full of what was, and in the end there will be nothing left but a heap of rubbish.

We know Armageddon is close because we live in a Den of Iniquity, and Father says there is nowhere for the Righteous Man to put his foot, quite literally sometimes. We also know we are near the end because there are wars and earthquakes and famines and people having "no natural affection," so they strap explosives to themselves or stab someone because they like the watch they're wearing or film one another cutting people's heads off. There are Sheep (Brothers like us) and Goats (unbelievers) and Lost Sheep (Brothers who have been Removed from the congregation or have fallen away).

There are Weeds in the Wheat (people who pretend to be Brothers but aren't), False Prophets (leaders of other religions), the Wild Beast (all world religions), Locusts (us with our stinging message), a rise in Immoral Relations (sex), and signs in the sun, moon, and stars (no one knows what they mean yet).

But in the real Land of Decoration, there won't be any unbelievers or any war or any famine or any suffering. There won't be any pollution or any towns either. There will be fields, and those who have died will come back to life and those who are living will never die at all and there will be no more sickness, because God will wipe out every tear from our eyes. We know this because God has promised.

Father says it's only a matter of time before someone blows the world up anyway or money becomes useless, or a virus wipes us out, or the hole the size of Greenland in the ozone layer becomes the size of Australia. So it's a good thing Armageddon is coming and nothing of this old world will be left.

And I think it's good, because polar bears are starving and trees are dying and if you put a plastic bag in the earth it will never go away and the earth has had enough of plastic bags. And because in the new world I will see my mother.

Moving Mountains

ON SATURDAY MORNING I woke from a dream in which I was swimming in a gigantic toilet bowl and Neil Lewis was reeling me in on a line. As I came through the water, I woke up. The bedside clock said 9:48. In forty-seven hours and twelve minutes I might be dead.

I practiced holding my breath that day and got to twenty-eight seconds. At bedtime I had a stomach pain and had to have Gaviscon and crackers. On Sunday I woke up as if I were coming through water again, and my clothes were sticking to me and the pain was worse. I looked at the clock. There were now twenty-six hours to go.

I couldn't eat breakfast, but Father didn't notice. He dropped an armful of wood beside the Rayburn stove and swigged his tea. "Ready?"

I was. I had on my best pinafore and the blouse with the roses on the collar and my black shiny shoes. My hair was in plaits. I'm not sure how even they were. Father grabbed his sheepskin coat and cap and I put on my coat.

Outside, it was very still and very cold. The air was misty and the sky was one block of cloud the color of feathers. No one was about, except the dog from number 29. We went over the round-about and turned down the hill. I could see the town, the aerials and chimneys and rooftops, the river, and the electricity pylons striding like lonely giants down the valley. And at the bottom of the valley was the factory, a great black thing with funnels and towers and ladders and pipes and above it huge clouds of smoke.

At the foot of the hill we passed the multistory car park, the bingo hall, the Labour Club, the unemployment office, the betting shop, and the pub where bleach mixes with the beer smell. On weekends there are water balloons on the pavement and sometimes nappies stained red. Once I saw a needle and we had to cross over.

In our town nothing seems to be where it should. There are car engines in gardens and plastic bags in bushes and shopping trolleys in the river. There are bottles in the gutter and mice in the bottle bank, walls with words on and signs with words crossed out. There are streetlights with no lights and holes in the road and holes in the pavement and holes in exhaust pipes. There are houses with broken windows and men with broken teeth and swings with broken seats. There are dogs with no ears and cats with one eye and once I saw a bird with not many feathers.

We passed Woolworths, the pound shop, Kwik Save, and the Co-op grocery store. Then we went through the tunnel beneath the bridge where the walls are dark green and trickling, and when we came out we were on a piece of wasteland and there was the Meeting Hall. The Meeting Hall is a black metal shed and has three windows down each side. Inside there are a lot of red seats and on each windowsill bowls of yellow plastic roses with pretend droplets of water stuck onto the petals at regular intervals.

Father and Mother helped to build the Meeting Hall. It isn't very big but it belongs to the Brothers. There weren't many people in the congregation then, only four or five. Without Father and Mother, the congregation might have fizzled out, but they kept preaching, and eventually more people got baptized. It was wonderful when they finally had a meeting place of their own. It took three years to build and every penny was donated by the Brothers.

Inside the hall, it was cold because the radiators hadn't warmed up yet. At the front of the hall, Elsie and May were talking to old Nel Brown in the wheelchair.

May said: "Well, if it isn't my little treasure!"

Elsie said: "Well, if it isn't my little love!"

"Ah, she's a lovely girl!" said May, hugging me.

"She's a blessing, that's what she is!" said Elsie, kissing my cheek.

May said: "Auntie Nel was just telling us about the time she and the priest had a dustup."

"Grape?" Nel said. Her chin wobbled as she chewed, because she doesn't have teeth. Her top lip was whiskery. Her bottom lip was spitty.

"No thanks, Auntie Nel," I said. I was too worried to eat, and even if I hadn't been I wouldn't have fancied one, because Auntie Nel smells of wee.

Uncle Stan came up. Uncle Stan is the Presiding Overseer. He drinks milk because of his ulcer and he's from "Beemeengoomb." Apparently Beemeengoomb is an even bigger Den of Iniquity than our town. It's where he got his stomach ulcer, though some people say he got it because of Auntie Margaret. Stan put his arm round Auntie Nel and said: "How's my favorite Sister?"

Nel said: "That carpet looks like it could do with Hoovering."

Uncle Stan stopped smiling. He looked at the carpet. He said: "Right."

Stan went to find the Hoover and I went to find Father. He was in the book room, sorting out last month's surplus magazines with Brian. There are small white flakes on the shoulders of Brian's jacket and in his hair. "H-h-h-how are y-y-y-you, J-J-Judith?" Brian said.

"Fine thanks," I said. But I wasn't. The pain in my stomach was coming back. I'd stopped thinking about Neil for a minute, only to remember again.

Alf came up. His tongue was flicking in and out at the corners of his mouth like a lizard. He said to Father: "Report cards in?" Father nodded. Alf is what Father calls "Second in Command." He's not much taller than me but wears little boots with heels. He is almost bald, but his hair is combed over and sprayed in a lid. I saw it lift once in the wind when we were preaching, and he jumped into the car and said: "Run and buy me some hairspray, kid!" and wouldn't get out until I had.

Uncle Stan appeared, lugging the Hoover. He looked gray. "The speaker's not here," he said. "I don't feel like giving the talk if he doesn't turn up."

"He will," said Father.

"I don't know," said Alf. He hoisted his trousers. "The last speaker we were supposed to have got lost." Suddenly he saw me and stopped frowning. "Josie's got something for you."

I didn't like the way he was grinning. "What is it?" I said.

Father said: "It's polite to say, 'Thank you,' Judith." He frowned at me as if he was disappointed, and I flushed and looked down.

But Alf said: "I couldn't tell you what it is, could I? That would spoil the surprise."

Josie is Alf's wife. She is very short and very wide, has a long white ponytail and a mouth like a slit, where creamy saliva collects in the corners and stretches like a concertina when she talks. She wears funny clothes and likes to make them for other people. So far she has made me: a crocheted dress with blue and peach roses, which she asked about until it shrank in the wash, a turquoise skirt with ribbon around the edge, which reached to the ground, a crocheted Cinderella-doll toilet-roll holder, which Father refused to have in the bathroom so I made it into a hill for the Land of Decoration, a toilet-seat cover, which now keeps drafts out at the foot of the back door, bright blue leg warmers, an orange bodysuit, two cardigans, and a balaclava. Josie must think either that we are very poor, that I am much bigger than I am, or that I am very cold. One day I will tell her that she is wrong: that we aren't rich but we have enough money to buy clothes, that though I may appear to be older because I read the Bible well and talk to the grown-ups I am ten, and four foot four, and that most of the time I am just the right temperature.

I scanned the crowd but couldn't see any sign of her. To be on the safe side, I went to stand behind the sound equipment with Gordon. There isn't anyone my age in our congregation, so although Gordon is a lot older than me, I chat to him. Gordon was testing the microphones, making a *pock-pock* sound.

I looked at the clock. There were now exactly twenty-three hours until Neil Lewis put my head down the toilet. There was nothing for it. Gordon was setting up the microphones. I said to him: "Have you got a mint?" Gordon rummaged in his pocket. He unrolled the top of a packet and dropped a dusty white tablet into my hand. "Thanks," I said. I only ask for Gordon's mints in emergencies. Gordon took two and went back to untangling cables.

Gordon has not long come off heroin; he got hooked on heroin because he Got In with the Wrong Crowd. He Battles Depression, so he does very well coming to meetings. It was really serious for a While. It looked like Gordon might have to be Removed. He was marked as a bad influence. They say that God shone His light into Gordon's heart, but I think his recovery is to do with the extra-strong mints. Father said heroin makes people happy because it takes away pain; the mints make you happy because when you have finished eating one you realize you're not in pain anymore. It comes down to the same thing. The trouble is, Gordon is getting used to them. He can already knock back four in a row. I don't know what he will do when he manages to get through a whole packet, because they don't make them any stronger.

There were a lot of people in the hall now, or a lot for our congregation anyway—nearly thirty, I would say. There were even some faces we don't usually see. Pauline, the woman who had the poltergeist Uncle Stan exorcised last spring, and Sheila from the women's refuge. Geena from the mental home, with scars on her arms, and Wild Charlie Powell, who lives up the Tump in a wooden house among the fir trees. It felt as if something special was going to happen but I couldn't think what.

On the platform, Alf tapped the microphone. "Brothers and

Sisters," he said, "if you'd like to take your seats, the meeting's about to start."

So the speaker hadn't made it. I imagined his car tumbling down the mountain, his cries getting fainter and fainter till the battered hunk of metal disappeared into the mist. "See you later," I said to Gordon, and went to my seat.

Father and I sit right at the front, so our knees are almost touching the platform. My neck gets a crick looking up. Father says it is better than being Distracted. Distraction leads to Destruction. But the front row has distractions of its own. The smell of Auntie Nel being one of them. I was glad of my extra-strong mint.

We stood to sing "The Joys of Kingdom Service." Father sang loudly, bringing the sound deep from within his chest, but I couldn't sing, partly because thinking about Neil and partly because the extra-strong mint had vacuumed all the spit out of my mouth. Father nudged me and frowned, so I stuck the mint into my cheek and shouted as loudly as he did.

We had to do the magazine study first because there was no speaker. It was called "Illuminators of the World" and was all about how we weren't to hide our light under a bushel, which turned out to be a kind of basket. Alf said the best way we could do this was to fill in a report card. Father answered up and said what a privilege it was to be God's mouthpieces. Elsie answered and said we met skeptics, but if we didn't tell people how would they know? Brian said: "Th-th-th-th-th-the thing. Th-th-th-th-thing is—" But we never found out what the thing was. Auntie Nel waved her hand about but it turned out she was only telling May she had wet herself.

By that time my mint had gone, so I put my hand up and said how happy God must be to see all the little lights shining in the darkness, and Alf said: "Well, we can all see your light is shining, Sister McPherson!" But it wasn't, and I didn't feel happy, and just then I wished I wasn't one of God's lights, because if I wasn't, Neil Lewis wouldn't put my head down the toilet.

When the magazine study was over, Father got onto the plat-

form and said: "Now, Brothers, due to unforeseen circumstances . . ."
I could see Uncle Stan collecting his papers and wiping his neck
with his hanky. Then a rush of air swept into the hall and we heard
the outer door close.

I turned round. A man was coming through the foyer doors.
They seemed to have blown open, because they held themselves
wide as he passed through, then closed behind him. The man had
caramel skin and hair the color of blackbirds. He looked like one of
the Men of Old, except that he wasn't wearing a robe but a suit of
dark blue and, where the light shone, it glistened like petrol in a
puddle. The man came right up to our row and sat at the end, and
I smelled something like fruit cake and something like wine.

Alf hurried up to him. He whispered to the man, then nodded at
Father. Father smiled. He said: "And we are very glad to welcome . . ."

"Brother Michaels," said the man. His voice was the strangest
thing of all. It was like dark chocolate.

Father said: "Our visiting speaker, from . . . ?" But Brother
Michaels didn't appear to have heard. Father asked again and Brother
Michaels only smiled. "Well, anyway Brother, we're very glad to have
you," Father said, then got down.

There was a lot of clapping, then Brother Michaels got onto the
platform. He didn't seem to have notes. He took something out of
his briefcase and put it on the rostrum. Then he looked up. Now
that he was looking at us, I could see just how dark his skin was. His
hair was dark too, but his eyes were strange and pale. Then he said:
"What beautiful mountains you have here, Brothers!"

I could feel how surprised everyone was. No one ever said anything about our valley being beautiful. Brother Michaels said: "Don't
you think so? I was coming over them today in my car and thinking
how lucky you are to live here. Why, from the top I thought I could
see right into the clouds."

I looked out the window. Brother Michaels must either be crazy
or need glasses; the clouds were even lower now—you couldn't see
more than three feet in front of you.

He smiled. "The theme of our talk today is 'Moving Mountains.' What do you think you would need, Brothers, to move that one over there?"

"Dynamite," said Alf.

"You couldn't," said Uncle Stan.

"A pretty big digger," said Gordon, and everyone laughed.

Brother Michaels held something up between his finger and thumb. "Do you know what this is?"

"It isn't anything," I whispered, but Father smiled.

"Which of you believes I'm holding anything at all?" said Brother Michaels.

Some people put up their hands; lots didn't. Father was still smiling and he put up his hand, so I did too. Brother Michaels held a piece of paper out just below the microphone. Then he opened his finger and thumb and we heard something fall. "Those of you who guessed I was holding something, give yourself a pat on the back," he said. "You were seeing with Eyes of Faith."

"What is it?" I said, but Father only put his finger to his lips.

"That, Brothers, is a mustard seed," said Brother Michaels. He held up a picture of a mustard seed blown up. It was like a tiny yellow ball. "It's the smallest of seeds but grows into a tree that the birds of heaven sit in." Then he began to talk about the world.

He said that many difficulties would befall God's people before the system ended. He said the Devil was roaming the earth, seeking to devour someone. We read about how the Israelites stopped believing they would get to the Land of Decoration, how they scorned God's miracles and the miracle workers. "Never let us be like that," he said. "Faith is not a possession of all people. The world laughs at faith. They wouldn't think of telling that mountain to move. But turn with me in your Bibles, Brothers, and see what Jesus says."

Then he began to read, and as he did my heart beat hard and it was as if I was catching light.

"For I say to you truthfully, if you have faith the size of a mustard seed, you will say to a mountain, 'Move from here to there,' and it will move and nothing will be impossible for you."

"Of course," he said, "Jesus was speaking metaphorically. We can't really move mountains. But we can do things we think are impossible if we have faith. Faith sees the mountain as already moved, Brothers. It isn't enough to think what the new world will be like, we have to see ourselves there; all the while we're thinking what it will be like, we're still here. But faith has wings. It can carry us wherever we need to go."

Then he began to talk, and it was like listening to a great story unraveling, and I knew the story but didn't remember having heard it before, or not told this way.

In the beginning, Brother Michaels said, all of life was miraculous. Humans lived forever and never got sick. Every fruit, every animal, every part of the earth, was a perfect reflection of God's glory, and the relation between the humans was also perfect. But Adam and Eve lost something. They lost faith in God. So they began to die, the cells in their bodies began to deteriorate, and they were expelled from the garden.

"After that there were only glimpses of how things used to be: a sunset, a hurricane, a bush struck by lightning. And faith became something you prayed for in a room at midnight or on a battlefield or in a whale's stomach or in a fiery furnace. Faith became a leap, because there was a gap between how things were and how they used to be. It was the space where miracles happened.

"Everything is possible, at all times and in all places and for all sorts of people. If you think it's not, it's only because you can't see how close you are, how you only need to do a small thing and everything will come to you; miracles don't have to be big things, and they can happen in the unlikeliest places. Miracles work best with ordinary things. Paul says: 'Faith is the assured expectation of things long hoped for, the evident demonstration of realities though not beheld,' and if we have just a little, other things will follow, Brothers. Sometimes more than we dreamed."

The talk was finished, but for a second there was no clapping; then there was a storm of it. I felt I had woken up. But I had been sleeping longer than the talk; I felt I had been sleeping all my life.

I couldn't wait for the song and prayer to be over. I thought Brother Michaels would be just the person to talk to about Neil Lewis.

AFTERWARD, I STOOD by Brother Michaels and waited for Uncle Stan to finish talking to him. But when Stan went away, Elsie and May came up. Then Alf. Brother Michaels shook hands with them, he listened, he nodded; he smiled and smiled. None of them wanted to go.

I was beginning to think I would never talk to him, but at last there was a gap and he turned round to put his papers in his briefcase and saw me.

"Hello," he said. "Who are you?"

"Judith," I said.

"Are you the one who gave the lovely answer?"

"I don't know."

"I think you were." Brother Michaels held out his hand. "Good to meet you."

I said: "I liked your talk," but my voice didn't seem to be working properly. "I don't think I've ever enjoyed a talk so much."

"Thank you."

"I was wondering if I could see the mustard seed?"

Brother Michaels laughed. "You can," he said. "But I'm not sure it will be the same one." He took a small jar from his bag and it was full of seeds.

I said: "I've never seen mustard like that before!"

"This is what it's like before they grind it up."

I said: "I wish I had some."

Brother Michaels shook a little pile of seeds into my hand. "Now you do."

I stared at the seeds. I was so pleased I almost forgot what I was going to ask him. "Brother Michaels," I said at last, "I came to talk to you because I have a problem."

"I knew it," he said.

"You did?"

He nodded. "What sort of problem?"

"Someone—I'm afraid that—" I sighed. Then I knew I must tell him exactly how it was. "I think that soon I may be no more."

Brother Michaels raised his eyebrows.

"I mean: not exist."

Brother Michaels lowered them. "Are you ill?" he said.

"No."

He frowned. "Has someone told you this or is it just a feeling?"

I thought about this. "No one has told me," I said. "But I'm pretty sure."

"And have you told anyone?"

"No. There's nothing they can do."

"How do you know?"

"I just do," I said. Grown-ups seemed to think that you could tell a teacher everything. They didn't see it only made things worse.

Brother Michaels didn't say anything for a minute. Then he said: "Have you tried praying?"

"Yes."

"Sometimes prayers take time to be answered."

"I only have until tomorrow."

Brother Michaels inhaled. Then he said: "Judith, I think I can safely say nothing is going to happen to you before tomorrow."

"How do you know?"

"What you're facing is simply fear," he said. "Not that there's anything simple about fear; fear is the most insidious enemy of all. But good things come from facing it."

I said: "I don't see how anything good will come from this."

"Start looking at things differently, then. When we look at things from another vantage point, it's amazing how problems we thought were insoluble disappear altogether."

My heart beat hard. "That would be nice," I said.

Brother Michaels smiled. "I've got to go, Judith."

"Oh," I said. I suddenly felt afraid again. "Do you think you'll be coming back?"

"I'm sure I will sometime."

Then he did a strange thing. He put his hands on my shoulders and looked into my eyes, and warmth traveled all the way down my arms to my fingers and right across my shoulders and back. "Have faith, Judith," he said. Then he looked up. Father was calling me.

"In a minute," I said, but Father tapped his watch. "OK!" I said. I turned back and the row was empty.

I ran up the aisle. "Where did Brother Michaels go?" I said. Alf shrugged. I ran into the foyer. "Uncle Stan," I said, "have you seen Brother Michaels?"

"No," said Stan. "I was just looking for him myself. Margaret and I wanted to invite him back for lunch."

I ran into the car park. Gordon was showing the other boys his new spoiler. "Where did Brother Michaels go?" I said, and I felt my eyes prick.

It was colder now but there still wasn't a breath of wind. The mist had lifted, but the sky was thick with cloud.

A hand on my elbow made me turn. Father handed me my coat and bag. He said: "The roast'll be burned to a crisp." Then he said: "What have you got there?"

I had forgotten.

"Seeds," I said. I opened my hand and showed him.

Why Faith Is Like Imagination

I KNOW ABOUT faith. The world in my room is made out of it. Out of faith I stitched the clouds. Out of faith I cut the moon and the stars. With faith I glued everything together and set it humming. This is because faith is like imagination. It sees something where there is nothing, it takes a leap, and suddenly you're flying.

Circles of paper from a hole punch become saucers for tea parties when you press the end of a pen into them. Glue that has hardened into bubbles becomes a bowl of soapsuds for a pair of aching feet. An acorn cap becomes a bowl, toothpaste caps funnels for ocean liners, twigs knees for an ostrich, an eyelet a small pair of scissors. Matches become logs, drops from the griddle tiny Scottish pancakes, cloves oranges, orange peel a slide, orange tops rows of plants in a garden, the net bag fencing for tennis courts, the bar code a zebra crossing.

Everything is pointing to something, and if we look hard enough for long enough we can see what those other things are. The real Land of Decoration pointed to the way the world would be again one day, after Armageddon. This is called Prefiguration. Father says Prefiguration is showing on a small scale what will happen on a grand scale, it's like soaring above things and seeing it all. But we can only see the possibilities with Eyes of Faith. Some of the Israelites stopped seeing with Eyes of Faith and they died in the wilderness. Losing faith is the worst sin of all.

Once a girl came to my room and said: "What's all this rubbish?" Because to her that was what it looked like. But faith sees other things peeping through the cracks just itching to be noticed. Every day the cracks in this world get bigger. Every day new ones appear.

Snow

THAT AFTERNOON I planted the mustard seeds in a pot on the kitchen windowsill. I asked Father if they would grow, and he said he didn't know. Then he turned off the electricity to save money and went into the middle room to have Peace and Quiet. Peace and Quiet is another Necessary Thing. I went upstairs and sat on the floor. The clock said 2:33. Less than nineteen hours to go till Neil drowned me.

I imagined them finding my body on the school bathroom floor, my hair spread out like a mermaid's, my eyes staring, my lips as blue as if I'd been drinking a blueberry Jubbly. Neil would be looking on too; he'd have raised the alarm; no one would know. I saw the funeral. Elsie and May would be crying. Stan would be praying. Alf would be saying that at least I had been spared the Tribulation. Gordon's neck would be sunk in his suit collar deeper than usual. I couldn't imagine what Father would be doing.

I knew that Brother Michaels said I should have faith that God would help me, that things we thought were impossible were possible with God. But I didn't see how, short of magicking the school or Neil Lewis away. If I was God, I would bring a hurricane or a plague or a tidal wave that would wipe out the town and the school. I would bring Armageddon, or an asteroid to make a hole in the earth where the school used to be or, if it was a very small asteroid and fell in just the right place, flatten Neil Lewis. But I knew none of those things would happen.

I began to feel like I did the other evening when the cloud swallowed me up. I went to the window and leaned my head against the glass, and my breath kept clouding it and I kept wiping it away. Outside was a row of houses. Above those was another row and above those another. Above the houses was the mountain. Above the mountain was the sky. The houses were brown. The mountain was black. The sky was white.

I looked at the sky. It was so white it might not be there at all. It was like paper, like feathers. Like snow. "It could snow," I said aloud.

There had been a lot of snow once before and school had closed. I looked at the sky. It could be full of snow this very minute, just waiting to fall. It *could* snow; it was even quite cold. Brother Michaels had said that if we had a little faith, other things would follow, sometimes more than we dreamed, and I thought I *did* have a little faith, and perhaps a little was enough.

I began thinking about snow; I began thinking hard, about the crunchiness of it and the clean smell of it, the way it muffles everything and makes the world new. How the air comes alive when the earth is asleep and things listen and hold their breath. I saw the town laid out under a blanket of snow, the houses asleep and the factory covered and the Meeting Hall and mountain white, reaching into a sky that was white, and from the sky more whiteness falling. And the more I thought, the heavier the sky seemed and the colder the pane beneath my fingers.

I turned back to the room. I had an idea, though I couldn't explain it. I didn't even know where it had come from, except it was as if a giant hand had written "Snow" on a blank piece of paper. I could see the way they had written the "S," the tail coming back to the "n" so it looked more like an "8." And the hand was writing other things, and I began hurrying to do as it said before the sheet was wiped clean.

I went to the trunk in the corner of my room, which used to be Mother's. Inside were materials and beads and threads she had and all then things I have found. I searched and I took out white cotton. I cut up the cotton and draped it over the fields and hills of the Land of Decoration.

"Good," said a voice. "More!"

Something hot licked my spine. My scalp pricked. "Who's that?" I said. No one answered.

My hands were shaking. I felt my heart in my throat. I took sugar and flour and sprinkled them over sponge treetops and paper grass and heather hedges.

"Faster!" said the voice. And although I didn't know where the voice was coming from, I knew it was real this time and meant for me, and I didn't care who or what was speaking.

I ran to the bathroom. I ran back. I squirted shaving foam along windowsills and eaves and gutters. I let glue dry clear in small drops around eaves and on branches and on bandstands and streetlights.

"More!" said the voice.

There was a drum in my brain. The whole room was pulsing. I made a fire in a caramel keg with gold sweet papers on the side of the lake where tall firs stood. I made frankfurters and marshmallows on sticks with pieces of plasticine. I made a polystyrene-ball snowman, a line of white paper geese. I hung them on a string across the moon. I took some down from my leaky duvet and shook it above, and it fell over the towns and seas and hills and lakes.

I snowed in houses and shops and post offices and schools. I iced roads and blocked bridges and strung white pipe cleaners along telegraph wires. I set cardboard skaters on a tinfoil lake and on the hill a woolly tobogganing party.

I grazed my hand and didn't feel it.

My foot went to sleep.

I stamped around and sat down again.

WHEN I OPENED my eyes the light was gone and the Land of Decoration was glowing whitely in the darkness, the line of geese tiny arrows in the sky. I was curled on my side, at the edge of the sea. My cheek hurt because it was pressing on the edge of the mirror. I sat up. Then I heard Father calling me. I held my breath. I heard him come to the foot of the stairs.

My heart was beating so fast it hurt but I didn't know why. He called again and I shut my eyes tight. At last Father went back into the kitchen and closed the door. He must have thought I had gone to bed.

I was shaking. I got up and went to the window. I couldn't see the mountain now, and the sky was black. Behind me the room was still. I could feel the stillness all around me, like water. I took a deep breath, turned back to the room, and I said: "Snow." I looked at the sky and I said: "Snow."

A car flashed by. It lit me up, then left me in darkness. The sound of that car pulled me after it. I thought it had gone but it came back again. I listened to the sound of that car, then I closed the curtains and got into bed.

I heard the clock chime nine times in the hall. I heard Mrs. Pew call her cat, Oscar, for his supper. I heard Mr. Neasdon come home from the Labour Club and the dog from number 29 begin to bark. I heard the bell from the factory toll the night shift and Father come upstairs, his steps hollow on the boards of the landing.

The Stone and the Book

THAT NIGHT I had a wonderful dream. I dreamed I was walking in the Land of Decoration. I was passing Glacier Mint ice palaces and tinsel fountains and Rolo Giant causeways and calico trees where jeweled fruits clustered and birds with long tail feathers sang. I wished I had time to stop and look at it all, but a voice was calling me. The voice led me to a field.

The air was warm and smelled of summer. I went walking, leaving a trail in the grass. Sometimes I went this way and sometimes I went that. Sometimes the sun was in my face and sometimes it was at my back. The hedges were filled with tissue cow parsley. Paper birds flew up under my nose. Paisley butterflies fluttered away. There were sweet-paper gnats and down dandelion clocks and glittering hat-pin dragonflies darting then stopping quite still in the air.

In the middle of the field there was a tree. Beneath the tree was an old man with a beard. His skin was like caramel and his hair was very black. He was dressed in a white robe and held his hands behind his back. He said: "Welcome, child. This is a great day. You have been chosen to receive a gift of inestimable value." And his voice was like dark chocolate.

"Thank you," I said. Then I said: "What does 'inestimable' mean?"

"Something whose worth can't be estimated," he said.

"In one hand I hold a stone that contains more power than any-one has ever possessed, and its fruits are sweet but the aftertaste is bitter. In my other hand I hold a book the wisest seek to read, and its fruits are loathsome but it gives the reader wings."

I said: "Why are you holding them behind your back?"

"Because the sight of them might influence you," said the man. "Now you must choose. Think carefully, because much hangs on your decision."

It was difficult. Because I wanted to have all the power in the world, and make Neil Lewis disappear, and never go back to school again. But I also wanted to find out what the secret was that even the wisest seek to read. And I would definitely like to have wings. And there was a moment when I thought perhaps I shouldn't choose at all and should go away through the long grass and not look back.

But I didn't. I said: "I'd like the stone please." And when the old man took his right hand from behind his back and gave it to me, it glinted many colors in my palm and I felt myself swell and become heavy, and when I spoke I thought it had thundered.

It could have been a long time or it could have been a short time that passed, I couldn't tell but I know that I said: "Could I look at the book?"

The old man pursed his lips. I thought he wasn't going to let me. But finally he said: "All right. But you can't touch it," and he brought a small brown book from behind him. The spine was com-ing away and the pages were dog-eared, and when he opened it it was full of letters I had never seen before.

I said: "Why are the pages wrinkled?"

And the man said: "They are wet with the tears of all those who have tried to read it and failed."

Suddenly I felt cold. "Would I have been able to?" I said.

He smiled. "We will never know now."

And then I woke up. But it wasn't morning. It was dark and I was shivering. The air was stirring and full of the sound of beating wings.

I pulled the blankets higher and wriggled down. I shut my eyes and tried to find the old man. I wanted to ask him about the aftertaste of the stone. But the air was no longer filled with gnats and dandelion clocks. It was filled with feathers, as if someone had shaken a giant pillow somewhere above my head, and as I watched, the feathers grew thicker.

It wasn't easy to see with the air so full of swirling. I sheltered beneath the tree in the middle of the field as the air got colder. The stone grew hot in my pocket and I warmed my hands on it, but soon it grew too hot to hold and I had to put it on the ground, and it grew brighter and brighter while all around the world grew white.

When I woke it was morning. The air was still and it was heavy. It pressed close to me like a blanket, and the blanket was cold. I got out of bed. I pulled back the curtains. And the whole world was white.

The First Miracle

I STARED AT the snow and wondered if I was still dreaming. But the houses weren't made out of cardboard and the people weren't made out of clay: Mr. Neasdon was trying to start his car, Mrs. Andrews was peeping through her curtains, little kids were building a snowman, and the dog from number 29 was lifting his leg against a heap of snow and trotting off to the next. I blinked and it was all still there. I pinched myself and it hurt. I sat on the bed and looked at my knees. Then I got up and looked out the window again. Then I pulled on my clothes and ran downstairs and opened the front door.

The snow wasn't cotton wool or pipe cleaners or felt. It was real. I turned my face to the sky. Whiteness sealed my eyes and my lips. The cold was like silence around me. I went back inside.

The back door crashed as Father came into the kitchen. His cheeks were red and his mustache bristled. He put down a bucket of coal and poured himself tea. "Put plenty on," he said. "It'll be cold until the house heats up."

"Aren't you going to work?"

"There isn't any," he said. "The power's down at the factory. There'll be no school for you either. The road's closed; even the gritter can't get through."

Then I sat down at the table and kept very still, because something was fizzing inside me. Father was saying: "I've never seen anything like it. Not in October," and it was as if he was a long way away, and everything was now new and strange: the clank of the Rayburn stove lid, the shunt of the scuttle, the wheeze and pop of the porridge. I was standing in a high place but I didn't want to get down. I wanted to go higher. I said: "Perhaps the snow is a sign of the end! That would be exciting."

Father said: "The only exciting thing around here is that our breakfast is getting cold." He put two bowls of porridge on the table, sat down, and bowed his head. He said: "Thank you for this food, which gives us strength, and thank you for this new day of life, which we intend to use wisely."

"And thank you for the snow," I said under my breath, and I reached out and put my hand on his.

Father said: "Through Jesus's name, amen." He moved his hand away and said: "The prayer is for concentrating."

"I was concentrating," I said. I tucked my hand into my sleeve.

"Eat up," Father said. "I want to get down to the shops before they sell out of bread."

WE PUT ON wellies and coats. We walked in the road, in the pink trail left by the gritter. It wasn't snowing anymore; the sky was fiery and sun flashed in each of the windows. And all the things we usually saw—the dog mess and cigarette butts and chewing gum and gob—had been washed away. Cars were tucked up beneath snowy eiderdowns. There was nothing except people carrying bags or shoveling snow or blowing on their hands.

At the top of the hill, the town spread out before us. I knew it was all there, but today you had to look hard to be sure. We passed the multistory car park and the bus station and the main street, and they, too, were deep under snow. I said: "I like this. I hope we have more."

Father said: "There won't be any more."

"How do you know?"

"The forecast is clear."

"They didn't forecast this, did they?"

But he wasn't listening.

THE CO-OP WAS busy. Hot air was blowing and people were pushing. "Have you ever seen anything like it?" they said. "No mention on the forecast," and "In October too." There were no newspapers by the tills and not many loaves of bread left. We paid for the groceries, Father took four bags and I took one, and we began walking home.

Halfway up the hill I said: "Father, how would you know that a miracle had happened?"

"*What?*" He was puffing, his face red.

"How would we know if a miracle happened?"

"A miracle?"

"Yes."

"What are you talking about?"

"I think the snow might be a miracle."

"It's just snow, Judith!"

"But how do you know?"

Father said: "Now, look, we don't want a long discussion, OK?"

"But how do you know that lots of things aren't really miracles?" I said.

I ran to keep up. "I don't think people would believe a miracle happened even if it was right in front of them, even if someone told them. They would always think it was caused by something ordinary."

Father said: "Judith, where is this going?"

I opened my mouth, then closed it again. "I can't tell you yet," I said. "I need more evidence first."

"*Evidence?*"

"Yes."

Father stopped walking. "What did I just say?"

"But—"

Then Father frowned. He said: "Drop it, Judith. Just drop it, OK?"

Evidence

BETWEEN THE KITCHEN and the front room is the middle room. The middle room is Father's room. It's dark and smells of leather and sheepskin. There is a moth-eaten tapestry of creepers and snakes, a clock with no pendulum, and a chaise longue with no springs. There's a threadbare fur rug and a picture of angels and a coat stand made from a tree. There's a large black fireplace with birds-of-paradise tiles. And on either side of the fireplace is a cupboard.

In one cupboard there are photographs of Father and Mother before I was born, cards and piles of letters and lots of photos of people I don't know—Mother and Father's families before they came into the religion. Now the family doesn't speak to us, all except Auntie Jo, Father's sister, who sends us a Christmas card she has made every year inviting us to visit her in Australia. It annoys Father a lot because she knows we don't celebrate Christmas, but he can't bring himself to throw them out.

In the other cupboard there are a lot of books. There are books about the planet and the universe that have pictures of superclusters and black holes and cells and things. Father gets these out sometimes. But most of the books are written by the Brothers and these have titles like: *Then They Will Know, The Lord's Day and*

You, and *You Know Not the Hour*. I knew I would find out about miracles in one of those books.

The problem was, the cupboards were Father's and I should ask before going in there.

I waited for him to go out all afternoon, but he didn't. He stoked the fire and made an omelet. He read the paper. He made dinner. He washed up. Then he got the look he gets when he's about to make something and went into the garage. In a while I heard sawing, and I went into the middle room and closed the door.

My heart was banging as I opened the glass doors. This was a sin, but a sin in service to a greater good, so in the grand scheme of things it could be overlooked.

The first book I took down was called *The Gentile Times Have Ended*. It was full of charts and numbers, and I put it to the side. The next book was called *Gog of Magog: The Arch Deceiver*. That didn't talk about miracles either. I took down another. A pile began to form beside me on the carpet. I could still hear Father sawing. Every so often there was the sound of the blocks toppling to the floor. My heart was beating so loudly that the room was vibrating.

I was beginning to think I would never find anything about miracles, when I came to a book with a dark-green jacket and a bush, pale green and burning, pressed into the cover. It was called *Gifts in Men*.

Inside, there were pictures of people walking on water and the dead coming to life. A man was praying in the belly of a fish. Another in a fiery furnace. Another in a lion's den. The book spoke of *gifts* and *signs*, of *messengers* and *callings*. Miracles, it said, were God's calling card, His credentials, seals of divine mission. It said: *For where miracles are, there certainly God is.* I sat cross-legged on the floor.

What is possible with God is seldom possible with men, the book said. *From times of old, faithful ones have known this. God knows no order of difficulty. There are no limits to His ability to intervene on behalf of His loyal ones. Age is no barrier to the outworking of God's purpose. Remember the Midianite maiden who far from home afforded the cure of Naaman's leprosy and the child Samuel who heard God's voice night after night in the temple, warning of the downfall of Eli's household. There is no knowing whom God will deem a suitable vehicle for the manifestation of His powers, nor how He will choose to reveal them.*

My heart was still hammering hard but my blood was singing now and I felt very light, as if I was hovering a few inches above the carpet. *The greatest period of miraculous activity was when Christ walked the earth, I read, but the Lord's Day will also afford limitless possibilities for God's expression of His Kingship. Christians should be on the watch for signs in the sun, moon, and stars and other supernatural indications that the end is at hand. This will be a time when to discerning eyes God's hand will be seen at work in the lives of His servants.*

God has been known to intervene in lives on more than one occasion when the supplicant is earnest and real faith has been demonstrated. It should be remembered that to skeptics acts of God will always be attributed to earthly sources. This should not deter faithful ones from taking heart. They are lights shining in the darkness, and the darkness is afraid of light. I held the book to my chest and closed my eyes.

I DON'T KNOW how long I sat there, but after a while I realized I couldn't hear sawing anymore. I opened one eye. A pair of legs were standing in front of me. I opened the other eye. The legs were attached to Father's boots. Father's voice said: "What are you doing?"

"Reading," I said, and stood up.

Father said: "How many times have I told you to ask before getting these books out?" He bent down and began piling the books one on top of the other. He opened the cupboard doors and slotted them back into place, *thwack, thwack, thwack.*

"Father."

Thwack.

"Father."

Thwack.

My breath caught me and hurt inside. "Father, it says here that we can still see miracles today."

He sighed sharply. "What is all this miracle nonsense?"

I bit my lip hard, then I said: "I think something happened on Sunday. I mean last night. I think the snow was a miracle."

Father looked at me, then he took the book and blew on the pages. He shut it with a snap and put it back with the others.

I said: "The book said we may meet with disbelief, that we shouldn't be downhearted! It says most people don't realize they have seen a sign—"

"*Sign?*"

Father shut the cupboard, took me by the elbow, brought me outside, and closed the door. He said: "I'm getting just a bit tired of this. It snowed because it does sometimes. Even here. Even in October. Now, that's an end to it."

My heart was making it difficult to breathe. "I heard a voice as well!" I said suddenly. "Like Samuel in the temple. It told me what to do."

"This is making me cross now, Judith. You know how serious it is to lie."

"I'm not lying!" I said. "I don't know where the voice came from but I heard it!"

Father's face was flushed and his eyes were very black. He said: "Judith, you're always imagining this or that. You live in a complete fantasy world."

"Well, this is real," I said.

Father looked at me for a moment. Then he said in a low voice: "I don't want to hear any more about this, d'you understand?" and he went into the kitchen and the door shut behind him. I looked at the door for a long time. Then I went upstairs and sat on the floor in my room and I looked at the Land of Decoration.

And though I was sad to begin with because Father didn't believe me, after a while I was glad I hadn't said any more, because it would be best to wait until I had more proof and for that I would do a test, to find out whether the snow was a coincidence. "And then we shall see," I said to no one in particular.

"We certainly shall," no one said back.

Why Seeing Really Is Believing

PEOPLE DON'T BELIEVE in very much. They don't believe politicians and they don't believe ads and they don't believe things written on packets of food in the grocery store. Lots of them don't believe in God either. Father says it's because science has explained so many things that people think they should be able to know how everything happens before they believe it, but I think there is another reason.

I think people don't believe things because they are afraid. Believing something means you could be wrong, and if you're wrong you can get hurt. For instance, I thought I could climb the whole way round my room without touching the floor, and it hurt when I fell down. All the important things, like whether someone loves you or something will turn out right, aren't certain, so we try to believe them, whereas all the things you don't have to wonder about, like gravity and magnetism and the fact that women are different from men, you can bet your life on but you don't have to.

I used to worry when Father said we shouldn't believe in God blindly because the type of evidence for God is either too much (the apostle Paul says it is "inexcusable") or not enough (Richard Dawkins, a scientist the Brothers like to argue with, says it is "superstitious bosh"). I used to worry it meant that I was thinking for myself. But believing isn't just about evidence, and here's why.

People take the same bit of evidence and jump to different con-
clusions. Mr. Williams, the headmaster, said I was "extremely
bright" for my age, which is why I am a year younger than everyone
else in my class and Mr. Davies says I have the best grasp of language he has ever seen in a ten-year-old. But Neil Lewis says I am a
"spastic." Mr. Davies told us about fossils and he said: "This is how
living things evolved," but Father says: "Mutations never survive."
Mr. Davies thinks religion is a mirage. He and Father had a debate
at the last parents' evening. Mr. Davies said I should be taught the
facts about how the world came to be, and Father said those were
only the facts as Mr. Davies sees them.

There are mirages in space, crosses and arcs and circles that are
the reflections of galaxies that existed billions of years ago and that
show us what happened in the past, and Father says that scientists
want to see things as much as religious people, he says they make
leaps all the time. The fossil record for evolution isn't that good, but
the scientists had already decided creation wasn't an option so they
made fake fossils and covered them up. And you would think, being
scientists, they wouldn't. But scientists make leaps of faith all the
time, because there's a lot of guessing and waiting, and some of the
best discoveries, like Albert Einstein's, were made that way. Father
says the only people who don't leap at all are agnostics.

Scientists say miracles couldn't happen because they are miraculous, but that doesn't make sense, because they believe in plenty of
"miraculous" things, like the universe coming from nothing, and
the odds for that are mathematically impossible. Years ago people
thought an eclipse of the sun meant God was angry with them, but
it isn't a miracle now because we understand it, and neither is radio-
activity or an airplane or germs, though things like bees are, because
we still don't understand how they are able to fly. One day someone
will explain it, and then bees won't be a miracle either.

It makes you think lots of things are miraculous, like the chances
of me hitting exactly the same bit in my mouth with the toothbrush
that I did a few seconds before, or of my tomato squirting Father on

the nose at dinner, or the chance of me being me instead of millions of other people. But they are very small chances, and a bee isn't a miracle either, only a wonderful thing, because miracles are *made* to happen.

Evidence isn't all there is to believing, and neither is being able to explain it. Even if people can't explain something—like seeing a ghost or being healed—once they have experienced it, they believe it, though they might have spent their whole life saying it was nonsense. Which means that people who say something is impossible have probably just never experienced it.

Of course, they might still want to explain it away and look for a rational explanation. But they are doing what Father is doing and missing the point. Which is that miracles are what you see when you *stop* thinking, and they happen because someone made them and because someone, somewhere, had faith.

The Test

WHEN I WOKE on Tuesday, the sky was blue and empty and the sun was winking in the windows. Already the snow piles by the front doors and along the sides of the road were softening. I said: "Now for my test."

I went to the trunk and I got out my materials. I rolled up the sky in the Land of Decoration and in its place I hung gauze. I unhooked the clouds and in their place put a blizzard funnel of wire mesh and tiny polystyrene balls. I removed the cotton fabric and laid cotton wool over houses and steeples, railway lines, mountains, and viaducts.

"Colder!" said a voice, and again I felt as if I had caught light.

I put the tiny people inside their houses. I bundled them in blankets and coats. I put hot cups of cocoa in their hands. I lit hurricane lamps. I sprayed frost on windows and made ice for the roads with sheets of Plexiglas.

"Colder!" said the voice.

I tore the paper lighthouse beam and on top of the waves laid shards of floating plastic ice. I glued icicles to the masts of the ships, turned on the fan, and flurries of paper hail stung sailors' hands and faces. Snowmen sneezed. Polar bears shivered. Penguins danced to keep warm.

Then I said: "Snow," just like before. And I saw the town and the steelworks and the mountain sewn up in it, heaps of snow, more than anyone had ever seen here or ever would again.

I said: "Now I must wait."

I waited through breakfast. I waited through lunch. I waited as Father and I brought in the last of the wood to dry in the lean-to and we pondered Jesus dying to save the world. I waited as we sat by the fire that evening and Father listened to Nigel Ogden playing his organ. I waited all night, checking and looking out at the stars and the white waste of the moon. I ran to the window next morning, but the sun was shining so brightly it hurt my eyes and a steady dripping was coming from above my window.

I felt sick and sat on the bed. I said: "What did I do differently?" I said: "Perhaps I just have to be patient."

THAT MORNING WE went preaching. Father said it was the ideal time for it. What he meant was that people would be in. Getting people in is a problem for us, because though we are trying to save people, they will do almost anything to avoid it. They don't answer the door, they tell lies ("My grandmother just died," "I've got a war wound and can't stand up for long," "I'm on my way to church"), they get nasty (shouting, letting the dog out, threatening to call the police), they run away (this is a last resort, but it does happen; once someone took off running when he saw us at his door and dropped some of his shopping in the road). These are all what Father calls Tactics of Evasion. We have tactics of our own, which include asking thought-provoking questions, turning Conversation Stoppers into Conversation Starters, and knocking twice the same morning (though once someone threw a bucket of water over Father's head when we did this, so perhaps that was not such an effective tactic after all).

We met the group at the corner of King Street. There were small hills of snow on either side of the road. Elsie and May were there, Alf and Josie. Stan, Margaret, and Gordon. Josie was wearing a fur hat and a cape and a knitted all-in-one suit that came down to her shins. She said: "I looked for you on Sunday. I brought you something."

I went round to the other side of Father. "We must have missed each other," I said.

"What do you think of this snow?" said Uncle Stan. "Beats everything, doesn't it?"

"The Tribulation is on the way!" said Alf.

Elsie said: "My joints don't like it." She offered me a Ricola Locket.

"Nor my chilblains," said May. She offered me a Werther's Original.

"Well," said Father, "we've got a good show of spirit in any case."

Uncle Stan said the prayer and we started. Elsie worked with Margaret, Stan worked with Gordon, Josie worked with May, Alf worked alone, and I worked with Father. It was cold. Our steps rang on the pavement. Father said hello to passersby. Some of them nodded. Some said hello. Most ducked their heads and kept walking. Despite the ideal circumstances, not many answered. Sometimes a curtain moved. Sometimes a child came and said: "No one's at home," and when that happened there was laughter.

The sky was incredibly blue. The blueness bothered me. "It could still happen," I said to myself. "It could still snow." But two hours later, when we met on the corner, the sky was just as blue as before. "We don't seem to be having much success," said Uncle Stan. I couldn't have agreed with him more.

Father and I said goodbye to the group and went on Return Visits. Return Visits are people we always call on; they don't hide from us. Mrs. Browning sat up bright as a pin with rollers in her hair and invited us in for tea and butter puffs. There were dog hairs and grease on the plate, and the cups were brown inside. Usually I can't drink the tea, which is made with condensed milk and only just warm, but today I swallowed it without thinking. Then Father asked me to read the scripture and Mrs. Browning said: "Such a bright girl! I bet you're looking forward to going back to school."

Father raised his eyebrows. "I wouldn't bank on it."

We left Mrs. Browning and went to see Joe and his dog, Watson.

Joe leaned against the porch as he always did, there was a stain on the wall he had done it so long. Watson dragged his bottom across the step.

Father said: "Any day now, Joe."

And Joe said: "I'll believe it when I see it."

Father said: "You have to believe it or you *won't* see it."

Joe laughed, and a chain rattled in his chest. We left some magazines with him, then Father said we'd have to get back or the fire would be out.

I could see my legs going in and out beneath me all the way up the street. There was a lollipop stick lying in the gutter. I usually made garden fences with them but this time I stepped over it. "I won't make anything ever again," I said to myself. "It would have been better for me never to have made the snow at all if it was just a coincidence." Suddenly going back to how things were before was too terrible to think about.

We went up the mountain road in the tracks left by the cars, and the sun was coming through the fir trees in long molten strokes, stammering and jabbering through the branches. Father took long strides. His boots splattered slush sideways in little showers. I listened to the crunching of boots and the flapping of sheepskin and my Bible bag bumping about on my back and I wanted everything to stop. Father said: "Come on! What are you dawdling for?"

"I'm not dawdling," I said. "I'm tired."

"Well, the quicker you walk, the sooner we'll be home."

The mountain seemed higher than I remembered. We reached a curve in the road and it went up again. We reached another and it went up still further. The higher we climbed, the whiter it got. The whiteness got into my clothes. It pierced the stitching, the buttonholes, the wool of my tights. I shut my eyes, but it pricked through my eyelids and made patterns there.

We reached the top. Father kept going, but I stopped in the road. I listened to his footsteps as they went away, and for a minute I didn't mind if they never came back. I put my hands over my eyes and stood very still and all I could hear was the emptiness around me and for the longest time I didn't think anything at all. Then a cold gust buffeted me and I opened my eyes.

The sky wasn't bright anymore. It was thick and it was whirling. Something was drifting in front of me. Something was lighting on my coat and my nose and my cheeks, touching me then disappearing over and over. I stood very still, and somewhere inside me a bolt slid home.

There were tears in my eyes but not from the cold. And then I was running down the steep mountain road, running and shouting: "Wait for me!"

I ran past him and swung right round, slipping and laughing and just staying up. "It's snowing!" I shouted.

"I had noticed."

"Isn't it wonderful?"

"It's a pain in the neck."

I began running again, blinking, spreading my arms like a bird. Father said: "Watch you don't fall!" And I ran even faster to show him I wouldn't.

Snowflakes and Mustard Seeds

MIRACLES DON'T HAVE to be big, and they can happen in the unlikeliest places. Sometimes they are so small people don't notice. Sometimes miracles are shy. They brush against your sleeve, they settle on your eyelashes. They wait for you to notice, then melt away. Lots of things start by being small. It's a good way to begin, because no one takes any notice of you. You're just a little thing beetling along, minding your own business. Then you grow.

High in the heavens snowflakes are born. When they fall to earth they are so light they fall sideways. But flakes find brothers and when they do they stick together. If enough of them stick they begin to roll. If they roll far enough they pick up fence posts, trees, a person, a house.

A mustard seed is the smallest of seeds, but when it has grown, the birds of heaven lodge in its branches; a grain of sand becomes a pearl; and prayers that begin with very little or nothing at all are spoken, because if there is enough of something it begins to grow, and if there is more than enough a great thing will happen which was there from the start in the smallest of ways.

Which comes first, the prayer or the particles? How can the smallest of things become the biggest of all and the thing that could have been stopped unstoppable, and something you never thought would amount to much amount to it all? Perhaps it's because miracles work best with ordinary things, the more ordinary the better. Perhaps it's because they begin with odds and ends—the greater the odds, the bigger the miracle.

A Skeptic

THAT AFTERNOON THE sky grew dark with the weight of the snow. It kept spiraling down, wondering which way to go. I sat and watched. I could have watched it forever. I didn't eat dinner. My hands felt hot or other things felt cold and my skin was prickling all over. Father asked if I had a temperature; I told him I had never felt better.

The next morning it was still snowing. Drifts reached to the sills of windows, cars were small white hillocks, my breath formed clouds, and the floorboards creaked with the cold. Father was rubbing his hands by the Rayburn when I came down. He said he'd had to dig a tunnel to get out the back door.

I decided the time had come to tell him what was happening. I took a deep breath. "You know I was asking about miracles?"

He banged the fire door and said: "Not now, Judith. I've got to saw more wood and I have to see if Mrs. Pew is all right. In fact, you could do that for me."

"But I have to talk to you!" I said. "It's important."

"Later," Father said. He swigged the last of his tea.

I stared at him. "Do I really have to go round to Mrs. Pew?"

"Well, it would help me."

"What if I don't come back?"

"Don't be silly, Judith. There's nothing wrong with Mrs. Pew."

"Her head wobbles."

"So would yours if you had Parkinson's."

* * *

Snow came over the top of my wellingtons as I waded through the front gate. My legs were wet by the time I got next door to Mrs. Pew's front door. The bell went on for a while. I shuffled from foot to foot. The little kids in the street say Mrs. Pew invites children into her house and they're never heard of again; they say that's what happened to Kenny Evans. Though some people said he went to live with his father. I looked up and down the street to see if there would be any witnesses if Mrs. Pew tried anything.

The door opened a crack and I smelled something strong and musty, heard the latch turn, old hats and gloves from secondhand shops. Then I saw a black dress, a high collar, and a white face with red lips, drawn-on eyebrows, and little black curls that shook and glinted greasily. Spider eyes peered at me. There were lines around her mouth, and the red of her lips ran into them. It looked as though she was bleeding. "Yes?" Mrs. Pew said in her cracked-china voice.

I swallowed and said: "Hello, Mrs. Pew. Father told me to come and see if you needed anything."

She turned up her hearing aid and leaned closer, and I backed away and said: *"Father said: Do you need anything?"* I was about to say it a third time when she shook her head, tweaked my sleeve, and pulled me into the hallway. I turned round, as the door shut. My heart began to beat very fast indeed.

Through the doorway, a television was blaring. A woman was standing in front of a lorry on a motorway, saying: *"Yesterday a blast of Arctic weather brought snow and ice to much of the country for the second time this week. The first taste of winter came just two days ago, when a mild October was shattered by an eight-inch fall of snow. The weather is causing problems on the roads and at sea. Four sailors, including a fifteen-year-old boy, had to be rescued yesterday after their yacht capsized off Plymouth. Both falls of snow have confounded weather forecasters . . ."*

Mrs. Pew turned the sound off, then came back and said: "Now, what is it? Speak up, child!"

"Father said: DO YOU NEED ANYTHING?"

"Oh!" she said. "There's no need to shout! That's kind of your father. But you can tell him I'm well provided for; I've enough tins in my pantry to feed the army."

"Good," I said, and turned to undo the door.

"Wait, young lady! Have you seen Oscar?"

"What?"

"Have you seen Oscar?"

"No."

"He didn't come in for his cat food last night," she said. "It's most unlike him. Usually he doesn't set foot outside if it so much as spits with rain. He holes himself up somewhere. If you see him, let me know, won't you?"

My legs were shaky as I went to the gate. I turned back to say goodbye, and then I stopped. Mrs. Pew was dabbing her eyes with her handkerchief, but her head was wobbling too much to do it properly. She said: "I can't help thinking something terrible has happened to him."

I looked down. I said: "I have to go now."

Father was on top of the wall at the side of the lean-to, raking off snow. "Mrs. Pew has enough tins to feed the army," I shouted, "but Oscar is missing. Can I talk to you now?"

"Can't you see I'm busy?"

"Yes."

"Later!"

BUT AFTER CLEARING the roof he was busy shoveling snow, and after that he was busy chopping wood, and after that he was busy reading the paper, listening to the forecast, and getting dinner. I played in the garden. I made a snow cat and a snow man and a snow dog, and by then the day was almost over. At dinnertime he was only busy eating, so I laid down my knife and fork and said: "Father, I've got to tell you something." I waited for him to speak, but he didn't, so I said: "On Sunday I made snow for the Land of Decoration." I said: "I wanted it to snow."

He went on chewing. I could see the muscles in his jaw move. He must be playing it cool.

I said: "Father, I made snow for the Land of Decoration and then it happened. It was a miracle! It happened twice, just as I wanted it to. But you mustn't tell anyone yet, because it might scare them and I've only just found out myself."

Father looked at me for probably the longest he has ever looked at me. Then he began to laugh. He laughed and laughed. When he had finished laughing he said: "You're a star turn. So this is what all the miracle business has been about?"

"Yes," I said. I hoped the laughter was due to shock. "I've been wanting to tell you. And I did it a second time, just to make sure—and it happened again! Even though you said that it wouldn't. Because I had faith!"

Father said: "It's because you spend too much time in that room." Then he sighed.

"Judith, whatever you made for your model world has nothing to do with the real one—you're always making this or that. It's a *coincidence*."

"It's not!" I said, and I felt strange, as if I was getting a temperature. "It wouldn't have happened without me."

Father said: "Have you been listening to a word I've been saying?"

"Yes," I said. But my head began to feel full again like it did on the day I made the snow, as if there were too many things in it.

Father said: "Judith, ten-year-old girls do not perform miracles."

I said: "How do you know if you're not a ten-year-old girl?"

Father pinched his eyes shut with his finger and thumb. When he opened them, he said he'd had enough of this ridiculous conversation.

He took my plate, though I hadn't finished, and put it on top of his own and went to the sink, ran the tap, and began to wash the dishes.

I stood up. I tried to speak calmly. "I know it's hard to believe," I said. "But it wasn't just once—"

He held up his hand. "I don't want to hear any more."

"*Why?*"

Father stopped washing the dishes. "*Because!* Because it's dangerous, that's why!"

"Dangerous to who?"

"Dangerous to *whom*."

"Dangerous to whom?"

"It's dangerous to think you have that sort of power. It's . . . presumptuous—it's *blasphemous*." He stared at me. "Just who do you think you are? It was a coincidence, Judith."

I heard what he said, but my head was getting too hot to think about what the words meant. I looked down and said quietly: "You're wrong."

"I beg your pardon?"

I looked at him. "It wasn't a coincidence."

Father reached up and banged the cupboard door hard. Then he leaned on the sink and said: "*You spend far too much time in that room!*"

"I have a gift!" I said. "I made a miracle happen!"

Then Father came up to me and said: "I want you to drop this right now, d'you understand? You do *not* have a gift. You can *not* make miracles happen. Is that clear?"

I could hear our breath and the drip of the tap. There was a pain in my chest.

Father said: "*Is that clear?*" For a minute the pain in my chest was too great to breathe.

And then it was as if a switch had been turned off and I didn't feel hot anymore. The pain went away and I was cool and separate from things.

"Yes," I said. I went to the door.

"Where are you off to?"

"To my room."

"Oh no, you're not; the less time you spend in that room the better. You can dry the dishes, and after that there's some other things you can do."

So I DRIED and then sorted out Bible magazines. I put the oldest ones on the top of the pile and the latest at the bottom. I brought in four bucketfuls of sticks and two of coal and stacked them by the Rayburn.

Father said how well I had stacked the sticks, but that was just because he felt guilty he had shouted, like he always does. I didn't say anything back, because I wasn't going to let him off that easily.

I waited till nine o'clock, then I said good night and went upstairs and got out my journal and wrote all of this down, everything that had happened since Sunday. Because it was too important not to, and if I couldn't talk about it I would have to write it somewhere instead.

A Secret

I HAVE A secret. The secret is this: Father doesn't love me.

I don't know when I first guessed, but I have been sure for a while now. He'll say: "That's a good answer," or "I liked the way you used that scripture," or he'll come to my room and stand in the doorway and say: "Everything all right?" But he sounds as though he is reading the words from a sheet, and afterward he tells me how I could have done the presentation better, and though I tell him he can come into my room he doesn't.

These are the reasons I know Father doesn't love me.

1) He doesn't like looking at me.
2) He doesn't like touching me.
3) He doesn't like talking to me.
4) He is often angry with me.
5) He is sad because of me.

1) Father doesn't look at me if he can help it, and when he does his eyes are black. They are actually green, but they look black because he is angry. There is a verse in the Bible where it says God's spirit *is sharper than a two-edged sword and divides even the soul*

from the spirit, and joints from their marrow, and knows thoughts and secrets of the heart. That's how it feels when Father looks at me. It looks like he doesn't like what he sees there.

2) Father doesn't touch me. We don't kiss good night or hug or hold hands, and if we are sitting too close he will suddenly notice and clear his throat or move away or get up. Sometimes when we are together, something in the air changes and it is as if we are the only people in the universe, but instead of there being lots of space, as there would be if we really were, we are locked in a very small room and there is nothing to talk about.

3) Father doesn't like talking to me. This may be because I ask a lot of questions, such as: "What will it be like in the new world?" and "Does God know everything that will happen in the future?" To which Father said: "God can decide what to know and what not to know." To which I said: "Then He must know what's going to happen in order not to want to know about it," and Father said: "It's a bit more complicated than that."

So I said: "Does God let bad things happen because He can't see them or because He doesn't want to stop them?"

"God lets bad things happen in order to prove that humans can't rule themselves. If God stopped everything bad happening, then people wouldn't be free. They would be little puppets."

I said: "I suppose so. But if everything we do is already written out somewhere, are we free to do what we want or do we just think we are?"

Father said: "We can't understand God, Judith. His ways are unsearchable."

"Then why ponder them?" I said.

Father raised his eyebrows and closed his eyes.

I said: "Perhaps you can ponder too much."

And Father said he thought you probably could.

But most of the time I don't say much to Father and he doesn't say much to me, and this is the biggest problem we have, because all the time we are not saying things, the air is filled with the things we could. I am always trying to hook one of these things down, but they are usually out of reach.

4) Father is often angry with me. This is because there is a list of things he approves of, which must be done a certain way, such as:

a) speaking (not mumbling)
b) sitting (not slouching)
c) walking (not running)
d) thinking (not daydreaming)
e) saving (not spending)

and an even longer list that must not be done at all, such as:

a) crying
b) playing with food
c) leaving food
d) running around (including hopscotch in the hall, which breaks another rule too; see f)
e) scuffing shoes
f) noise in general
g) leaving doors open
h) not paying attention

And sooner or later I am bound to do one and forget to do the other.

Sometimes, though, I don't know why Father is angry with me. Once I asked him what I had done wrong.

He said: "*You?*"

"Yes."

"What makes you say that?"

"You always seem cross."

"*Me?*"

"Yes."

"*I'm* not cross."

"Oh."

"You'd know if I was cross!"

"That's all right, then."

He said: "Cross indeed!" And he was angrier than he had been to start with.

5) But worse, much worse than Father being cross, much worse than Father not talking to me or not wanting to look at me or not wanting to touch me, is when he is sad.

Sometimes when I was younger, I used to come downstairs at night to get a drink and the light would be on under the kitchen door. I would see Father through the glass panel, sitting at the table, not doing anything, just sitting there. I stood by the door waiting for him to move, and if he did it was like stepping into warm water. If he didn't I would go back to bed with a pain in my chest and promise to be better and wait for the light to come.

That was when I thought I could make Father love me, but I don't anymore. Because the reason he doesn't happened a long time ago and I can't do anything about it now, even though without me it wouldn't have happened at all.

A Voice in the Dark

WHEN I HAD finished writing in my journal, I put it under the loose floorboard beneath my bed. I would have to hide it for now. Until Father came to his senses and saw what was staring him in the face.

I suddenly wondered what Brother Michaels would say if he knew what had happened, and I wished I could tell him how right he had been, that I could make things happen just like he said.

I got into bed. My head still felt hot and I was feeling even stronger than before. I could see myself in bed as if I wasn't in my body. I'd fainted once and it felt similar. I was thinking about Father and the argument, thinking how surprised he would be when he finally did realize I could perform miracles, but it was as if it had all happened to someone else now, as if the little body lying in the bed and the house and our street and the town and the whole universe was pouring into my head and my head was big enough for it all, but it went on getting hotter and hotter, and it was all so strange I just lay back and let it happen. Then I heard something.

"So, you can make it snow," said a voice. "What else can you do, I wonder?" Something shot up my spine and into my hair, and it felt like something inside me had melted.

"Hello?" I said, but no one answered. I waited.

Then someone sighed. I was sure of it.

I sat up in bed. I was breathing very hard. I pulled the blankets around me and took a deep breath. "Who's there?" I whispered.

Everything was silent again. Then the voice said: "I said: 'What else can you do?'"

I gasped. "Who are you?" I said.

"Now, there's a question."

I opened my mouth. I shut it again. "Where did you come from?"

"There's another."

I said: "I want to know—"

"You already do," said the voice. It sounded quite close.

I shook my head. "Where *are* you?" I said.

"I'm all around," the voice said. "Inside things and outside them too. I was, and am, and will be."

Then my heart beat once, very hard, and I said: "You're God, aren't You?"

"Shh," said the voice.

I swallowed. "Can You see me?"

"Of course," said God. "I've been watching you for some time. You could be very useful to Me."

I sat up. "What do You mean?"

"Well," said God, "you've got a great imagination. I need someone like you to be My Instrument."

"Your Instrument?" I said.

"Yes."

"What for?"

"Miracles, that sort of thing."

I put my hands over my face and then I took them away. I said: "I *knew* I was meant to do something important!"

"Shh!" said God. "Not so loud. We don't want to wake your father." He paused. "But there's one condition: You have to have complete faith; you have to be prepared to do whatever I ask, no doubting, no grumbling, no asking why."

"OK," I said. "I won't."

"You mean it?"

"Yes!"

"All right," said God. "We'll talk later. Right now I have to get on with some other things."

"What other things?"

"Well, this is a busy time in heaven right now. Four horsemen are straining at the bit, there're some winds that are very restless, and there are a lot of locusts that are getting under everyone's feet. Oh, and some seals that have to be opened. In the meantime, no blabbing, all right?"

"Can I carry on using my powers?"

"Yes," said God. "I'll let you get used to them for a bit."

"Do you think I could make things happen to people and animals as well?"

God said: "Judith, it's all a matter of faith."

"The mustard seed!"

"Precisely."

"I won't say any more to Father."

"Very wise."

"But he'll believe me in the end?"

"Yes."

"Because I'll do more and more things and he'll have to see. He will have to see I am doing something special."

"No doubt about it," said God.

Then God went wherever it is that He goes and I lay down and thought two things. The first was that I had been silly to expect Father to understand about the miracles but I didn't have to worry because it would all come right in the end.

The second thought was strange. It was that this had been waiting to happen to me, and thinking that made me happier than anything I had thought before in my whole life. The miracles had been waiting all this time, and so had I. And now the waiting was over, and things could begin.

The Long-Distance Call

FATHER SAYS THAT God is the voice in every Christian's head helping him to do the right thing. He says that the Devil tells the Christian to do the exact opposite. This means we must be careful which of them we listen to. Up until yesterday, I hadn't heard God's voice but I had been talking to Him. I think I must have been saving up things to say, because for a long time I didn't talk at all.

WHEN I WAS small, Father took me to see a doctor because I didn't do anything but stare straight in front of me. There is a photograph of me taken by Father at that time. It's a warm day and I am sitting beneath the cherry tree he planted for Mother in the front garden. The grass is littered with blossoms. I am wearing a blue T-shirt and shorts that come down to my knees. There is a scab on the right one. My legs stick straight out in front of me. My hands are in my lap.

I can't imagine Father thinking it was a good idea to take me to the doctor, because he never goes to them himself, but he did. I remember that the doctor's room smelled funny. I remember there was a chair with a leather seat and in the corner a box of plastic blocks and a big red bus. I played with the bus and Father talked to the doctor.

The doctor did tests and made a plan and came to a conclusion. The conclusion was that we were both missing Mother, and the plan was that Father should read to me. So he did, and I learned all about the Nephilim, and the Ark of the Covenant, and why circumcision must be performed on the eighth day, how to clean an infected house of leprosy, what not to say to a Pharisee, and how to remove the sting of a gadfly. And as I began to read I began talking, and in a while I was talking as much as anyone—though perhaps not about the same things.

There weren't many people to talk to except Father, so I began talking to God. I always supposed it was just a matter of time before He answered me. I used to think of it as a long-distance telephone call. The line was bad, there were birds sitting on it, there was heavy weather, so I couldn't make out what the other person was saying, but I never doubted I would hear them eventually. Then one day the birds flew off, the rain cleared up, and I did.

The Third and Fourth Miracles

I DECIDED TO use my power to help people, and first on my list was Mrs. Pew. I had been thinking about her since I saw her crying. I didn't think she could be the type of person to kidnap children if she was so upset about Oscar; it was quite disappointing to think that Kenny Evans probably did go to live with his father after all.

Oscar is a large ginger cat who sits in Mrs. Pew's front-room window between a bowl of hyacinths and a yellow china dog. I didn't know why he had decided to disappear. Perhaps he was tired of the dog, who didn't do anything but grin in an empty way, or perhaps he was tired of the view. Anyway, all that mattered was that I bring him back. So on Thursday when the snow came down in flurries, I made a cat with marmalade wool. Father called: "What are you doing?" and I called back: "Reading!" The lie was justified: I was now God's Instrument and had work to do.

I gave the cat a blue collar and one white paw and took a chip out of his ear, just like Oscar, though I couldn't remember which ear and hoped it didn't matter. I made an old woman in a black dress and gave her a high lace collar and little black boots and pushed very small beads in the sides of the clay for buttons. I gave the lady black curly hair, glued pieces of cut-up staple in her hair for clips, painted her face white and her lips red. I made a trail of cat prints leading through the snow to the old lady and put the cat on her lap and made sure he was curled up and didn't look like he was going to get up again. I sewed his eyes closed and tucked his paws in. Then I said: "Come home Oscar."

When I had finished, I wondered what might actually happen if the miracle worked. Would Oscar's whiskers be singed after being flown back from wherever he was at the speed of light, or would his fur stand on end after being brought back to life with a bolt of lightning? Anyway I went round to Mrs. Pew's and knocked on the door. I saw her wobbling head and smelled the secondhand-shop smell and felt a bit queasy, but I stayed where I was and when she opened the door I said: "Don't worry about Oscar, Mrs. Pew. I have a feeling he'll be home very soon."

She turned up her hearing aid and I said it all over again, and then she said: "Oh, I do hope so. I do hope so!"

I said: "Have faith, Mrs. Pew."

Then she said: "Pardon?"

And I said: *"HAVE FAITH!"*

Her hand fluttered at the base of her throat and she said: "Oh. I certainly will."

She watched me go down the garden path. When I was at the gate she said suddenly: "You're Judith, aren't you?"

"Yes."

She said: "Thank you, Judith. It was nice of you to come by."

I said: "You're welcome, Mrs. Pew."

When I got back, I wrote up the miracle in my journal, then turned over three pages and wrote: *Has Oscar come home yet?* and then I wrote the same on the next.

I WAITED FOR Oscar all that day and the next day too but it just went on snowing. In the meantime I decided that even though I didn't want to go back to school, because of Neil Lewis, the snow would have to go. Father kept talking about how much work he was missing and accidents were happening on roads and old people like

Joe were getting sick. Father said Joe had gone into the hospital and Watson was being looked after by a neighbor. So that afternoon I undraped the gauze and peeled back the cotton wool and blew away the flour and broke the icicles off the houses. I rolled up the cotton and dismantled the blizzard and packed up the snowmen and wiped away the shaving foam and put the blue back in the sky and turned on the sun.

On Saturday night the wind dropped. The next morning, blue sky appeared. By the afternoon the sun was quite warm. Icicles dripped outside my window like someone playing jars of water. The snow in the street became slushy and broke into platelets of ice. Father said: "I knew it couldn't last." I didn't say anything but went and stood on the pavement and listened to water running into the drains at the side of the pavement and said: "Thank You, God. You have me again."

But there was no Oscar. I waited all day and I waited all evening. I said: "Did I do it right, God?" But God must still have been busy with the four horsemen or something, because He didn't answer.

I sat up in bed that night and watched clouds crossing the moon and veiling and unveiling the Land of Decoration. I watched the sun come over the mountain and blink a bleary red eye, striping the sky pink and yellow like a stick of rock. But there was still no sight of Oscar.

I WAS STANDING in the garden with Father after the meeting the next day when the fourth miracle happened.

Father was clearing the paths and I was helping him. Little birds had left prints here and there on the bird table and on the top of the walls. A trail of larger prints that belonged to some larger animal led from the garage doors. The buddleia bushes and golden cane bowed beneath a foam of snow, and the cherry-tree branches were black and dripping. There were open patches of ground here and there where the earth and a little sodden grass were beginning to show.

Father was drinking tea, looking around with his hand on his hip, his breath a pink cloud in the air. He said: "I think it's going to be pretty next spring when your mother's cherry tree is out. And a few more weeks and we'll have the first Christmas roses." That's when we heard tapping and looked up to see Mrs. Pew standing at her kitchen window. She was beckoning me.

When I got to the wall, she opened the back door and pointed. By her feet, bent over a bowl of cat biscuits, cracking them with his teeth, turning his head this way and that, and making hungry noises, was Oscar. Mrs. Pew said: "I looked up and there he was on the windowsill!" Her head was wobbling twice as fast as usual. She said: "I thought he was dead, and here he is, right as rain, eating for England!"

I climbed over to Mrs. Pew's and reached out to stroke Oscar's head. I was pleased to see that not one bit of fur was singed and all his whiskers looked perfectly straight. "I told you he'd come home," I said. Mrs. Pew was smiling and nodding. Her eyes looked watery. At that moment I didn't feel afraid of her at all.

She said: "Judith, would you and your father like some jam tarts?"

A vision of Father and me rolling around clutching our sides, with smears of jam and pastry crumbs on our faces, flashed before my eyes. Then I said to myself: "Don't be silly." Out loud I said: "Thank you, Mrs. Pew."

She wrapped a plate in a tea towel and gave it to me. "Come and have tea with me one afternoon," she said.

When I got back, Father had gone inside. I could see him through the kitchen window, getting tea. I didn't go in straightaway. I stood on the path, watching the sky redden, smelling the earth, and feeling the warm plate in my hands.

I suddenly saw how everything would get better and better, and wondered why God had helped me like this. And though He didn't answer and had gone wherever He goes, He must have known what He had done, to make me happy so suddenly, to make everything begin changing.

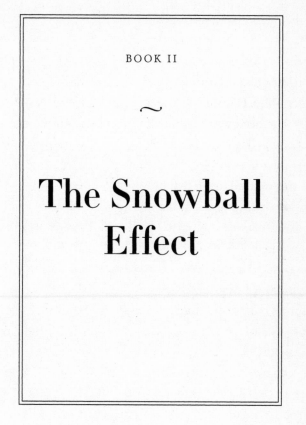

BOOK II

~

The Snowball
Effect

Monday

On Monday it rained. Rooftops rang, drainpipes sang, and little pieces of snow coasted along gutters like islands setting to sea. Drips fell from Sue Lollipop's hat as she crossed me over the road to school. I wondered if she knew just who she was crossing over but I didn't say anything, because God had said not to talk about being his instrument.

Sue said: "I'm off to the Bahamas. Any day now, kid, I'm going to get the ticket." I asked if I could come with her, and she said she would stow me away in her suitcase.

In the classroom I sat and waited for them to come in from assembly. I don't go to assembly because Father says they sing to false gods. The smell of the classroom was making my stomach twist, so I forced myself to think of the snow I had made. And now it was turning to water. Two buckets were collecting drips from the ceiling, and rain battered the window. Drops falling from the sky stood out pale in the fluorescent light. They looked like tiny sparks, appearing and disappearing. I tried to follow them as they fell but it made me dizzy, and in the end I just put my head on the desk and closed my eyes.

The door banged against the wall and I jumped. They all poured into the room and a wave of sound came with them; they were laughing and pushing. Neil was jumping on Hugh's back and shouting. I slipped down in my seat. Then I made myself sit up again. "There's nothing to be afraid of," I said. "Not anymore."

Gemma, Rhian, and Keri sat down at the table. They didn't say hello. They were looking at a magazine Gemma had. When Gemma saw me looking, she held it up so I couldn't see.

Gemma has blond spiral hair and skin that is brown all year round. She can do the splits. She has two sets of gold earrings in each ear; gold rings on her fingers; wears high-top trainers with ankle socks; and has a spangly leotard. I have never had a leotard. I am not good at PE. I wear boots and long socks. I wore some trainers to school once, but they had a Velcro strap and Gemma said: "I had a pair like that—when I was *four*," and everyone laughed. Gemma is good at making people laugh. But Gemma was just jealous of my trainers because they lasted longer than hers. And I wouldn't be caught dead in a leotard, even if it did have spangly bits on it.

Gemma and Keri began to giggle. I was getting out my reading book to show I wasn't interested. Then a pie hurtled past our heads. A bag of crisps followed and a few seconds later a pair of football boots. I turned around to see Hugh, on the floor and picking things, while Neil shook his bag out. Suddenly the door slammed. Mr. Davies said: "What in God's name do you think you are doing?"

There was laughter and scraping of chairs. Neil sat down, then got up again and took a handful of the back of Hugh's sweater. Mr. Davies shouted: "NEIL LEWIS! Do you think what I say applies to everyone but you?" Neil sat down and grinned as if Mr. Davies had paid him a compliment.

Mr. Davies passed his hand over his eyes and walked toward his desk. He got halfway then lifted his foot. He said: "What the—" Then his face turned dark and he shouted: "This is the limit! The absolute limit! How did this pie get here?"

Neil said: "It flew, sir."

Lee said: "Hugh threw it, sir."

Mr. Davies shouted: "I will not tolerate this sort of behavior! I will NOT, do you hear me?"

He took off his shoe and went to the sink and got two paper towels. As he came back, he tripped over the bucket that was collecting the drips. He stood up and his glasses were steaming. "Someone get some paper towels and CLEAR UP THIS MESS!" He sat down at the desk, loosened his tie, and opened the attendance book. "Right," he said. "Right! Scott! Robert! Stacey! Paul . . ."

Mr. Davies had got to "Rhian" when there was a squeal from the back of the room. We turned to see Neil hoisting Hugh over the back of his desk by his tie. Mr. Davies stood up. "NEIL LEWIS," he roared. "LET HUGH GO!"

Neil let Hugh go so suddenly he fell off his seat. Mr. Davies sat down and wiped his head with his handkerchief. His hand shook. It moved toward the drawer of his desk. He seemed to consider something a moment, then went on with the attendance.

When he had finished, Mr. Davies said: "Page seventy in your English books! Exercise eleven!" There were groans and opening and shutting of desks and slapping of books on desks. Mr. Davies said: "Is it possible to do it quietly please?"

AT TWENTY PAST ten, Mr. Davies banged on the top of the desk, the drawer shot forward, and he took something out. He stood up and said: "I'm going out for five minutes. When I come back I'll expect you to have finished the exercise."

"*Five minutes!*" he said, poking his head round the door.

As soon as the door shut, a waterfall of noise broke over the room. Chairs screeched, cupboards banged, someone began to draw on the blackboard, someone else got onto a table. Gemma put down her pen and yawned. She rolled onto Rhian's shoulder and giggled. Then she sat up and looked at me sleepily. To Rhian she said: "Neil Lewis is sex on a stick." But she was looking at me.

Someone said to Gemma: "All right, babe?" and I felt a wave of heat pass over my body. Neil was standing behind Gemma. He said: "Hiya, spaz. How's life in Freaksville?"

I looked down at my book. "You are God's Instrument," I said to myself. "There is nothing to be afraid of."

Gemma stretched back in her chair. She said: "Judith, your father is nuts. I saw him knocking on doors the other day."

I said: "The world is going to end; we have to tell people."

Gemma said: "You're nuts too." She turned to Neil. "Her father came to my house and asked my mum if she thought God would do anything about the trouble in the world!"

"He called on my house once and my dad told him to fuck off," said Keri. "He had a hat on. He always wears that hat." She laughed suddenly. "I bet it really smells!"

Neil said: "If he ever calls on my house, my dad will kick the shit out of him."

I gripped my pen tightly. I said: "We have a commission. People have to be warned."

"Oh God," said Gemma. "She's starting again."

Then something happened very quickly. Neil pulled my head back and stuffed something into my mouth. The thing had edges. Neil pushed it so far I thought I was going to choke. He held on to my arms.

Gemma, Rhian, and Keri burst out laughing. I could feel the heat in my face. I wanted to shut my face up and lock it away but I couldn't, and they went on laughing. Then someone ran in and said: "He's coming!" Neil cuffed the back of my head and sauntered to his seat.

I pulled the thing out of my mouth. It was paper. The paper made a soggy lump on the desk. I scooped it into my drawer and bent my head over my book.

"Have you all been behaving yourselves?" said Mr. Davies. He opened the drawer of his desk and closed it again. His voice was stronger now. He said: "Let's check these answers."

But I couldn't think about answers. Something was creeping

down my arms and into my fingers, rising up my neck into my hair. My head felt hot and full again, like it did the day of the snow, and the room was vibrating slightly. Specks appeared in front of my eyes.

I wasn't sure whether I was frightened or angry; if I was angry it had never happened before.

Tuesday

WHEN I GOT home that evening, I made a sandwich and watered my mustard seeds. I thought perhaps they needed more light, so I moved them to the other windowsill and prodded the soil a bit. Then I went upstairs and sat on the floor in front of the Land of Decoration.

I thought of making a model of Neil and sticking pins in him, but in the end I made a banana boat with lots of paddles and six little men with bones through their noses. I intended them to look happy, but they all looked quite fierce.

ON TUESDAY NEIL opened his mouth and rolled his eyes at me. He pushed his tongue in and out of his cheek and lapped. He flicked paper balls and they bounced off the top of my head.

I thought of hailstones and balls of fire rolling down streets. I thought about earthquakes and lightning. I thought about people screaming and buildings falling and rivers of molten lava. Then I heard someone saying: "Hello! Earth calling Judith!

"Well," said Mr. Davies, when I looked up, "now that we're all here . . ."

Neil's lip curled and his eyes smiled.

At eleven o'clock, I went up to the desk for my work to be marked. I watched the army of black hairs move back and forth in Mr.

Davies's nose and smelled the sharp tobacco smell coming down it and waited for him. He handed my book back to me and said to the class: "Listen everyone, we have someone here who has already finished." When I went back to my seat, Neil's eyes followed me.

One by one everyone else came up to the desk with their books to be marked. At half past eleven Mr. Davies said: "You three at the back—the rest of the class is waiting for you." Then Neil, Lee, and Gareth came shuffling to the front with their exercise books and slouched in a line.

Neil stood right behind our table. I could hear the rustle of his Puffa jacket and the silky sound of his warm-up pants and smell the sickly smell of his skin. Gemma was smiling, but I couldn't see why. A minute later I heard a noise like a little trumpet and something landed on my hand. I looked down and saw a perfectly round plug of snot, pale green and circled with red. It must have fitted the inside of Neil's nose exactly.

Gemma said: "What's that?"

Keri said: "Gross!"

Rhian said: "Oh my God."

My head began to get hot. I looked for something to get rid of it but I couldn't find anything, so I wiped my hand against the underside of the chair, bent my head over my book, and began writing very fast but I couldn't remember what.

Mr. Davies finished marking Gareth's book and began to mark Lee's. The line moved forward. Neil stayed where he was. I heard him shuttle a slug of snot to the back of his nose. Then I felt something in my hair.

"Oh my God," Gemma said. "Judith, what's in your *hair*?"

I put up my hand and my fingers came away covered with green paste.

I felt dizzy. I tried to tear a page from my exercise book, but my hands were shaking and it tore wide.

Neil said: "Judith tore her exercise book, sir."

Mr. Davies looked up. "Judith, did you tear your book?"

Neil made a chopping motion with his hand.

"I didn't mean to," I said.

"She's lying, sir," said Neil. "She did it on purpose."

"Be quiet, Neil," said Mr. Davies.

"It's true, sir," said Gemma. "I saw her."

Mr. Davies frowned. "Judith, I'm surprised at you. We don't deface school property here." He turned back to marking Lee's book.

My head was very hot now. After a minute I tried to wipe away the snot, but the paper only spread it. Gemma said: "Sir, I don't want to sit next to Judith."

Mr. Davies said: "What *is* going on at that table?"

Rhian said: "Judith needs a tissue, sir."

Mr. Davies said: "Judith, if you need a tissue, then go to the toilets and get one. I wouldn't have thought I would have to tell you that."

When I didn't move he said: "Well, go on."

As I got up, Neil smiled.

"And wash your hands!" Mr. Davies called after me.

The Other Cheek

I SAT IN front of the Land of Decoration for over an hour that evening. The little people looked at me with their painted-on smiles. I knew every one of them. The two little people I had made to begin with, years ago—a pipe-cleaner doll with a green sweater and a kite, and a fabric doll with brown hair, dungarees, and flowers—stared at me hardest of all. They seemed to be asking something, but I didn't know what.

"God," I said, "I'm finding it really difficult having this power and not using it to punish people." But God didn't answer.

AT TWENTY TO six I heard the front door slam. Father called up to me, then he went into the kitchen. I heard Mike with him. Mike is not a believer, so we shouldn't associate with him, but Father says he is a good man so it's all right.

Mike and Father work in the factory together. Most of the people in town do. Inside the factory they make steel for things that fly. Mike says as factories go it's not such a bad place. In the next valley is a factory where they kill chickens, and someone got so tired of killing chickens he put his hand in the machinery. And not long ago in the paper, there was a factory where people began getting ill because their gloves weren't protecting them from the chemicals they were using, though the factory said it was nonsense. But Father has never liked our factory much and is always in a bad mood when he comes home, unless Mike is with him.

I got up and went along the landing. When I got to the bottom of the stairs, I stopped to tie up my shoe. And that was when I heard Mike say: "Doug's a bad lot. I'd keep out of his way if you can help it. I know it's easier said than done."

Someone moved a chair and Father said something I didn't catch, then Mike said: "Aye, I heard about that."

Father put something on the Rayburn. "Jim and Doug go to the Social together. They're like that."

"Aye. Well," Mike said, "I'd say something."

"It's cutting the hours that's done it," said Father. "It's getting to some of them."

"Extra meetings for the union."

Father said: "The union's a joke."

Then Mike said: "It might be a joke, but if they do strike I'm not looking forward to it." He sighed. "If it wasn't this it would be something else. They'll get this sorted and something else'll pop up; it's like molehills."

Father said: "I didn't read my contract properly," and I could tell he was smiling.

Then they were quiet, and I went to the door and opened it and Mike said: "Top of the morning to you!" which is what he always says even when it's evening. And I said: "How're the hens laying?" which is what I always say back.

He said: "What have you been up to, Fred?"

I thought for a minute and then said: "Making things."

Mike said: "Good for you. Why did the chicken cross the road four hundred and seventy-eight times?"

"I don't know."

"Because his suspenders were stuck to the lamppost."

"Good one," I said. I sat at the table and peeled a tangerine.

They went on talking, but not about the factory. After a minute I said: "What's a bad lot?"

Mike looked at Father, then he said: "A bad lot is someone you should stay away from."

I put a piece of the tangerine in my mouth. "What's the union?"

Father said: "Judith, don't you know better than to listen to other people's conversations?"

Mike laughed. "The union is a group of people that hang around with one another."

"Oh," I said. I thought about Gemma and Rhian and Keri, and Neil and Gareth and Lee. I knew about gangs. "Why is it a joke?"

Father shook his head and got up. Mike said: "I suppose they just aren't very good at what they do."

"What do they do?"

Mike said: "Talk about the third degree! Well, they organize things so that us workers get a fair deal; that's the theory anyway."

LATER, WHEN FATHER and I were having tea I said: "Why isn't the union any good?"

Father said: "You don't give up, do you?"

I was just about to ask again when he said: "The union's too disorganized to do anything."

"Oh."

He was eating quickly. I could see that a lump of potato was traveling down his throat. He said: "It's nothing for you to worry about."

"So why do they want to strike?"

"They don't think our hours should be cut."

"Should they?"

The muscles of Father's jaw and temple were moving up and down. "It's not important what I think, Judith. What's important is that we honor the civil authorities as God's representatives on earth. Jesus said: 'Pay Caesar's things to Caesar, God's things to God.'"

"But is cutting the hours unfair?"

"Jesus said: 'Turn the other cheek.' We have to leave things in God's hands," Father said. "Most things aren't worth getting wound up about. Most things are small stuff."

Smoothed my potato down. "Small stuff is important too," I said.

Father put down his knife. He said: "Are you playing with that food or eating it?"

I stopped mashing.

"Eating it," I said.

The Present

ON WEDNESDAY, NEIL Lewis put a worm in my curry and threw me in the bin and I had to bang till Mr. Potts, the caretaker, heard me. When Father saw my clothes, he was angry and said he had enough to do without this, but I didn't say anything about Neil, because I didn't want Father to have to go to the school. I just went up to my room and told a story in the Land of Decoration.

On Thursday, Neil pulled my chair from under me and tried to start a fire in the playground with my bag. When Father saw my bag he said: "Damn it, Judith, money doesn't grow on trees!" and I knew he was very angry because he had sworn. I went upstairs and played with the Land of Decoration and told a story about an umbrella that had a pattern of flamingos on it; if it had been opened, each flamingo would have taken flight, but it never was, because the little girl it belonged to loved it so much she didn't want it to get wet.

On Friday, I kept my head bowed over my work and didn't look up once, because if I had seen Neil I wouldn't have been able to hide how angry I was. And it was strange how I didn't remember being angry, only frightened, before I discovered my power, but now that I had, I was angrier than I had been my whole life and felt as though something was racing round inside me, like the Road Runner trying to get out.

Mr. Davies's face was the color of putty that morning. He adjusted his glasses and his hand shook. Sweat glistened on his forehead. At ten to eleven he banged on the desk, fumbled in the drawer for a bottle inside, and stood up. He said: "I'll be back in five minutes. Get on with your work quietly and remember: I'll be checking spelling and grammar!"

When he had gone, pandemonium broke out. I bent over my book and leaned my head on my hand. We were doing creative writing in our news books. I like creative writing, but the subject was "Presents" and was difficult for me to write about. The Brothers don't celebrate Christmas or birthdays, and Father didn't buy presents, because he said the world was full of materialism and we didn't have to add to it. I suppose I could have written about one of Josie's presents, but I didn't want to.

Gemma was saying: "I'm getting a pony for Christmas."

"I'm getting a trampoline," said Keri.

"I'm getting a pair of Rollerblades," said Rhian.

Then Gemma said: "You don't celebrate Christmas, do you?"

"No," I said, "because it's not Jesus's birthday. It's the birthday of the Roman sun god."

Rhian said: "You don't have birthdays either."

"No, because they were pagan celebrations, and on the only birthdays recorded in the Bible, people were beheaded."

Keri said: "You don't have television either."

"No," I said, "because when my mother and father got married, my father said: 'It's either me or the telly.' My mother made the wrong choice."

They didn't get the joke. They gave me the "weird" look, which is one eyebrow raised, chin drawn in, and a frown. Then Keri said: "You don't have a mother, do you?" And I said nothing.

Gemma said: "Anyway, Jesus *was* born on Christmas Day. Everyone knows that." And one turned her back on me and leaned on her arm and forced me over the edge of the desk.

But suddenly I knew what to write about: I would write about the snow. It was easily the best present I ever had, better than any Christmas or birthday present, and it was safe to write about too, because Father had only said I shouldn't talk about the miracles and no one would read my news book except Mr. Davies, who wrote *Good work* at the bottom of everything—once I wrote I would rather die than go to school and he wrote *Good work* at the bottom of that too.

I drew a margin with my ruler. I wrote the date. I closed my eyes and the noise of the classroom faded. I could hear the wind rising. I could feel the air getting colder. Whiteness was filling my eyes. Everything got darker.

I DON'T KNOW how long I had been writing when I felt something behind me. When I turned, Neil Lewis was standing there looking pleased, as if he had just found something he had forgotten about. He said: "What you doing, spaz?"

"Nothing," I said.

I opened the drawer to put my book away, but he was faster.

I grabbed at the book, but Neil held it higher. I grabbed at it again and he lifted it above my head. Then I sat very still and looked at my hands.

Neil found the page I had been writing on. He read in a loud voice: "*I had the best present I found out I have a gift it was magic it happened on Sunday I made it snow—*" He frowned. Then he laughed and shouted: "Oi! Everyone! Judith's got magic powers!"

There were hoots. There were shouts. They gathered around.

Neil began to read again. "*I made it snow I made it in my room I made it from cotton wool and sugar—*"

There was shouts.

"*God showed me how to make it—*"

There were hoots.

"*It was a mi-mir-a-mira-c-mira—there was no other ex-exp-expa-...*" Neil cleared his throat. "*...other explan-... explan-...*" Neil frowned. "*As we appro-appro- the con-conc-conclu- we must be vigi-...*" He was getting red. "*As we ap-ap-*

appro-appro- the con-conclusi- . . . we must be vigi- . . . we see an
inc-inc-incre- in sup-erna- occ-occu- . . ."

People were staring. Neil said: "What the *fuck?*" and he hurled
the book at my chest.

"Thank you!" I said, like it was all a big joke, but my hands were
shaking too much to open the drawer.

Neil's face was dark. He bent close to me and I saw again how
blue his eyes were. He said in a soft voice: "So you've got magic powers. So you made it snow."

I tried to smile, but the smile wobbled.

He came closer. His voice rose. "But you're scared really, aren't
you? You're scared now. You're shitting your little pants." His lip
curled. "The end of the world. Ooh. I'm scared."

There was laughter and shouting. Neil stood up and grinned.
Then he sauntered away. And as he did, something rose inside me. It
rushed down my arms and into my fingers. It crawled up my neck
and into my hair. I heard a voice say: "You will be." I think it was me.

Neil said: "What?"

Someone else said: "Oh my God."

I said: "You will be." And this time I knew I had spoken.

Neil's face was thickening with something, as if he had smelled
something foul, like when Gareth did one of his farts. He came
close to me and said in a low voice: "You are such a waste of space."
And all of the words were heavy and slow, as if they were too enormous to be spoken.

My head was too hot to think. It was too hot to see. I said: "At
least I can read."

For one second there was complete silence. Then someone
laughed. The sound bounced up as if released by a spring. It bub-
bled somewhere beneath the fluorescent strip light, then the silence
reached up and strangled it.

Neil's face was peculiar. It changed, then changed again as I
watched, as if something was passing through it. He said: "*You are
such a fucking loser.*"

I stood up and there was a roaring sound and my body was full of shaking blood. I said: "It's you that's the loser. You're the biggest loser I've ever met. Stay away from me, Neil Lewis, or you'll be sorry."

"What are you going to do?" someone shouted. "Turn him into a frog?"

"I might," I said. "If I want to." I looked at Neil and I said quietly: "I can do anything I like."

Then three things happened. Neil lunged forward, I stepped backward, and the door opened.

Mr. Davies said: "Why is everyone out of their seats?" Neil and I stared at each other. Mr. Davies said: "Perhaps you two didn't hear me!"

Neil walked over to his desk. Mr. Davies said: "*Thank* you."

I sat down, and I was glad to, because my legs didn't feel solid anymore.

Gemma said: "Oh my God."

Keri said: "He's going to kill you."

Rhian said: "Can you really do magic?"

I bent over my book. I tried to find my page. But two invisible strings were attached to my back. Whenever I moved, the strings moved too. When I turned, Neil was staring at me. And as I watched, he took a pencil in one hand and, without taking his eyes from me, snapped it.

A wave of heat rushed over me and I was falling. But I felt something else too. I felt my whole body pricking as if it was catching light, like it did when Brother Michaels told us about the mustard seed, like it did when I saw the snow.

And as I turned back to the front, I thought about the snow, of how it came softly at first, of how the flakes melted and left no trace. But how soon it covered roads and houses and wiped the town clean and flattened ditches and made the mountain disappear and shut down the factory and turned off the power and shouted from the page of every newspaper in black six-inch letters. Of how it came from nowhere, while I was sleeping, and turned the world white.

A Decision

WHEN I CAME out of school that afternoon, something happened that had never happened before. Neil and Lee and Gareth were waiting for me on bikes by the gate; they followed me all the way home.

I made myself walk slowly and didn't look round. When I turned into our street, they circled, and Neil rode so close to my feet that gravel sprayed up. They waited to see which house I went into, then they cycled away. I went upstairs and lay on the floor and stared at the ceiling.

I like the ceiling in my room. There are small stains and gray furry balls in the corner where spiders live that are like a little cluster of huts. There are old cobwebs that hang like tired party streamers. And there is a hot-air balloon lamp shade. My mother made the lamp shade. She liked making things too. When I look at the hot-air balloon, I think of her and I think of traveling somewhere and leaving this town behind. I was looking at it now, but for the first time I wasn't really seeing it. God, I said: "I wish I could do something."

"Like what?" said God, and I was so pleased He had spoken to me again. I had the feeling of fire along my back and my hair, as if someone had flicked a switch.

I sat up. "Well, what's the point of having this power if I don't use it?" I said.

"Your father said it was dangerous," said God.

"You use Your power."

"Yes," said God. "But I am the Almighty."

"I've only used my power for good things so far, haven't I?"

"Yes," said God. "So far . . ."

"But this was what I wanted it for in the first place," I said. And suddenly I was shaking. *"I hate him!"*

"Aren't you forgetting forgiveness?" said God.

"Yes."

We were quiet for a while.

Then God said: "Of course, there is another way. . . ."

"What?"

"There's the Old Testament as well, you know. Have you heard the saying 'an eye for an eye'?"

"That's the Law."

God said: "I see you've been paying attention. 'Soul will be for soul, eye for eye, tooth for tooth, hand for hand.' I got tired of being messed around, you see. If people hurt Me, I hurt them back. It's My Fundamental Law. But you don't need Me to tell you; you know all this."

"What are You saying?"

"That someone needs to be paid back," said God.

"Do You think so?"

God scratched His head—or it could have been His beard. I heard Him scratch something. "Yes," He said at last.

"Really?"

"Yes," said God. He sounded more certain. "Something has to be done."

"I'm so glad You agree!" I said. "But what about Father?"

"He doesn't believe you can do anything anyway," said God. "I wouldn't worry. What were you thinking of doing?"

"Oh, something little," I said. "Nothing much. To begin with."

"I like it," God said. "I like your style."

My heart began hammering. "And it will be OK?" I said.

"Of course," said God. "That is: I think so. As you said, it's a small thing. I can't see any problems with that. A taste of his own medicine will do the boy good."

"*Hooray!*" I jumped up.

"I'm just saying, I can't give you a guarantee it will all turn out as you expect."

"OK."

"So are you going ahead with it?"

"Yes!"

God laughed. "Then what are you waiting for?"

How to Make a Man

THIS IS HOW to make a man. You will need:

> mohair
> cotton
> umbrella/nylon fabric
> all-purpose glue
> modeling clay
> pipe cleaners
> paint (acrylic)
> Wite-Out
> toothpicks
> wool

1. Make shoes and shins and hands and arms and a head and neck from modeling clay using the toothpicks. Make holes in them for wire with the toothpick. Let the clay harden.
2. Glue pipe cleaners into the holes and bend them into a figure. The spine must be thin enough to bend but not thin enough to break.

3. Give the man a nose (upturned, in this case), two eyes (blue, for example), a mouth (big teeth), and whatever else you fancy (freckles).
4. Give the man mohair hair (yellow, cowlick). Give him a mood (a frown, tears).
5. Wrap wool around the pipe cleaners. Measure the wool, then cut it off.
6. Paint the man's shoes (or trainers). Give him trousers (or warm-up pants: black cotton and Wite-Out stripe). Give him a coat (or Puffa jacket: umbrella material).
7. Breathe into his lungs and stand him up.

A Knock at the Door

I PUT THE man I had made in the middle of a group of people. The people stood around and pointed. The man tried to break through the ring, but the people didn't let him. He walked around, but the people wouldn't let him pass. He sat down and put his hands over his ears. I felt better just looking at him. I had no idea what was going to happen yet, but whatever it was, I didn't think Neil Lewis was going to like it.

Then I wrote up my journal. When I heard the front door shut I hid it under the loose floorboard and ran downstairs. My legs felt like I had just run a race and my heart was beating in my ears.

THAT EVENING FATHER lit the fire in the front room, which meant he was in a good mood. The front room is where all of Mother's things are: the black piano with the gold candleholders, the Singer sewing machine with the pedal underneath, the three-piece suite she made white-and-pink covers for, the lupine and hollyhock curtains, the cushions she embroidered. I will be allowed to use Mother's sewing machine when I am older.

It was nice in the front room, like being in a boat. Dark and rain buffeted the windows but couldn't get in. The wind clamored and the waters rose higher and spray spattered the sides, but we were safe and dry. Father sipped his beer and poured me a lemonade and listened to Nigel Ogden while I lay on my belly in the half circle of firelight.

I was drawing the angel standing on the earth from the Book of Revelation who gave the apostle John the little scroll that was sweet and then bitter. That was what the old man in the dream said about the stone I had chosen, and I still didn't know what he meant. I wondered if it mattered whether the sweetness came first or the bitterness did and tried to remember which way round it had been but couldn't.

I liked Revelation. It was mostly about the end of the world and the last few chapters were about what it would be like afterward, in the Land of Decoration. "What will Armageddon be like?" I said.

"The biggest thing the world has ever seen," Father said, and his voice was calm and good-tempered. He was settled deep in the chair and his legs were stretched out.

I sat up on my knees. "Will there be thunder and lightning?"

"Perhaps."

"Earthquakes?"

"Maybe."

"Hailstones and balls of fire rolling down streets?"

"God will use whatever He sees fit."

"But it's strange though, isn't it?" I said. "Killing all those people . . ."

"Not really," Father said. "They will have been warned for years, remember."

"But what if one or two didn't get the message," I said, "and it couldn't be helped? Like—what if they didn't listen because someone had told them not to? Would God let them off?"

I looked at my drawing. The angel's face was stern. Muscles bulged from his arms. He didn't look like he would let anyone off.

"God can read hearts, Judith," Father said. "We have to leave these things to Him." I felt better when I remembered that and went back to drawing the angel.

When I had finished, I showed it to Father. The angel had blue eyes and hair like the sun. He had one foot on Egypt and one foot on Algeria. "There's the Great Rift Valley," I said, in case Father missed it.

Father said: "Very good." Then he said: "Why are both the angel's feet on the land?"

"What?"

"One of his feet is supposed to be in the sea."

"Is it?"

I turned to Revelation, Chapter 10. Father was right. But if I colored over Algeria with blue, then it would end up purple and it would be the wrong shape. I said: "Does it matter a lot?" But I knew that it did, because the angel wasn't just a parable but symbolic, which meant it had a larger significance, like Prefiguration, and even the smallest detail had much bigger meaning. So I picked up the eraser. And then our letter box crashed. Three short bangs.

Father went to the door. He opened it, but I didn't hear any voices.

"Who was it?" I said when he came back.

"No one." He put some more wood on the fire and took a sip of beer.

"No one?"

"No."

"Oh," I said.

I began to erase the angel's foot, but the drawing underneath just got messy.

I sighed. "Maybe the angel moved around a bit. Maybe his foot got cold in the sea." And as I spoke, the letter box crashed again, three short bangs.

This time, just before Father opened the front door, I heard the gate click and laughter. I peered through the curtains but couldn't see anyone.

When he came back I said: "Who was it?"

"Boys playing games." He put more wood on the fire.

"Oh," I said.

Father was being very calm but I knew he was angry; he hated people knocking on the door hard or even slamming it, because the door had a beautiful picture of a tree in the colored glass, which Mother had restored. He often commented on how pretty it was.

I took a new piece of paper and drew the angel's head. I didn't want to think anymore about what Father had said, I had just begun coloring the face when the letter box crashed again.

This time Father went to the back door. I heard a shout and the sound of running feet, then the garden gate clicked.

A minute later Father came into the front room, laughing. He said: "I surprised them!"

"Who?"

"The kids."

A wave of heat passed over my body. "What were they doing?"

"Making nuisances of themselves."

"Have they gone?"

"Yes. They ran off when they saw me. They didn't expect me to come up the lane."

I looked down at the angel. "What did the kids look like?" I said.

"Boys. No older than you, I should think. One had blond hair. Big kid. D'you know anyone like that?"

I had felt hot but now I felt cold. The angel's blue eyes looked back at me. "No," I said. "I don't know anyone like that at all."

Sunday

SOME THINGS EVEN miracle workers can't get out of. Today I discovered Josie has knitted me a poncho.

May said: "No, it's a shawl."

"No, no," said Elsie. "It's a poncho."

"Orange with shells and tassels," said May.

"Were they shells?" said Elsie. "I thought they were pearls."

"Shells," said May. "The small ones you can thread."

"Anyway, she's looking for you," said May.

"Aren't you lucky?" said Elsie.

I spent the rest of the time before the meeting hiding in the toilets.

ALF GAVE THE talk. His tongue was in fine form, flickering at the corners of his mouth. "What is God asking us to *do*, Brothers?" he said. He glared around, his face red, his eyes bulging. After half an hour it made my head ache to listen to him, but it could have been the fumes coming from Auntie Nel; they were stronger than usual this morning. Even the yellow plastic roses were looking the worse for wear.

Alf's voice got louder. His arms thrashed. I thought he was going to get them tangled in the microphone cable. "What is God asking us to *do*?" he repeated. When he said it a third time I couldn't bear it any longer and stuck up my hand and said: "Fill in our report cards?" because this is usually the right answer. But everyone laughed. Father explained afterward that Alf was asking what is called a rhetorical question, which is just meant to hang there and no one is supposed to answer.

Alf said I was right—of course, God did want us to fill in our report cards, but He also wanted us to have faith.

I pushed my nail into the side of my Bible. *I* had faith. More than anyone knew. I'd made things happen they couldn't even imagine. If they knew, they wouldn't laugh at me. If they knew, they would be amazed.

I couldn't help thinking it was strange no one had noticed I was God's Instrument. I'd expected it to be showing by now. I decided that I would ask Uncle Stan for Brother Michaels's address. I was sure *he* would take me seriously.

AFTER THE MEETING, I went up to Uncle Stan and tapped him on the arm. I said: "I wondered if you could give me Brother Michaels's address. Or his phone number."

"Brother Michaels?"

"Yes."

"Why's that, pet?"

"I need to tell him about the mustard seed and how a miracle happened."

He smiled. "Right you are."

"What?"

"Well, I'll get it for you."

"Oh . . ."

"Remind me if I don't bring it next meeting," Stan said. He began putting papers in his bag.

Perhaps he hadn't heard what I had said. "Uncle Stan," I said, "I made a miracle happen! I made it snow!"

"Did you?" he said.

I said: "What do you mean, 'Did you?'" The heat was coming back.

"Judith . . ." he said, and put a hand on my head.

"I'm not making it up!" I said. "I wasn't going to tell you, but then it just slipped out—that's why I need Brother Michaels's address. This is serious. I need to know what to do next. With my power."

"Well, I'm sure Brother Michaels will be able to advise you, sweetheart," said Uncle Stan. "Now I've got to see Alf about something . . ."

But he needn't have worried; I saw a bright pink hat with peach feathers coming toward us. Josie was scanning the room.

"I have to go too," I said, and slipped to the end of the row. It looked like if Josie didn't get hold of me soon, she would send out a posse.

The Fifth Miracle

WHEN I WALKED into the classroom on Monday, a woman was standing by Mr. Davies's desk. It was difficult to know how old she was, because she was quite small, but I thought she must have been about Father's age. She had red hair pushed back with a hair band and round glasses and small hands that looked raw. Her hands were as red as her hair. I liked her hair. I thought how good it would be to make it for one of my little people. I would use bright orange wool and tease the strands apart.

The woman was trying to open the drawer and the whole thing was moving forward. "You have to bang the top," I said.

"Oh." She frowned, banged hard, and the drawer slid open. She beamed at me. "Thanks. Who are you?"

"Judith."

"I'm Mrs. Pierce," she said. "I've come to replace Mr. Davies for the time being."

"Oh," I said. "What's happened to him?"

"He's not very well. But he's going to be fine." She smiled again. She had very small teeth, and at either side one of the top teeth lay sideways so that the edges stuck out. I liked Mrs. Pierce's teeth. I liked her voice too. It reminded me of green apples.

She said: "Don't you go to assembly, Judith?"

"No. I have to stay separate from the World."

"Oh," said Mrs. Pierce. She blinked. "What's wrong with it?"

"It's a Den of Iniquity," I said.

Mrs. Pierce looked at me more closely, then she sniffed and said: "Well, you're not missing much." She banged the desk again and the drawer shot out and caught her elbow. She closed her eyes and said something under her breath. Out loud she said: "This will take some getting used to." At that moment the door opened and everyone came in.

They stared at Mrs. Pierce. She sat on top of Mr. Davies's desk and crossed her legs. "Good morning, class eight," she said. "My name is Mrs. Pierce. I'll be looking after you for a while."

"Where's Mr. Davies?" said Anna.

"He's not well," said Mrs. Pierce. "But I'm sure he'll be better soon. In the meantime we're going to have to get used to one another. I have my own way of doing things, so there'll be a few changes around here."

There was scuffling at the back of the room. A second paper airplane hit my head. On it was written *LOSER*. Mrs. Pierce sniffed and reached for the attendance book. "For a start," she said, "we'll have you three boys—yes, you—sitting at the front. Would you mind telling me your names please?"

"Matthew, James, and Stephen, Miss," said Neil.

Mrs. Pierce smiled. "Fortunately, Mr. Williams has drawn me a seating plan; it wouldn't be Gareth, Lee, and Neil, would it?"

"Yes, Miss," said Matthew. "I'm Matthew, and that's James, and that's Stephen."

Mrs. Pierce jumped off the desk. "Come on, boys." She began to move two tables together. "On your feet!"

"I can't, Miss," said Neil.

"Why is that?"

"I can't find my bag, Miss."

"Oh," said Mrs. Pierce. "When did you lose it?"

"Don't know, Miss," said Neil. A smile slunk across his face. There was laughter.

"Well, you can still come and sit here," said Mrs. Pierce.

Neil pretended to be caught on the chair and tugged this way and that at his coat. "Oh dear," said Mrs. Pierce. "It is difficult standing up, isn't it? Can someone give Neil a hand?" Everyone laughed again but this time with Mrs. Pierce.

Neil freed himself from the table and swaggered to the front. Mrs. Pierce held out a chair and he sat down backward, looking at the class. Everyone laughed again.

Mrs. Pierce smiled. "You're quite a comedian, aren't you, Mr. Lewis? There's just one problem. You're in my class now and I don't have time for jokes. Now, would you get your books out? You see, we are waiting for you to begin."

Neil rubbed his head. "I can't, Miss."

"Why is that?"

"Lost them, Miss."

"Your books?"

"Yes, Miss."

"What, all of them?"

"Yes, Miss."

"Do you often lose things, Neil?"

"Don't know, Miss."

There was more laughter.

Mrs. Pierce walked to the back of the room and pulled a bag out of the corner. "They wouldn't be in your bag, would they?"

"No, Miss. That's not my bag." Neil turned to Lee and grinned.

"Oh," said Mrs. Pierce. "Well, in that case, I shall keep this bag and its contents until the owner claims it. In the meantime, I will expect you to replace the books and equipment you need by the end of the week." She threw Neil's bag into the art cupboard, slammed the door, turned the key, and pocketed it.

Neil said: "Hey!"

"Yes?"

Neil scowled and turned to the front again. He shoved the desk. "I don't want to sit in this crappy seat!"

"Cheer up, Neil," Mrs. Pierce said. "This way you can see the blackboard more easily."

I laughed out loud. I put my hand over my mouth, but it was too late. Neil turned round and his eyes flashed. But for some reason, instead of looking away I looked right back.

"Well, now that's sorted out," Mrs. Pierce said, "let's get on with our lessons. We're going to be reading poetry today."

"*Poetry?*" Gemma said.

"That's right, Gemma," Mrs. Pierce said. "Nothing wakes you up like a good poem. That's because poets never say exactly what they mean—or not the best ones. Instead they find other ways of saying it. They paint a picture or they talk about it as if it were something else. We use pictures in everyday speech too—for instance, we say 'the leg of a table,' 'a sunny disposition,' 'I wouldn't bank on it,' 'an icy stare,' 'boiling hot.' "

She wrote the phrases up on the blackboard. "See if you can spot how many pictures this poem uses to describe the sun: It's by Robert Louis Stevenson and it's called 'Winter-Time':

Late lies the wintry sun a-bed
A frosty, fiery sleepy-head;
Blinks but an hour or two; and then,
A blood-red orange, sets again. . . .

"So," said Mrs. Pierce when she had finished reading, "did anyone spot the pictures?"

"Yes," said Anna. "The sun in bed."

"Good. And how does that help us understand what the poet is trying to say?"

"Because the sun gets up later in the winter," said Anna.

"Good," said Mrs. Pierce. "Yes. There's less daylight. Anything else?"

"The sun is a blood orange," said Matthew.

"Great," said Mrs. Pierce. "And why is that applicable?"

"Because of the color."

"Yes," said Mrs. Pierce. "Have you noticed how much redder the sun can be in the winter? There are brighter sunsets too. Anything else?"

"The wind like pepper," said Rhian.

"Yes," said Mrs. Pierce. "Now, that's strange. Why do you think the poet wrote that?"

"Because it hurts your nose in the cold?" Rhian said.

"Yes. Excellent," said Mrs. Pierce. "I can see this class is full of budding poets! The wind also tickles sometimes too, have you noticed that? And I suppose the poet could even be referring to hail. Now do you see how the pictures make the poem richer, more interesting?"

"There's the picture of his breath like frost," said Stephen.

"Yes, the patterns his breath makes in the air are like the patterns the frost leaves." Mrs. Pierce smiled. "There's one more picture the poet uses to help us see more clearly."

"The land frosted like a wedding cake," said Luke.

"Excellent," said Mrs. Pierce. "And how does that help us see more clearly what the poet is saying?"

"Because the snow is like icing sugar," said Luke.

"Yes," said Mrs. Pierce. "Or it could be frost. Sometimes frost is very heavy and as thick as snow." She turned to the blackboard and wrote up each phrase. "Now"—she turned back to us—"does anyone know what those pictures the poet uses are called?"

She waited, then picked up a piece of chalk and turned back to the words on the board.

"Metaphor," said Gemma. She looked at me and smiled.

"Well done!" said Mrs. Pierce. "Yes. Metaphor is when we talk about something as if it was something else. Can anyone give me another example of a metaphor?"

"A leap of faith," I said. I looked at Gemma.

"Excellent!" said Mrs. Pierce. "Though that might be a little bit difficult to explain: Faith is believing in something. To say faith is like a leap is to say it's like stepping into thin air, to leap from one place to another without getting hurt. Is that how you would describe it, Judith?"

I nodded.

"OK," she said. "But in fact, going back to our poem, only four of the five 'pictures' Robert Louis Stevenson uses are metaphors; the last picture, the one where the poet compares the wintry landscape to an iced cake, is in fact a 'simile.'" She wrote the word "simile" on the blackboard. "Can anyone see the difference between the metaphors and the simile?" said Mrs. Pierce.

I stared at the poem. I didn't see what Mrs. Pierce was getting at. And then suddenly I did. I put up my hand.

"Yes, Judith."

"The land is *like* a wedding cake," I said. "It isn't one."

"Indeed," said Mrs. Pierce. "Can you explain that to us, Judith?"

"The sun is in bed; it *is* a blood orange; the wind is pepper. But the land is only *like* a wedding cake."

I felt Gemma's eyes on me.

Mrs. Pierce's cheeks were quite pink. "Did everyone get that?" she said. "A simile says something is 'like' something else. But a metaphor says something really 'is' the thing you are comparing it to. So, we have similes and metaphors, both pictures, both interesting ways of saying things. But"—and now her voice became quieter—"one is stronger than the other; one is much more powerful. Which one do you think it is?" She raised her eyebrows encouragingly. "Don't worry, I wouldn't expect you to know this."

Was one more powerful? I wondered. The similes and the metaphors seemed to be the same. But I looked again and there was something about the line that said the sun was a blood orange that was missing from the line that said it was like a wedding cake. And then I knew why: It didn't sound as good.

Mrs. Pierce beamed when she saw my hand. She said: "Yes, Judith."

"The metaphor is stronger," I said.

"Why do you say that?"

I flushed. Now I looked stupid, as if I had guessed. I hadn't; I just couldn't explain why I knew for certain.

I could feel Gemma looking at me. Neil too. But it was no use; I couldn't explain. Mrs. Pierce turned back to the board.

"There's a clue in the word. 'Metaphor' is made up of two Greek words: *meta*, which means 'between,' and *phero*, meaning 'to carry.' So metaphors *carry* meaning from one word to another."

And then I remembered something someone had said: that it wasn't enough to imagine what the new world would be like, we had to be there. It was Brother Michaels. He said faith could do that for us. "Because we're there," I said suddenly, without putting my hand up. Everyone turned to look at me. I flushed. "I mean, *it's* there. I mean—it's not side by side." My cheeks were hot. "Metaphor isn't imagining, it's the thing itself."

Mrs. Pierce's eyes were so sharp they should have hurt, but they didn't. They were like a current of electricity passing from her to me, and the current flared and warmed me.

"Yes," she said at last. "The words aren't talking *about* something; they become the thing itself." She put down the chalk, and we looked at each other for a moment, and it was as if I was flying. Then the moment passed and she dusted off her hands and said: "Right, class, I'd like you to write poems using metaphor."

LATER THAT MORNING, while Mrs. Pierce was organizing the stationery cupboard, a ball of paper landed beside Gemma's elbow. I didn't know how the paper had got there, but I saw Gemma's hand close over it. She kept the paper underneath her hand for a minute, then unrolled it. She giggled and drew something, rolled it up again, and flicked it to Neil Lewis. Neil opened it and grinned. He passed the paper to Lee, and Lee's shoulders shook. Lee passed it to Gareth.

Mrs. Pierce looked up. She said: "Is something funny? If there is, I am sure the whole class would like to hear it."

Everything was quiet for a minute or two, then the paper shot back to our table. This time Gemma squeaked she was trying so hard not to laugh. She wrote something, rolled it up, and flicked it back to Neil. Neil then wrote something and flicked it back. Gemma slapped her hand down on the paper too loudly and Mrs. Pierce put her hands on her hips. She said: "Whatever is going on over there had better stop!"

Nothing happened for four whole minutes. Then Neil flicked the paper to Gemma. The paper shot wide and landed by my feet.

Mrs. Pierce put down the tubes of paint she was holding. She said: "Pick up that piece of paper. Yes, you, Judith! Read it out please."

I picked up the paper and unrolled it. What I saw didn't make sense. At the top was the word "METAPHOR." Beneath it was a picture of a girl kneeling in front of a man. Something was coming out of the man's trousers. It looked like a snake. A wave of heat passed over me and after the wave sickness. At the bottom of the picture there were four words. One of them was my name.

"Go on," Mrs. Pierce said. "Read it out."

I looked at her.

"Read it, Judith!" she said. "I won't have any secrets in my class!"

"*Judith gives good head,*" I said.

A breath rippled through the class.

Mrs. Pierce looked like someone had slapped her. She walked up to me and took the paper. "Sit down, Judith," she said quietly. Then she went to her desk.

"All right," she said brightly. "Let's get these fractions marked. Who can start us off with the answer to number one?"

Strike

"HOW WAS SCHOOL?" Father said when he got in.

"We've got a new teacher," I said. "She read us poetry."

"Good," Father said. He filled the kettle.

"She read out a poem about winter."

"Did she now?" He put the lid on the kettle and switched it on.

"And we talked about metaphor."

"Good."

"Then we all wrote poems and Mrs. Pierce liked mine."

"Good," said Father. "That's good." He placed both hands flat on the worktop and looked at them. Then he said: "Judith, I'll be coming home later next week. A bus is bringing me and it might take a bit longer."

"A bus?"

"Yes." Father took his hands off the worktop. "They're striking."

"But you're still going to go to work?"

"Of course." He got potatoes from the box under the sink.

"Caesar's things to Caesar, God's things to God."

"But why do you have to be brought home in a bus?"

"All the people who aren't striking are going to go to work in a bus," Father said. He ran the tap.

"Why?"

Father turned the tap off the wrong way, and the water came out in a spurt. He began to wash the potatoes. "Well, some people think we shouldn't be working," he said. "And they want to stop us."

"Stop you?"

"Yes, Judith! Look, I'm just telling you so you don't wonder why I may be a bit late."

I knew he wanted me to stop asking questions but I also knew there was something he was hiding. I said: "What do you mean 'stop us'?"

Father said: "I just mean—Look, it's no big deal, OK? It's nothing for you to worry about."

"OK." I looked at Father. "Aren't you afraid?"

Father put down the potato peeler and looked at the taps. He said: "No, Judith. There's nothing to be afraid of; the strike will be over in a week or two and everything will be back to normal."

"Is Doug striking?"

Father said quietly: "You've got a memory like an elephant," then more loudly: "Yes, Doug is striking."

I looked at Father and knew I couldn't ask any more. I wandered to the windowsill. "Nothing is happening to these mustard seeds," I said. "Do you think it's because I don't believe they will grow?"

"No, Judith," Father said. "It's probably because you don't know how to grow mustard seeds."

THAT NIGHT, THE Bible reading was about the Harlot sitting on the waters. Father said the waters prefigured rulers and nations and the Harlot was causing civil unrest. "Like the strike?" I said.

"Well," Father said, "it's all part of the sign of the end."

And then the door crashed. Three short bangs like before. Father went out and I heard a shout in the street. He didn't come back for twenty minutes.

When he did, he was panting and his face was shining as if he'd been laughing. He said it was the same boys as the other night. He had chased them down the hill. He caught the blond boy at the top of the multistory car park. Father said: "He was saying: 'Don't hurt me, don't hurt me, mister!' As if I would hurt him! I frightened him though. He lost one of his shoes."

"What did you do to him?"

"I just told him to clear off," he said. Father shook his head and laughed. "I don't think we'll have any more trouble."

Neil Lewis Learns a Lesson

THE NEXT DAY, while the others were in assembly, I asked Mrs. Pierce what the note meant. Mrs. Pierce turned over some papers on her desk. Then she said: "It didn't mean anything, Judith. It was nonsense."

I said: "It must have meant something."

"Do you know who wrote it?"

"I think it was Neil . . . and Gemma."

Mrs. Pierce nodded. "I thought as much." She sighed, then she smiled at me. "How would you feel if we moved you from that table?"

"I'd like that."

It was strange sitting with Anna and Stephen and Matthew. No one whispered or giggled or looked sideways at me. No one whispered or pushed my arm or hid my pen or took up all the space or threw things at my head or dropped things in my hair. I wondered why Mr. Davies had never moved me.

Neil came in late that morning, carrying a plastic bag over his shoulder. His feet made a funny sound on the floor, and when I looked down I saw that he was wearing a pair of daps like we wear for PE, except they were too big for him. "Neil Lewis," said Mrs. Pierce, "where are your shoes?"

Neil said: "Shoes are for wankers."

Mrs. Pierce said: "One hundred lines."

"What the fuck?" said Neil.

"Three hundred lines," said Mrs. Pierce.

Neil opened his mouth.

Mrs. Pierce said: "I asked you a question: Where are your shoes?"

Neil sat down and threw his bag under the table. His face was dark red. "Lost them."

Mrs. Pierce said: "You lost your bag yesterday; today it's your shoes. Have you replaced the books you lost yet?"

Neil frowned so much, his eyebrows hid his eyes. Suddenly he said: "*My dad gave me a right bollocking 'cause of you!* You got no right to take my bag!"

"Oh, so it *was* your bag," said Mrs. Pierce.

Neil's face grew purple. He said: "My dad's going to come and see you!"

"Is that supposed to scare me?" said Mrs. Pierce.

Neil's leg jigged up and down. He seemed to be thinking of something.

Mrs. Pierce sighed, got up, and sat in her usual place on the edge of her desk. "Now, what do you normally do on a Tuesday morning, class eight?" she said.

"Grammar," said Hugh.

"Well, from now on we'll be doing Art." There were murmurs of surprise. "Gather round, everyone."

She held up a postcard. In the postcard there was a café lit with yellow light. There were lamps in the ceiling and the lamps looked like little planets. The lines in the painting were warped, as if they had been painted by someone who was drunk, but Mrs. Pierce said the interesting thing was that the man who painted it could draw perfectly well. He had painted this way deliberately, to heighten "the emotional charge" of the picture.

Then she told us all about how pictures could make us happy or sad, comfortable or uncomfortable, excited or sleepy. She said pictures, like poems, were charged with electricity. There was laughter. Mrs. Pierce said: "Well, pictures make us feel emotions. Emotions are just electricity. How does the picture make you feel?"

"It makes me feel seasick," said Gemma.

Mrs. Pierce looked at Gemma. She pursed her lips: "You're quite an artist yourself, aren't you, Miss Butler?"

Gemma said: "What?"

"Yes," said Mrs. Pierce. "I saw an example of your artwork yesterday. Tell me, do you often draw your classmates?"

Gemma flushed. "I don't know what you mean, Miss."

"I think you do," said Mrs. Pierce. "But perhaps the picture I saw was a joint masterpiece—with Mr. Lewis. Is that right?"

Neil scowled.

"I expect you both thought it was quite amusing, though I'm afraid I didn't. And your grasp of human anatomy was sadly lacking." Mrs. Pierce picked up a ruler and got down from the desk. "Would you like to know where your picture is now?" She said a little more loudly: "I *said:* Would you like to know where your picture is now?" Then there was a crack like a whip and Neil jumped. He wasn't slouched over his desk anymore.

Neil had turned red. "Mr. Lewis!" said Mrs. Pierce. "I asked you a question." Neil folded his arms and stared at the desk, but his chest was rising and falling.

Mrs. Pierce began walking again. "The picture is in a safe place," she said. "Where it will stay until I decide what to do with it—and what to do with the people who drew it." She frowned and put her hand to her chin. "Perhaps," she said, "I should include it in the work I show to parents on parents' evening. It would make interesting viewing, don't you think?"

Gemma's eyes were filling. She said: "I don't know what you're talking about, Miss!"

"A liar too," Mrs. Pierce said. "Well. It takes all sorts. Doesn't it,

Mr. Lewis? Yes," she said as she walked back to her desk, "it takes all sorts." Suddenly she sounded tired. "All right, everybody, let's get painting."

I painted the field I had seen in the dream. But instead of me and the old man in the field, I painted the first two people I had made for the Land of Decoration—the pipe-cleaner doll with the green sweater and the fabric doll with dungarees. Mrs. Pierce said: "That looks interesting." I told her it was and that it was something I had made. "Really?" she said. "Out of what?"

"Rubbish," I said, and I told her about the Land of Decoration.

Mrs. Pierce said: "And who are these two people meant to be?"

"Father and me," I said. I hadn't known this before but saw now that was who they were. I said: "We're going to be there one day. When the earth is a paradise."

"A paradise?" she said.

"Yes. After Armageddon."

She said: "You really will have to tell me more about all of this, Judith. It sounds fascinating."

I was very happy for the rest of the morning. When I had finished, Anna and I went up to the sink to rinse our brushes. I was swilling out the jar when I turned to see Neil beside me. He said: "Still got magic powers?" And then he put his mouth close to my ear. "You're going to need them."

He turned, and as he did he knocked the jar out of my hands, splashing yellow water on my skirt and tights. "Oh. *Sorry,*" he said. "I must have slipped." He grinned. "You'd think you would have grown out of wetting yourself by now."

Neil went back to his seat. I saw him nudge Lee and Gareth. Lee said: "Judith's wet herself, Miss."

Mrs. Pierce looked up. "Judith, what happened?"

Neil mouthed: "I'll kill you." I looked back at Mrs. Pierce.

"Judith?" she said.

Neil made furious chopping motions with his hands.

"Neil threw water over me," I said suddenly. It was easy.

Neil stared at me.

"Yes, Miss," said Anna. "I saw him."

"Well, well," said Mrs. Pierce in a flat voice. "Why am I not surprised? Judith, go to the nurse and get some dry clothes. Neil, you seem to have some sort of problem with Judith. What is it? Can you tell me?"

WHEN I CAME back to class twenty minutes later, something was strange. I knew it as soon as I closed the door. It was as if something had landed in the middle of the room and no one could look at it. Mrs. Pierce was walking up and down between the desks with a bright, hard look on her face, and everyone had their heads bent over their books. I sat down and then I saw what the strange thing was. Neil wasn't in his seat. He was sitting with his back to us at a desk at the front of the room that hadn't been there before.

He stayed there for the rest of the day, as still as a stone. I wondered if he could tell I was looking at him, that everyone was now and then. I think he could, and whether or not it was because of him not being with us, or because Mrs. Pierce was on the warpath, everyone was quieter.

When it was time to go home, Mrs. Pierce said: "Neil Lewis, where do you think you're going? We have an appointment, remember?"

Neil's shoulders dropped. He said: "Oh, Miss, I've got boxing! My dad'll kill me if I miss it!"

Mrs. Pierce said: "That's too bad; you should have thought of that before you swore in my classroom."

"But, Miss!"

"No buts," Mrs. Pierce said. "Get your exercise book out."

She went to the board and in large chalk letters wrote: *I will not use foul language in Mrs. Pierce's classroom.*

Neil stared at her. Then he threw his plastic bag down, flung himself into his chair, and slapped his exercise book on the desk.

"Three hundred lines. No mistakes," I heard Mrs. Pierce say as I went down the corridor.

"YOU LOOK LIKE you've just won the lottery," said Sue as she crossed me over the road.

"I've won something better than the lottery," I said. I ran the rest of the way home. "It's working!" I said, and I jumped up and punched the air. "It's working!—And it's better than I imagined!"

"How was school?" Father asked when he got in.

"Great!" I said.

Father raised his eyebrows. "Wonders will never cease," he said.

More Knocking

AFTER I HAD gone to bed on Saturday night, the knocking began
again. Father went out, but the boys had gone away by the time he
got to the door. He went to the door four more times, but the boys
kept running away. I watched from the window. When the letter
box crashed a sixth time, Father went into the street, and Neil Lewis
and Lee and Gareth and some other boys rode round him on bikes.

When Father came inside, I stayed awake for ages but I didn't
hear him come to bed. The boys ran sticks along the railings and
threw stones at the windows. They laughed and did wheelies in the
road. "Why is this happening, God?" I said. But God didn't answer.

The next day, in the meeting, Father turned the scriptures in
little jerks with his thumb and first finger. His head looked shiny
and hot, as if there was too much blood in it. Uncle Stan gave the
talk about being separate from the world. He said that the Brothers
who were not striking merited the congregation's support and that
we shouldn't give funds to the strikers. He said: "Our leader is Christ,
not men." A prayer was said for the safety of the factory workers, and
Stan said we must have faith that God would help and we should not
be afraid. Being afraid was just like faith, he said, but it attracted bad
things instead of good. "If we're fearful, we're praying for the wrong
things," he said.

Afterward, everyone went to look at the new tracts we had been sent from headquarters. "It's a new initiative," said Alf. "We'll use them next week." Uncle Stan said we should preach in the main street.

I tugged at his sleeve. "Can I talk to you?"

I took his hand and led him to the side. I said: "I made another miracle happen. I wanted to punish someone. But something unexpected is happening."

Uncle Stan shook his head. He said: "What is all this miracle business? I'm glad things are looking up for you, pet, but does your dad know you're going around talking like this?"

I said that Father had said something to me, he had said it was nonsense but I thought that Uncle Stan would believe me.

"I do believe you, Judith," he said. His face looked kind and tired at the same time. "At least, I think *you* think you've made something happen."

I wondered whether to tell him about God speaking to me. I suddenly felt I couldn't bear it a moment longer if no one knew. And then something strange happened. I heard God say: "DON'T," very clearly. And it was peculiar, as if a bit of my brain had split off from the rest.

Uncle Stan frowned. "Are you all right?"

"Yes—"

"Are you sure?"

I put my hand over my eyes. "Yes," I said and made myself smile at him.

Uncle Stan said: "Oh, by the way, love, I wanted to ask you if your dad was all right. With the strike and everything, it must be pretty difficult at the moment. We're all thinking about him, but he never talks much. Is he OK?"

"Yes," I said. "But he's annoyed about the knocking at the door."

"What?"

"There are some boys knocking at our front door."

Uncle Stan frowned. "Your dad hasn't said anything about that. Nothing serious, is it?"

"I don't know," I said. "It's what I was trying to tell you, about what I did to the—"

And then God said: "STOP!" so loudly that I jumped.

"What's the matter?" said Stan.

And then I jumped again, because another voice said: "All right?" and I looked up and there was Father.

He and Stan began to talk and I slipped away. When I looked back, Uncle Stan had his hand on Father's back. I hoped he didn't tell Father I'd been talking about miracles. Then I jumped a third time, because two fat arms grabbed me and a voice said: *"Got-cha!"*

A whiskery face with a mouth like a slash and creamy bits of spit in the corners was grinning. "You've been avoiding me!"

"No, Josie! Honest!"

"Hmm." She eyed me suspiciously, then shoved a parcel into my arms. "Present!"

"Thank you."

"Well: Open it!"

"A poncho," I said.

There were more shells, there were more tassels, it was more orange than I could have imagined.

Josie's body shook with laughter. "Well, I know how you like these little things. I'm so busy making things for this one and that one, but I always find time to make you something extra special. Try it on! It should fit, but I made it a bit big to be on the safe side."

The fringe brushed my ankles. "Just right," I said.

"Why are you taking it off?"

"Keeping it for best."

I looked back to where Father and Uncle Stan were talking. Uncle Stan was talking and Father was looking serious.

"I want to see you wearing it next Sunday," she said.

"OK."

"Come on, cheer up!" she said. "Don't you like it?"

I looked back to Father and Uncle Stan and they were laughing. Suddenly the world was brighter. "Yes," I said, "I do. Thanks, Josie, I like it a lot."

One Good Thought

THAT NIGHT THE letter box crashed again. I know that's what it
was because as I woke I heard the boys laughing and the gate spring
shut. I got up and stood by the side of the window and looked
through the curtains. I couldn't see much without moving them, so
I slipped into the other front bedroom.

Neil and Lee and Gareth were down below, with Neil's brother
Tom, who I sometimes saw at the school gates, and some older boys I
had never seen before. When Father opened the door, they rode away.
But they came back about five minutes later. One of the older boys was
swigging from a can; the others were doing wheelies on their bikes and
spitting on the ground. The phone rang in the hall, and I heard Father
come out of the kitchen and the door slam behind him. The phone
stopped, and then I heard him say: "Mrs. Pew!"

"Yes," he said. "Thank you. I'm dealing with it."

He said: "Everything is being taken care of, Mrs. Pew. Please
don't worry."

I was cold then, so I went to bed.

When the boys came back they shouted: "Where's the witch?"
through the letter-box slot and threw chippings at the upstairs windows. I felt the noise in my chest like a shower of red-hot pellets,
and I wondered if this is what it felt like to be shot. I couldn't lie

there, because my body was on fire and I was shaking, so I got out my journal and wrote. But the noise went on so I put the journal away and sat against the wall. I sat there for a long time, until it was quiet in the street, until the hall clock struck twelve. Then I got up and opened the curtains.

It was very still and very bright. The full moon cast long black shadows from the houses and trees in the Land of Decoration. The shadows stretched right across the floor. I wondered what they reminded me of, and then I remembered that the graveyard in town looked like that when shadows fell from the headstones.

"God," I said quietly, "why is this happening?"

"Well," said God, "to Neil it looks like you're the cause of all his problems at the moment."

"I can't help it if Mrs. Pierce doesn't like him," I said. "What should I do?"

"I don't know."

"You're God!" I said.

"But you got yourself into this."

"*You* did," I said.

"No," said God. "It was you."

"But I've only done what You told me to do."

"You've done what you *wanted* to do."

"It's the same thing," I said.

"What?" said God.

"I don't know!" I said. I began to feel hot. "I don't know why I said that."

I didn't want to talk to God anymore, I didn't want to be in my room anymore, I was afraid the cloud would come over me again like it did the day I made the snow, so I went to the door, but when I got there I couldn't go out, and I sat back down. After a minute I went to the door again and this time I went down the stairs.

Halfway down, I screamed.

A figure was standing in the hall. The figure whirled round and Father's voice said: "*What the—*"

"You frightened me."

"What are you doing up?"

"Nothing. I—I didn't want to be in my room."

He turned back to the front door. He looked like a boy with the moonlight catching the back of his head.

I couldn't see any reason for him to be standing in the hall, so I said: "Are you all right?"

"Yes."

I suddenly wanted to say something to him very badly, but I didn't know what. "Don't worry about the boys," I said.

"I'm not worried!" He turned and his eyes flashed.

"Good," I said. "I was just checking."

"Everything's under control!"

"OK."

"They won't be back tonight anyway." He sniffed loudly and put his hands in his pockets as if that settled it, but he continued to stand there.

I said: "Are you sure you're all right?"

"I'm fine! You're the one who's all bothered! You should be asleep! What are you doing up?"

"I don't know."

"Well, get back to bed."

"OK."

AFTER A WHILE the boys came back. I heard Father go out. He stood in the street and they rode around him, calling him names and spitting at him.

At last he came back in. I heard him open the front-room curtains and saw the light stream across the road. I heard a creak and knew Father had sat down in one of the wicker chairs. I didn't understand what he was doing. Then I heard him begin to whistle, and I knew he was thinking good thoughts. The boys hung around for a while and then they went away.

My Perfect Day

FATHER SAYS WE should never underestimate the power our thoughts have to help us. He says that all we need is One Good Thought to save the day. I have a few good thoughts. These are some of them:

1) that the world is about to end,
2) that everything is actually quite small,
3) that I am in the Land of Decoration, having my perfect day.

The last is the best thought of all.

I HOPE THAT there are still things from this world left over in the Land of Decoration, because I am very fond of some of them. If I could have all of my favorite things in one day, that day would be perfect, and this is how it would be.

To begin with, there would be Father and Mother and me. I know Mother will be in the Land of Decoration, because God has promised to bring the dead back to life if they were faithful, and Mother is dead, and she is the most faithful person I know. They still talk about her in the congregation, about what an example she set, about how she died, about how she trusted. Margaret still has a dress Mother made for her, and Josie has a shawl.

I've tried so many times to imagine meeting Mother, but all I have are odds and ends. I know, for instance, that she had brown hair and eyes like me. I know she smiled a lot, because she is smiling in most of our photos. I know that she liked making things. But after that I have to use my imagination.

In my perfect day, it would be one of those days when you wake up to sunshine, with nothing to do and all the time in the world to do it in. This day would be like a bubble floating past your window. It would be like opening your hand and it landing right in your palm, the light touching it the way it does, so that only the surface seems to be spinning and the inside of the bubble is perfectly still.

The day would begin with Mother and Father and me having breakfast, and as we ate I would tell Mother all about my life in this world and how I had been looking forward to seeing her, and she would tell me what it was like to be dead and how she had been looking forward to seeing me. Then I would show her the things I have made with the things she left, and she would shake her head as if she couldn't believe it, she would hug me, and then we would go outside.

It would be one of those days when everything shimmers and the world is made up of jostling pieces of light. The air would be warm and smell of summer and the hedges would be filled with cow parsley and butterflies. There would be dandelion clocks and crane flies and dragonflies darting and stopping quite still in the air. There would be a field leading down to a river with grass long enough to wade through and a few flowers and some trees, and in the distance maybe the sea. Mother would take one of my hands and Father would take the other, and it would be difficult to believe it was really happening, because I had imagined it so often, but I would have to believe it because it would be true.

We would go walking in the field. There would be lots of different sorts of grass, and the grass would get inside our shoes and the cuffs of our trousers and inside our socks. And there would be a shaggy dog with one ear up and one ear down and he would bounce ahead of us. He would race ahead, and on this most perfect of days I would be able to whistle and bring him back.

But Father doesn't approve of dogs because he says they carry germs, so we would keep the dog away from him.

Then my mother would point and over the way there would be a Ferris wheel and music. But Father doesn't approve of Ferris wheels and fairgrounds, because they are dangerous and they are a Waste of Money, so Mother and I would go alone.

We would ride on the dodgems and shoot down the slide. And when we came home, there would be fish and chips for tea, and the chips would be fluffy and squidgy, and the fish would fall apart in moist flakes, and the batter would crunch when you bit it and then it would ooze, and Mother and I would eat with our fingers. But Father doesn't approve of fish and chips, so for him I guess there would be bitter greens or something.

And there would be television. This might seem a strange thing to have in paradise, but I like television. Father says television is softening to the brain, but he needn't watch it, Mother and I could, when the stars came out, in a gypsy caravan which would be our home now, with blankets pulled over us and a fire crackling outside and sausages on sticks and black-currant punch. And I have forgotten the main thing! Which would happen earlier: There would be a hot-air balloon.

One summer day when Father and I were in the back garden, a balloon came over. It was like a creature from the deep sea. I saw the shadow pass over, I heard the flaring, and I wanted to go where those people were going so much.

Yes, there would definitely be a hot-air balloon and we would take a ride. Or perhaps just Mother and I would, because Father doesn't approve of hot-air balloons either. He says they're dangerous and if anything happened to you in one of them there would be No Chance. He means if it exploded in the air, you would get fried or plunge to your death. But I think the feeling of flying would be worth the risk.

I DON'T KNOW what Father's perfect day would be like. I expect it would be full of Necessary Things like Bible study and preaching and pondering and Saving Electricity and Being Quiet and Wasting Not Wanting. In which case he has his perfect day all the time.

Or perhaps his idea of a perfect day vanished a long time ago and he has forgotten how to imagine a new one.

Neil Lewis Gets Angry

ON MONDAY NEIL looked at me and whispered a word which sounded like "blunt." Mrs. Pierce looked up as he turned round. She said: "Neil, if you would like Judith to help you with your arithmetic, you can ask her. You don't need to whisper." Then Neil looked as if he would like to murder someone. He bent his head over his desk.

Mrs. Pierce said: "*Do* you need help, Neil?"

Neil's fist tightened on his pen.

Mrs. Pierce said: "I'm sorry, Neil. I didn't hear you. Was that a 'yes'?"

Neil flung down the pen.

"Don't be embarrassed, Neil," said Mrs. Pierce. "No one is going to laugh if you are struggling. Would you like some help?"

Neil sat up so suddenly, the chair screeched on the floor.

"All right," said Mrs. Pierce. "Then you've no need to bother Judith, have you?" She raised an eyebrow at me, then went back to her marking.

Everything was quiet for about fifteen minutes, then something whizzed past my head and clattered to the floor.

Mrs. Pierce looked up. "What was that?"

"A ruler, Miss," said Anna.

"Whose is it?" Mrs. Pierce said.

Lee spluttered: "Neil lost it, Miss!"

"Judith took it!" Gareth said.

Lee said: "She can do magic, Miss." There were guffaws and giggling.

Mrs. Pierce turned to me. "Judith, did you take Neil's ruler?"

"No, Miss."

"What is your ruler doing by Judith's desk, Neil?"

"I don't know, Miss," said Neil.

"You can't remember why you left your ruler there?"

Neil scratched his head and looked round. Everyone laughed.

Mrs. Pierce said: "Really, Neil, I'm getting quite worried about you. On Monday you lost your bag. On Tuesday you told me you had lost your shoes. This morning you can't remember where you left the ruler you were using a few seconds ago. If this goes on, you should think about seeing a doctor."

Everyone laughed again and Neil scowled. "Pick up your ruler, Neil," said Mrs. Pierce. Neil came to the table and picked up the ruler. As he straightened he looked at me and his eyes were sleepy and slow, full of something I couldn't name.

AT LUNCHTIME I walked around the edges of the buildings, looking for things for the Land of Decoration. I collected five different weeds, three wrappers, two can tops, a straw, and half a plastic Kinder egg case, in which I planted the weeds. I showed them to Mrs. Pierce because she was on playground duty. "Are these for the model world in your room?" she said, and I nodded.

"I'd love to see the things you've made," she said. "Could you bring some in for me?" I said I would. Then I went to the toilets to water the weeds.

I was leaning over the sink when I heard a slippery sound, looked up, and saw a black jacket in the mirror. I didn't have time to see any more, because hands were dragging me toward the toilets and my legs were scrabbling on the floor. Someone said: "See if God can help you now, bitch!" My head knocked against the toilet bowl; my nose was burning, and water was filling it.

Then I was falling backward, and Mrs. Pierce was holding Neil by the back of his jacket and her voice was shaking, but I didn't think it was because she was afraid. She said to me: "Go to Mr. Williams, Judith, and tell him exactly what happened."

When I got back to the classroom, Mrs. Pierce and Neil were standing opposite each other. Mrs. Pierce was shouting: "*What makes you think you're different from everyone else? What makes you think you can get away with this sort of behavior?*"

Neil said: "I didn't do anything to her!"

Mrs. Pierce shouted: "Good *God*, boy! *I saw you!*"

I sat down.

"There's not one good thing I can say about you, Neil Lewis," Mrs. Pierce was saying. "Not one! And to top it all you are an incorrigible liar. Right now I don't know what to do with you! I don't even want to look at you!"

Neil picked up his coat and walked toward the door. He said: "I'm not staying in this fucking dump."

Then something happened to Mrs. Pierce. She was in front of Neil, blocking his way, her glasses were flashing, her cheeks two bright pink spots. I suddenly saw how small Mrs. Pierce was. Neil was almost as tall as her. I thought he was going to hit Mrs. Pierce, because his fists were clenched. Then I thought Mrs. Pierce was going to hit Neil, because her chest was rising and falling. And as I watched them, something seemed to be happening to me too, because my heart was beating so hard I was floating and something was flowing out of me as if there was a leak.

Nobody moved for what seemed the longest time. Then something, somewhere, snapped. The strings holding Neil were cut; Mrs. Pierce set her chin a little higher. It was difficult to say what changed exactly, but we all felt it. Mrs. Pierce said: *"Get!"* and

Neil went to his desk. He put his hands over his ears and he didn't look up.

And something about the way everyone was looking at him, something about the way he drew in his head and curled up, reminded me of something I had seen somewhere else, though just then I was too tired to remember what it was.

In the Classroom

AT HOME TIME Mrs. Pierce said: "Would you wait behind a minute, Judith, please?" so I sat at my desk while everyone trooped out, and after a little while the classroom was quiet.

Mrs. Pierce shut the door. Then she came to my table and sat down beside me. She said: "I'm sorry about what happened today. If it's any consolation, I think things are going to change quite a bit around here, so you won't have to worry about that sort of thing anymore."

I said: "They've changed a lot already."

Mrs. Pierce inhaled. She said: "And high time they did." Then she said: "Judith, there was just something I wanted to ask you. You see, something I overheard Neil say today in the toilets puzzled me—something about God helping you? At least that's what it sounded like. Perhaps I'm wrong. . . ."

I heard God say: "Be careful. Be very careful."

"Don't worry," I told Him.

"I don't remember," I said out loud.

Mrs. Pierce frowned. She said: "I thought I heard him say: 'See if God can help you now'—or words to that effect." She smiled. "I only mention it because it reminded me of something I read in your news book, about God making it snow. Is that right?"

"Get out of there," said God.

"But Mrs. Pierce is my friend," I said.

"I'm your friend," said God. "And I'm telling you to get out."

"I have to answer her," I said to God.

I said to Mrs. Pierce: "Yes, I did make snow in my model world. And then it really did snow. But it was just a coincidence. God didn't make it happen."

"Oh," said Mrs. Pierce. "I thought you wrote that a miracle had happened."

God said: *"Get out right now!"*

My hands felt slippery.

Mrs. Pierce said: "How did Neil know God 'helped' you, Judith?"

I looked down. "Neil read my news book."

"Ah," said Mrs. Pierce. "Then I *did* read it there."

"But it's all made up!" I said. "It's just imaginary. I'm a good storyteller."

"You are," said Mrs. Pierce. "Well." She smiled and folded her hands in her lap. "That explains that."

"Yes."

I thought she had finished, but then she said: "Judith, there was just one more thing. There was a conversation with God in your news book. It was so lifelike I wondered whether you ever heard voices or chatted to people—in your imagination, of course."

"Why are you still there?" shouted God.

"No," I said. "I mean yes. Sometimes!"

Mrs. Pierce bent her head so that she could see my face. "And is that person God?"

"GO!" shouted God.

I rubbed my hands back and forth over my knees. "Yes," I said to Mrs. Pierce. "But that's pretend too."

Mrs. Pierce's voice was very soft now. "What about seeing things, Judith? Do you ever see things other people don't, things that are invisible? Do you ever see things you can't explain?"

12

God shouted: *"She is going to ruin everything!"* and His voice was so loud it sort of flattened me and it took me a minute to feel three-dimensional again.

I heard Mrs. Pierce saying: "Judith, are you all right?"

She was saying something else too but I couldn't hear her, because it was like being turned round and round.

I heard Mrs. Pierce say: "It's all right, Judith, it's all right; let's stop talking about this. I didn't mean to make you uncomfortable. I was just interested, that's all."

Then God said: "GET OUT." And His voice was so deep and so strange I wondered if it was God at all, and it frightened me so much that I began to cry.

Mrs. Pierce said: "Judith! What's the matter?"

I walked to the door but I couldn't go out. Instead, I stood there, staring at the handle and it was as if my body was one big heart. I said: "I've never seen anything invisible, but I do believe in God. And sometimes I talk to Him," and it was as if the words were the burning coals the angel touched to Isaiah's lips, and saying them was like stepping off a cliff. There was a rush of heat and my blood frothed up inside me. But once I had said them I was glad, because Mrs. Pierce smiled, as if she had been hoping I would say something like this all along and knew I would manage it eventually.

She came up to me and said quietly: "Does talking to God make you unhappy, Judith?"

I opened my mouth and closed it again. I looked down at my shoes. "I don't know," I said.

"All right," said Mrs. Pierce. "Sometimes it's difficult to know what we feel, isn't it?" She put her hand on my shoulder. "You're a very special person, Judith, I want you to remember that. I also want you to remember that if ever you need to talk about anything—anything at all—you can come to me and talk to me in the confidence that whatever you tell me won't go any further. And though

I might not understand, I'll do everything in my power to help you."

* * *

God was silent as I walked home. It was like being in a room with someone you weren't talking to, but I couldn't go out of the room because it was my own head. In the end I couldn't bear it. I said: "Why were You acting so strangely? Mrs. Pierce is our friend."

"*I'm* your friend," said God.

"She was just being kind," I said. "She wants to help us."

"If you carry on blurting things out, there won't be any 'us,'" said God. "You'll be on your own. Don't you know how dangerous it is telling people everything like that? They'll try to separate us. They'll tell you you're not talking to anyone at all. They'll tell you you're imagining it and send you to some sort of doctor."

"I wouldn't listen if they did," I said. "*I* know what's real. I didn't tell Mrs. Pierce anything anyway."

"You told her far too much," said God. "Listen, young lady: Your power depends on you doing exactly what I tell you. That's the deal. You won't get far without Me."

"I'm sorry!" I said. "I'll try to be more careful. But I don't understand: You weren't like this when I talked to Father or Uncle Stan."

"That was different," said God. "I didn't foresee any problems with them."

"Father didn't believe me at all!"

"Precisely," said God. "I mean—more fool him." He coughed. "Listen," He said. "If that teacher tries to talk to you again—"

"Don't worry," I said. "I won't say a word."

Then I remembered something. "Oh, and God," I said, "please don't ever use that strange voice again."

"WHAT, THIS ONE?" said God, and it was like being wiped out in a flash of light.

"STOP IT!" I shouted out loud, and I put my hands over my ears.

"Sorry," said God in His normal voice. "Better?"

I leaned up against the railings. A woman on the opposite side of the road was staring at me. I felt like crying. "Was that really You?"

"Who did it sound like?" said God.

I shuddered. "The Devil," I said.

Trouble Begets Trouble

FATHER CAME HOME late from work that evening. I knew he was going to, but it seemed an awfully long time anyway. I peeled the vegetables for dinner and put them in the saucepan. I set the table and I watered my mustard seeds. Though I didn't know why I was bothering, as there was still nothing to be seen. Then I wrote in my journal and I told a story in the Land of Decoration about a dragon who loved roses and whenever he passed a rose tree would have to stop and sniff it but his breath charred the flowers. I couldn't finish it. In the end I just sat on the stairs and waited.

At five to six I heard the bus and ran to the front door. Through the stained-glass picture I could see the bus. It had grates on the windows, and some were slipping off. A tomato was caught in one and what looked like egg was smeared on the window. There were six men on board. Father came down the steps, and even through the colored glass I could see how pale he looked under the streetlight. He waved to Mike, then came through the gate and I ran into the kitchen; I didn't think he would have wanted me to see.

Father switched the kettle on. He said: "How was school?" He didn't look at me but began lighting the fire in the Rayburn. I knew then that I mustn't ask about work. I said: "Mrs. Pierce got cross with Neil Lewis because he tried to put my head down the toilet. But I don't think I'll have any more trouble with him."

Then Father did look at me. He said: "Are you all right?"

"Oh yes," I said. "It was nothing."

Father frowned. He said: "Is Neil Doug's son?"

I tried to think quickly. "I don't know," I said.

"Were you having trouble with him?"

"Sort of—but not anymore."

Father said suddenly: "That's not the kid who knocks on the door, is it?"

I looked at him and then at the fridge. "I don't know," I said.

Father straightened up. "Judith, you haven't been aggravating him in any way, have you?"

"No," I said, and my heart beat once, very hard.

"Are you sure?" Father said.

"Yes."

"Good," Father said; he turned back to the fire, "because trouble only begets trouble." He stood up and closed the Rayburn door to a crack to let the air in. "And there's more than enough of it to go round now lately."

WE READ THE Bible while we had tea instead of clearing the table first. The study was about God being jealous. It wasn't the way we thought of the word, Father said. It meant that God wanted people to serve only Him, that He exacted Exclusive Devotion.

My head was all tangled. I didn't know if I was being stupid or asking a proper question, but I said: "Why must God have Exclusive Devotion?"

"Because He knows what's best for us," said Father.

I thought again, but for some reason what Father said still didn't make much sense. I said: "Why?"

Father didn't get angry as he usually does if I say "why" too much. In fact, it looked as though he was thinking about something else. He was frowning and holding his breath. And then suddenly the frown went away and he blinked and said: "What?"

Then I, too, had to think to remember what we were talking about. "Why does God know best?" I said.

"Because He knows everything," Father said. And then he said quickly: "And He made us"—as if I should know this—as if *he* should know this—as if he should have thought of it before. Then he said: "Hang on," and got up and went into the hall. When he came back, I said: "What is it?"

"Nothing."

I looked at him, but he didn't say any more, and he began to read again.

When I went to bed, Father was sitting by the Rayburn in his overalls. After I had been in bed a little while, I crept back downstairs. But the kitchen light wasn't on, the middle room one was, and through the keyhole I saw Father at his desk, sifting through bills he kept there. I was pleased he wasn't staring at nothing like he used to and went back to bed.

But later, quite a lot later, when I was just dropping off to sleep, I heard the front door open, and when I peeped through the curtains he was standing on the pavement, the wisps of his hair catching the light. He stood there for a long time, though the street was empty.

Four Photographs

FATHER IS NOT the person he used to be. I know this because of four photographs. The first is in the album in the cupboard in the middle room. In the cupboard photo, Father is standing against a sign that says JOHN O'GROATS. He has jeans on and a belt that says LEVI'S and a T-shirt. He is smiling and his whole face seems to be shining. I have never seen Father's face like that. This was taken on Mother and Father's honeymoon, and Mother was taking the photo.

The second photo is in a silver frame and is a photograph of Mother and Father lying in grass. Mother is wearing blue dungarees and has long, curly brown hair, and the sun is in her eyes and all around her so that her hair looks like a halo. She is laughing so hard, all her teeth are showing. Father is holding the camera above them at arm's length and making a funny face.

The third photo is in the album again, and they got someone to take the picture for them and are standing on a pier against some railings. Mother's tummy is stretching her T-shirt; she has her arms around Father's waist and her head on his shoulder, and he has his arm around her neck, and both are smiling and look as if they have caught the sun, and their hair looks like it has been blown all day long in the wind.

I don't look at these photos often, because it feels so bad. It isn't just knowing Mother isn't here now but knowing she isn't here because of me.

The last photo is the worst of all. It's in another album and is quite different. Father is holding me in a white blanket. I am bound up like a little grub and all you can see is my face, which is crumpled and red because I am screaming. In the bed behind us is my mother. Her face is white and her eyes look very small and she seems to be in another place altogether, looking back at us. Father's face is dark and his eyes are blazing. And this is the Father I know.

The Snowball Effect

THAT WEEK FATHER came home at six o'clock on the bus every day. It was strange being in the house on my own. I didn't think it would be much different from when Father was there, because I am in my room and he is in his, but it was. May and Elsie offered to come and sit with me, but I asked Father not to let them, because it would be Bible stories all the way, and in the end he agreed, on the condition I didn't touch the cooker, the matches, or the kettle.

Father was gray when he got in. Sometimes he didn't cook the vegetables I had prepared but ate things like sausages and beans. Sometimes he didn't even light the fire in the Rayburn but sat by the oven with the range on till bedtime. But no matter how tired he was, he always made sure we read the Bible portion.

I wished Mike could have stopped by. "Why doesn't he?" I asked.

"He has to get home," Father said.

I didn't like to ask about the factory. Father didn't say much except that there were lines of people called picketers at the gates and they shouted and never went away. "It'll be over soon," he said. "I'll give them another week."

But the strike people seemed to think it would last. On Tuesday after school, Mrs. Pew invited me round for tea. While we were eating corned beef sandwiches and macaroons at her foldaway table, some people knocked at the door. I heard Mrs. Pew open it and a man say they were calling on everyone, warning against failure to support the union and contact with something called "scabs." He told Mrs. Pew to hang up if a scab tried to call, not to talk to them.

Mrs. Pew waited till he stopped talking, which was quite a while, then said: "I'm sorry?"

There was a pause, then the man said everything again and asked Mrs. Pew if she would like to make a donation for hungry strikers.

Mrs. Pew said: "Country bikers?"

"Hungry strikers."

"Yes, I thought that's what you said," said Mrs. Pew. "I'll get some money right away."

She got some change from the jar on the sideboard. I heard her give the man some money and close the door. "A biking event," she said as she came back into the sitting room. "I do like to give to a good cause. My husband, the late Mr. Pew, God rest his soul, was an ardent cyclist."

"WHAT'S A 'SCAB'?" I said to Father when I got home.

"Where did you hear that?"

"Someone knocked on Mrs. Pew's door, wanting money for the strikers, and told her not to talk to scabs."

"A scab is someone who's not supporting the strike."

"Then *you're* a scab," I said. "Why do they call them that? It's a funny name."

Later that evening, I was coming down the stairs when the letter box crashed and a water balloon fell through the slot and burst on the floor. I heard the squealing of bikes. I picked up the balloon. It wasn't colored like a balloon I'd ever seen but clear. It was a different shape than a balloon too, longer, like a tube and the hole was too big to blow through. Father came into the hall from the bathroom, without his shirt on and with a towel round his neck.

He said: "Drop that!"

I stared at him.

"Drop it!" he said. "Go and wash your hands!"

On Wednesday someone tipped the dustbin up and strewed rubbish all over the garden. On Thursday, Neil and his brother snapped some branches off Mother's cherry tree, and Father sat up till after midnight. On Friday night when the knocking began, he phoned the police. I heard him say: "Can't you just send a car up or something? It's getting beyond a joke. I'll be had up for assault if I go out there and do anything. . . . No, I don't know what started it."

Later, when I was in bed, a police car came down the street. I heard it stop outside and the policeman talk to the boys. After that it was quiet, and when I looked they had gone away.

"God," I said, "what's happening? Why won't Neil Lewis leave us alone?"

"Something to do with the fact that he has been getting into trouble in school every day because of you?" said God.

"Not *because* of me," I said. "Because of what he *does* to me."

"Swings and roundabouts," said God.

"It's not fair!" I said. "I didn't know any of this would happen. How could I know he would start coming to the house?"

"Not easy, is it?" said God.

"No. I've solved one problem and found another one."

"That's life," said God. "Things disappear and reappear some-where else. You stamp on them here and they come up over there. Like molehills. Now you know what it feels like."

"What?"

"Being Me."

"I thought I could say just what I wanted to happen."

"Yes, but can you *stop* things happening?" said God. "Did you think about that?" God laughed. "Thinking is a dangerous thing at the best of times."

"But what's going to happen?" I said. "With Neil and everything?"

"I don't think it would be helpful for you to know at the moment," said God. "In any case, it depends on you."

* * *

IT WAS STRANGE that Neil kept coming to the house, because he didn't come near me in school. He didn't tell me he would kill me and he didn't draw his finger across his throat and he didn't hit me or put my head down the toilet or pull away my chair. He wasn't doing a lot of the things he used to do. Mrs. Pierce made him move to Kevin and Stacey and Luke's table so he didn't sit with Lee and Gareth anymore, but so often when I looked up, his blue eyes were fixed on me, and they were strange, as if he wasn't seeing me at all but something on the other side of me.

Mrs. Pierce kept him in detention four times that week. At home time, when he'd hoist his bag onto his shoulder, she would say: "Neil, where are you going?"

"Home, Miss."

"I thought you and I had an appointment."

"My dad'll kill me if I'm late again."

Mrs. Pierce would say: "It's no fun for me either, you know, so the sooner you learn how to behave, the better for both of us. Sit down and get your books out."

Neil didn't follow me home once that week, but some of the other boys rode their bikes past me very fast and yelled swear words. On the following Wednesday, when I came out of school, I had seen a man with a shaved head and denim jacket waiting by the school gates. He was covered in tattoos. His arms were folded and his chin jutted out and his mouth was set in a tight line. As I went by, he opened the side of his mouth and a jet of saliva landed on the pavement.

"Sue," I said, as Sue Lollipop crossed me over the road, "who's that man with the shaved head?"

"That's Doug Lewis," she said in a low voice. "He's on the war-path about something."

So now I had a face to put to the "bad lot."

On Thursday Doug was there again, huddled up against the wind. This time he was smoking. And as I went by, I noticed something I had missed before: On the backs of his hands, writhing to and fro and over and under one another, were lots of green snakes.

What Happened in the Co-op

ON SATURDAY WE went preaching in town with the new leaflets. We stood in the main street opposite the Baptist church and Margaret held a placard that said: CAN YOU READ THE SIGNS? on one side and CHRIST DIED FOR YOU on the other. Uncle Stan had a loudspeaker, and Father and Alf wore boards over their jackets with THE END OF ALL THINGS HAS DRAWN CLOSE on them. Nel insisted on having a placard too, so we propped it up against her wheelchair, even though you couldn't see her over the top of it. The rest of us gave out leaflets.

It was very cold. Sun winked in each of the shop windows. A market seller said: "Go and proclaim the gospel somewhere else," but Uncle Stan said we had as much right to be there as anyone else, and after that it was a contest between us and the market seller as to who could shout the loudest.

Twice someone shouted: "Scab!" and a few spat on the ground as they passed us. Uncle Stan flushed but carried on shouting, and Margaret thrust her chest out and held the placard higher. Gordon's neck was deep in his collar, his eyes were half closed, and he was chewing hard.

Only two people took a leaflet, even though I held them as Father said to and didn't obscure them with my hand, and even though we employed thought-provoking questions. On the cover of the leaflet,

happy people were walking through a garden. Inside, there were lightning and hailstones, buildings falling, and cars disappearing. People
were shaking their fists at the sky. Some had their hands raised to protect themselves. The men wore headbands and tattoos and lots of
denim. Some had transistor radios. The women had miniskirts and
lots of makeup and high heels. It made me confused to look at the
picture because all the Brothers looked like the happy people, and not
everyone in the World carried a transistor or wore a miniskirt; Auntie
Jo, Father's sister, for instance, wore jeans and Dr. Martens in the
photos she had posted to us, and Mrs. Pierce didn't wear makeup.

At midday Uncle Stan said: "A good effort." He didn't seem to
notice we had as many boxes of leaflets as before. We carried them
back to his car near the dumpsters behind the Co-op, then Father
and I said goodbye to the group and we went into the Station Café
for a cup of tea.

We divided an ice slice between us. I licked the icing off my fingers and said: "Do you really think Armageddon's coming soon?"

"Yes," said Father.

"D'you think Mike will be saved?"

"Only God knows the answer to that."

"What about Mrs. Pew?"

"I've no idea."

"What about Joe and Mrs. Browning and Sue Lollipop?"

"Judith, it's useless speculating about these things. Only God
can read hearts."

"What about Auntie Jo?" I said, and I didn't look at him.

Father brought his hand down on the table. Then he said: "Judith,
you've asked this before—how do I know? Everyone will have had
a fair chance."

"How do we know?" I said.

"Because God has promised He will save everyone who deserves
to be saved."

"I'm glad I'm not God," I said, and I smiled at Father to show
him I didn't want to annoy him and wanted to be friends.

"So am I," said Father.

I laughed. "I wouldn't know who to save and who not to."

He smiled, but the smile was watery and tired. I thought it was better not to smile at someone than to smile like that. We finished and went to the Co-op.

We were pushing our cart to the checkout a few minutes later when two men appeared. They looked like they had just stepped out of the picture in the leaflet—it would have been quite funny if I hadn't been so scared. One had long hair and a headband, though he wasn't carrying a transistor. The other man was Doug Lewis.

The men's eyes gleamed like marbles. They reminded me of the eyes of the dog from number 29 when he sees Oscar on a wall. Doug jutted his chin. He seemed to be nodding. He put his hands on the front of the cart and said: "Scabs eat, I see."

Father's eyes were black, but when he spoke his voice was steady. He said: "Go and wait for me at the checkout, Judith," but my feet wouldn't move.

Father said: "Let me get on with my shopping, Doug. I'm not hurting you."

But Doug didn't take his hands off the cart. His face was red. He and Father looked at each other, and they kept on and on looking at each other until I wanted to scream. Then suddenly Doug shoved our cart sideways. It bounced, but Father didn't let go. Doug's chest rose and fell. The man with the long hair put his fist into his hand. Then he said to Doug: "Come on." Doug's nostrils flared. After a minute he slammed the cart sideways and followed his friend.

We walked to the till. My heart felt as if it had been plunged into hot lead, and my arms and legs were falling away from me. Father didn't seem to realize what had just happened. He began putting things onto the conveyor belt. Then he looked up and said: "All right, everyone, the show's over," and I saw that he did, and that the whole shop was watching us. To me he said: "Go and start packing," and I was glad, because I couldn't think what to do. Then he looked at me and smiled, a proper smile, but this time I couldn't smile back.

WE DIDN'T TALK about what happened for the rest of the day, and for the rest of the day my heart felt sick and my legs and arms didn't belong to me.

A Broken Window

"UNCLE STAN," I said at the meeting next morning, "have you got Brother Michaels's address?"

"Oh darn," said Stan. "Sorry, pet, I forgot. Keep reminding me."

"OK."

He said: "Are you all right?"

"Yes," I said. "I just really need to write to him."

"Look." Uncle Stan smiled. "I'll make a note." He took out a little piece of paper, wrote on it, then folded it up and put it under his wedding ring. "How's that?"

"Great," I said.

Uncle Stan frowned. "Are you sure you're all right, pet? How's everything at home?"

"Fine," I said. I couldn't tell him about what Doug Lewis had done yesterday. Father wouldn't want me to. In any case, what had happened felt like it was stuck in the middle of my chest and would hurt too much to pull out.

When we got home, I asked Father for a piece of his writing paper. "What for?" he said.

"To write to Brother Michaels."

"Who?"

"The Brother who came and gave the talk about moving mountains."

"Why on earth are you writing to him?"

"I liked him."

Father shook his head and went into the middle room. He took a piece of paper from his desk. "That's all you're having," he said. "So don't waste it."

I went upstairs. I thought I may as well begin the letter now, even if I didn't have an address yet. I wanted to talk to someone a lot. I wrote:

Dear Brother Michaels,

This is Judith McPherson, the girl you talked to after giving your talk about the mustard seed. You gave some to me, do you remember? I hope you are well.

I thought for a minute.

I am writing to thank you for coming to our congregation. Your talk changed my life. When I came home I made a miracle happen, and lots after that, but the first one was that night after you told us about faith. I made it snow by making snow for my model world. There is a world in my room made of rubbish. I made snow for it and then it really did snow, do you remember?

After that I made it snow again and then I made it stop snowing. Then I brought back our neighbor's cat and then I punished a boy at school. But now he is knocking at our house all the time and yesterday his dad threatened Father in the Co-op and called him a "scab."

I chewed the end of the pencil.

The police are not helping. Nobody believes I have done any miracles. I should say also that I have heard God's voice on numerous occasions.

"Cross that out," said God.

"I don't want to."

"It's dangerous," said God.

"But I've only got one piece of paper."

"Cross it out!"

I crossed the sentence out.

The thing is, now I don't know whether to try and make more miracles or not. Having power is not as easy as it looks.

You said that all we needed to do was take the first step, but now I don't know what to do next, and it doesn't look like I can go back to where I began.

Then Father shouted: "Dinner!" and I folded the letter up and put it inside my journal, put them both under the floorboard, and went downstairs.

A BIT LATER we were pondering the Fall of Man, which happened six thousand years ago—two thousand years from us to Jesus, Father said, and four thousand years from Jesus to Adam—and I was pondering the reason I had to eat bitter greens again and not saying anything at all. My face must have though, because Father said: "There are thousands of African children who would be only too glad of that dinner." I was about to say: "Then I wish we could send it to them," when we heard the sound of smashing in the hall.

Father said: "Stay here," and went out.

I didn't hear anything for so long that in the end I got up and went into the hall. The first thing that hit me was a gust of wind and rain. The second thing was that Father was standing with his back to me, and at his feet there were pieces of stained glass, in the midst of the glass was a brick, and where the stained-glass picture had been in the front door, there was a large hole. Beyond the hole was the night.

Father cleared his throat. He said: "Go back into the kitchen please."

I sat by the Rayburn and drew my knees up and put my chin on them. I said to God: "Please help Father."

In the hall I heard Father say: "I'd like to report a smashed window. . . . Yes . . . my front door . . . About five minutes ago . . . No, not now."

I peered into the Rayburn. The coals flickered and glimmered, but in the heart of them, where they were palest, they were perfectly still.

"I want someone here now," Father was saying. "I've reported other incidents and nothing's been done. . . . No, you listen. I've got a ten-year-old daughter—"

There were caverns in the fire. There were gullies and canyons and ravines. I imagined I was journeying to the center of the earth. Heat lapped at my cheeks. Heat sealed up my lips. I closed my eyes and heat bathed them.

Father went on talking. I went further into the fire. It was like being beautifully dead or asleep. My face began to sting, but I didn't move away. This was how a star felt, I thought, and what were stars but furnaces eating themselves up, then falling inward, getting redder and redder and cooler and cooler until nothing was left but a heap of gray ash?

A click told me Father had put the phone down. I pulled my chair back. When he came into the kitchen, you wouldn't have been able to tell from his voice that anything had happened. He said he was going to clean up this mess and then we would continue with our Bible reading.

He wouldn't let me help. I watched from the kitchen doorway as he pushed the glass into a dustpan. I watched him wrap it so the garbagemen wouldn't cut themselves. I watched him sweep the floor, then run his hand over it to see if there were any pieces he had missed. "Don't walk around in socks for a few weeks," he said.

"OK," I said. And then I looked up and screamed.

A face was peering through the hole in the front door, a wobbling white face with red lips and black hair and a plastic rain cap. Father jumped too. He said: "Mrs. Pew!"

"Oh, John! I saw it all!" Mrs. Pew said. She appeared to be dissolving. Small black snakes were making their way down her forehead, and her head was wobbling fantastically. "Three boys on bikes!"

"I know," said my Father. "I've spoken to the police. Everything's taken care of."

"One of them had a brick," she said. "How terrible! Why would they do such a thing?"

Father said: "I don't know, but don't worry now. You go back inside. It's too wet for you to be out here."

"Will you and Judith be all right?" she said as he took her arm.

When Father came back, he went to the garage and came in with pieces of plywood. One by one he nailed them to the front door. I couldn't bear to look, to see what he was doing to Mother's door. But I heard the wood splinter and squeak and the rain whip and the wind batter. Then finally the hole was boarded up and the hall was quiet again.

A policeman arrived as Father was drying the floor. He stood in our hallway and wrote in a notepad. Father waited for him to finish, his eyes glittering like two lumps of coal beneath the light.

The policeman said: "And you didn't see who did it?"

"No."

"All you found was the brick?"

"Yes."

"At approximately nineteen hundred hours?"

"Approximately."

The walkie-talkie on the policeman's shoulder burst into life and he said back to the crackling: "Yeah, all right, tell him to hang on. . . . No, just a domestic."

Father waited. The crackling petered out. He said: "So what are you going to do to them?"

The policeman said: "Who, Mr. McPherson?"

"The thugs who did this."

"You don't know who did it," said the policeman.

Father shut his eyes, then opened them. It seemed to me he was saying something without moving his lips. He said: "It's the same boys I've been making complaints about for the past month."

"But you didn't see them."

"On this occasion, no. I was in the kitchen with my daughter. We heard the crash, and when we got here they were gone."

"There you go," said the policeman. He put his notepad away.

"But our neighbor did see them."

The policeman said: "Could she identify them?"

A vein pulsed in Father's temple. "I don't know; why don't you ask her?"

The policeman said: "I'm trying to help you, Mr. McPherson. If I were you, I'd think about getting some cameras installed. A visual holds up well in court."

"Cameras?" Father gave a strange laugh.

The policeman said: "There's nothing we can do tonight. We'll keep this on file with the other complaints you've made. If anything else happens, you know where we are."

Father half-shook his head. He looked as though he was trying to get something out of it that had got loose. He said: "What—that's it?"

"All we can do is patrol the area now and then," said the policeman. "Good night, Mr. McPherson," and he went out, pulling our new door shut behind him.

I BIT MY lip. I could see the little hairs on the top of Father's head shining in the light. His arms hung by his sides. He scratched his eyebrow, then they went back to his sides again. He said: "Your mother loved that door."

I suddenly wanted to touch him.

"I'm sorry," I said. I was scared; Father never mentioned Mother.

He blinked as if he was waking. "Why are you sorry?"

Then he frowned and all the darkness came flooding back into his face. "It's nothing to do with you!" But the way he said it made it sound as if it had everything to do with me. He put the mop in the bucket, locked the door, picked up the bag of glass, and we went back into the kitchen.

And I ate all my bitter greens, every scrap, though they were cold now and slimy, so that Father would carry on pondering the Fall of Man that happened six thousand years ago and not the thing that happened forty-five minutes ago in our hall.

A Story

ONCE THERE WAS a man and a woman. When they met, sparks flew, meteors collided, asteroids turned cartwheels, and atoms split. He loved her from here to eternity, she loved him to the moon and back. They were two peas in a pod, heads and tails and noughts and crosses.

Something about her made him walk toward her. Something about him made her say hello. They got married in the town where they had grown up, and their families were so happy. Then someone knocked on their door and told them the world was ending. The man didn't know what to think to begin with, but the woman saw the light straightaway.

Believing meant giving things up; their families didn't want to know them anymore; they moved away, to another town where the need for preachers was great. They bought a small brick house. The man took work in a factory. The woman made dresses. The neighbors didn't like them. They didn't mind. They had each other.

They filled the house with things no one wanted: a door with a picture of a tree, a clock with no pendulum, a chaise longue with no springs, an old fur rug; a threadbare tapestry of creepers and snakes, a picture of angels; broken tiles of birds of paradise.

The woman took the paint off the door and cleaned the glass so that the tree could be seen and the light glinted in its fruit. They repaired the tapestry. They made a border for the fire with the broken tiles. The woman made curtains and covers from scraps of materials. The man dug up the concrete around the house and planted Christmas roses and golden cane and a cherry tree.

Sometimes I see them, her sitting opposite him in the evening in the armchair, her long hair on her shoulder, embroidering lupines and hollyhocks, wrapping silk around the needle and drawing it clean through the middle. Then I think they would be side by side and she would be mending something. Then I think, no, she would be at his feet while he read the Bible aloud. The woman is pregnant. The man is young. Every so often they smile at each other.

Then I stop imagining, because I don't want to see what comes next. But often, because I don't want to, I see precisely that.

A Bad Lot

ON MONDAY AFTERNOON, Mrs. Pierce was reading *Charlotte's Web* to us when the classroom door burst open and Doug Lewis appeared. A smell came into the room with him like rotten fruit, like the smell of Father's old wine bottles he keeps, for the bottle-recycling bank. Mrs. Pierce lowered her glasses. She said: "Can I help you?"

Doug said: "You can do more than that. I want my son! You kept him here every afternoon last fucking week!"

Everyone sat back as if they had been doused in cold water.

Mrs. Pierce said: "Would you like to come outside?"

Doug said: "No, I would not!" His voice was loud, and it was blurred as if his tongue or his lips weren't working properly.

Mrs. Pierce said: "I don't know how you got into the school in this state, Mr. Lewis, but no doubt someone is on their way to escort you out again." She went to the door and tried to take his elbow, but he shrugged her off.

I looked at Neil. Something strange seemed to have happened to him. The Neil I knew had vanished and in his place was a boy who seemed to be smaller, his face white and shut up, as if it had been wiped out. It was like one of those octopuses that change color even as you watch them so you can never be sure where they are.

"You're persecuting my son!" Doug shouted.

Mrs. Pierce said: "Two things, Mr. Lewis: Firstly, it is your son who has been persecuting other children in this school for God knows how long. Secondly, I don't like being threatened. I never have and I don't intend to get used to it now. Now, if you don't mind, you're disturbing my class, of which there's still another fifteen minutes; if you want your son, feel free to take him. I'd be only too happy for you to. He's nothing but a nuisance."

Doug Lewis came close to Mrs. Pierce. He said: "You stuck-up little bitch. I'll have you up before the authorities. You won't get a job anywhere!" Mrs. Pierce turned her face away. Doug seemed to consider something—we could hear him panting—then he decided whatever it was wasn't worth it and lunged at Neil. The chair fell over. Doug pushed him toward the door and Neil stumbled forward, pulling his sweater straight. His face was still very white.

Doug Lewis glared around as if he was looking for someone, then turned back to Mrs. Pierce, but she wouldn't look at him. Doug pushed Neil into the corridor, then followed, slamming the door so hard that the windows rattled.

Mrs. Pierce's shoulders drooped a little. After a moment she said: "Get on with your work quietly, class eight. I'll be right back." Then she went out too, and we were left in silence.

I THOUGHT ABOUT Doug Lewis the rest of the day and how Neil had changed before my eyes. I thought how strange the classroom felt after they had gone, as if some shameful thing had happened to all of us, as if we had seen ourselves with no clothes on and couldn't look at one another. The strangest thing of all was that I had wanted this to happen but now that it had I didn't feel how I expected to. In fact, I felt quite the opposite.

Rising Above

THAT EVENING AFTER we had finished dinner, Father said: "I want to have a talk with you, Judith."

"Oh," I said. Suddenly I needed to go to the toilet.

Father folded his hands on the table and looked at me sternly. "I expect you're worried about what's been happening at the house. Well, don't be. Sometimes God's servants become subjects of attack through no fault of our own. We shouldn't think that God has stopped helping us. It's a test of our faith, d'you see?" I nodded.

"It's never very pleasant being tested, but it's part of being a Christian. The harder the test, the more worthwhile it is." He frowned. "The point is, faith helps us to rise above these things. They don't seem so big anymore; we see them for what they really are. Only then can we see them as they really are: stepping-stones bringing us closer to God. Of course, it also helps to know the real reason behind the recent events."

My stomach felt as if I had gone over a humpbacked bridge. I said: "The real reason . . ."

Father said: "The real reason for things isn't always obvious; those boys aren't acting independently, although they think that they are; the unrest in the town isn't really caused by the factory; they are all pawns of larger forces. Someone is behind all of this."

"Oh," I said. The room had become terribly still.

"These things are signs of the end," Father said. "And we know who is roving about, like a lion seeking to devour someone."

"Oh," I said, and the room came back to life again. "You mean the Devil."

"He's our real enemy," Father said. "He's every Christian's real enemy."

"But don't you think those boys are bad, then?"

"Do bad people exist, or are there just bad actions?"

I thought. "Bad people," I said.

"That's not what Jesus said," said Father, and I could see he was pleased to correct me. "Jesus said it was the evil that proceeded out of a person that condemned them."

And then I saw what Father meant, because I couldn't have imagined feeling sorry for Neil before, but since I'd found out what Doug was like I wasn't sure what I felt about Neil; now I felt angry with *Doug*. But what if *Doug* had a bad father? Would I feel sorry for him too? And what about Doug's father—what about his *mother*? A long line of figures suddenly appeared, like paper cutouts. I said: "Then who's to blame?"

"For what?"

"Everything."

"The Devil."

"What if he was a cutout too?" I said quickly: "I mean—what if something made him that way too?"

"No," Father said. "The Devil had the same chance to be good as all the other angels."

"So we are supposed to feel angry with the Devil?"

Father said: "There's no need to feel angry with anyone. Jesus didn't feel angry. He said: 'Forgive them; they know not what they do.'"

"But God said: 'An eye for an eye,'" I said. "'A life for a life.'" I sat up straighter. "It's the Fundamental Law."

Father said: "Which would you prefer was applied to you?"

I didn't say anything.

LATER THAT NIGHT, after Father had gone to bed, I woke and heard voices below my window. Neil Lewis and Gareth and Lee and the other boys were underneath the streetlight on bikes and leaning up against the railings. Neil was riding on another boy's back. They were drinking from cans and crushing them and sticking them on the branches of Mother's cherry tree. The sound of their laughing was like donkeys braying and pigs snorting. Two of the boys came against our garden fence and undid their trousers. I saw two bright arcs of water catch the light, and a cold wave passed through my body. I sat down on the bed. I said: "We must rise above."

I said: "They know not what they do."

I said: "I forgive you."

It wasn't working.

Little Witch

ON SATURDAY WE went preaching to Hilltop. Hilltop is the poor neighborhood at the top of the town. There are no trees there. Wind whistles between the fences and pebble-dash houses, and beyond the houses there is nothing but mountain.

Strange people lived in Hilltop. There was Crazy Jane, who hugged children and cried; Jungle June, who invited strange men into her flat; Dodgy Phil, who wore a mackintosh belted around the middle and had a three-legged dog; and Caerion, who thought the government was spying on him, kept the orange-and-brown curtains of his house closed, and disguised himself when he went shopping. We'd talked to them all at one time or another. Father even started a Bible study with Caerion, but it was difficult because he kept getting up to look through the curtains.

Someone else lived in Hilltop. Neil Lewis. We'd never called on the Lewises, so I didn't know which house he lived in, but I was pretty sure it was one of the houses on Moorland Road, right at the top. I'd seen him riding his bike there. I didn't know what would happen if we called on Neil today. Now that he was knocking at our house. Now that there was the strike and Doug wasn't working. Now that Doug was angry because of what was happening to Neil at school. I didn't know what would happen and I didn't want to know.

We met in Stan's house. We sat on his red settee and the room smelled of aftershave because Gordon was there and of dog because the dog was there and of toast because Stan's house always smells of toast, and we read the day's text. Stan said the prayer, Margaret said we must all come back for pancakes when we had finished, then we went out. Stan worked alone, Father and I worked together, Gordon worked with Alf, Brian worked with Josie, and Elsie and May worked together.

Josie prodded me. "You're not wearing your poncho."

"It's too good for preaching," I said.

She seemed to think about this. "I suppose it is."

It was so cold I began to wish I had worn it. There was frost on the ground and small pieces of hail in the wind. The looks we got weren't much warmer. Banners hung from windows. They said: SUPPORT OUR STRIKE and A FAIR DAY'S WORK FOR A FAIR DAY'S PAY. But I was thinking about Neil.

There was a little hope: The hope was that if enough people invited us in, we might never reach Moorland Road at all. It might really be possible too because, unlike other places, for some reason Hilltop was full of people who deployed no Tactics of Evasion at all but on the contrary invited us into their houses. In fact, sometimes the trouble was getting out.

We got off to a good start with the first person we called on. He was a fat man in a shirt more yellow than white, with oily hair that rose up at the front. There were pictures on the living-room walls of a man in a white suit with his knees turned in and paintings of Hawaiian girls whose skin was strange shades of orange and green. The man pointed to the picture of the man in the white suit and said: "The King is alive!" Father told him another King was alive too and showed him the scripture from Revelation about Jesus on a white horse. He gave the man a magazine and said: "This will explain things more."

The man took the magazine but didn't look at it. He grinned at me in a sickly way and made snapping movements at my face with his hand, like a crocodile. He said he had a daughter about my age but he never got to see her. Father said: "Did you know that there is a time coming when families won't be divided anymore?"

Then the man began to cry. He said his wife wouldn't let him near his daughter. Father turned to another scripture but the man didn't look at it, he wiped his eyes on the back of his hand. He said he wasn't the one who had been drinking. It was her, that bitch, though she told the court it was the other way round. It was her, that whore, she'd been having it off with some man up the road. Many was the time he'd thought of taking the ax and putting it through the two of them. And now she'd taken his angel. She had it coming, he said, she had it coming and one of these days—but I never found out what she had coming, because around about then Father said it was time to go.

After that we had a lot of houses where people shut the door straightaway and then even more where no one was in and Father said we would call back later, and I began to think perhaps we would get to Moorland Road before twelve o'clock after all. Finally we got to a house where a girl came to the door. She was wearing pajamas and had bare feet. The house was warm and I could hear people talking and a door banging. It was my turn, so I said: "Hello. We are talking about the good news of the kingdom. Did you know that soon the whole earth will be a paradise?"

The girl stared at me, she stared at Father, then she stared at the Bible.

I said: "Would you like to live in a world where there won't be bad things anymore?"

The girl moved her feet back and forth in the carpet. The carpet was pink and fluffy. Her feet looked snug there. I said: "I'm sure you would. Can I share a paragraph with you from this book?"

The girl put her finger inside her left nostril and turned it.

I said: "This verse is talking about the future," and I read the scripture from Isaiah about how the lion will lie down with the lamb.

The girl took her finger out of her nostril and put it into her mouth.

I said: "This is God's promise, that the whole earth will be turned into a paradise. There are signs all around us that tell us it will happen very soon. Would you like to find out more about this?"

The girl took her finger out of her mouth and put it into her other nostril.

I began to feel hot. If she didn't say something soon, we would have to go. I wanted to take her head and make her read the words. I wanted to make her say something so that I could say something back.

Then a woman appeared. She had three gold hoops in each ear, a necklace with what looked like a gold tadpole on it, and gold rings on each of her fingers. She held a cigarette in her hand. She opened the door wider and said: "What d'you want?"

I opened my mouth but Father said: "Good morning. My daughter was just telling your little girl about a hope for the future. We've been asking your neighbors an important question: Do you believe God will step in and do something about the world?"

The woman said to the girl: "Get in the house." To Father, she said: "We're not interested, love."

Father said: "Did you know God has plans for this earth? Do you want to find out about a better future for yourself and your family?"

The woman waved and shouted to someone on the other side of the street: "All right, Sian! Aye! Don't forget it's bingo tonight!"

Father said: "Do you wonder what the world is coming to?"

The woman sucked on the cigarette, and her eyes half-closed and her bosoms swelled. "Not really," she said, and she blew smoke in Father's face.

"God said He would step in and bring an end to the wickedness we see," Father said. "Can I show you that?"

"You're wasting your time," the woman said.

"All right, well, thank you, we'll see you again," Father said, and we walked back down the garden path.

A few houses later we came to Moorland Road.

I BEGAN FEELING sick as soon as we turned in to it. The wind off the mountain hit us like a wall, and there were little bits of hail in it. There was a burned-out car in the road and a lot of boys on bikes and music thumping somewhere. I looked at the boys on bikes but I couldn't see Neil.

I said: "Do you think those houses we left might be in now?"

"We've only just called on them."

"So," I said, "they might be in now. There were some we missed altogether, you know—where the road went into that cul-de-sac. We should do them before we forget."

Father said: "I didn't think we missed any houses."

"Yes," I said. "And if we don't go back, we might forget about them and Armageddon could come tomorrow and they will never have got the message."

Father frowned. "Judith, why don't you want to work this road?"

"I do!" I said.

"Then come on."

At the first house we came to, the gate was hanging off. We knocked but we didn't need to; a bull terrier chained up next to a mattress in the front garden began snarling and yanking the chain. A volley of bikes went by and boys called: "Bible thumpers!"

Father knocked again. I edged farther away from the terrier, who looked like he was choking himself to death.

"Father," I said.

"Yes."

"Do we have to work this road?"

Father said: "Judith, these people deserve to hear the message as much as anyone else."

We walked down the path and went up the next one. The front

window of the house was taped over with packing tape, and the letter box was missing its flap. A door slammed upstairs and someone shouted: "Whoever it is, tell them to piss off!" This time an old man with eyes like a wild animal opened the door.

Father said: "Good morning, sir. We've been asking your neighbors a very important question: Do you believe God will step in and do anything about the situation in the world?"

The old man's eyes flitted from Father to me. He swallowed and his lips rolled over and under each other as if he was chewing.

Father said: "I expect things have changed since you were a boy. I expect you could go out without locking your door then. Things are different now, aren't they? It's not surprising so few people believe in God. But look what the Bible says will happen."

The old man's jaw moved up and down but no words came out. His eyes darted inside the house, then back to us again.

Father read a scripture and gave the old man a leaflet. The man's fingers were yellow and the paper rattled in his hand. Father said: "Look at that. That's the way God has promised to make the earth. Would you like to live in a world like that?"

A woman shouted: *"Tell them to piss off!"* The old man's Adam's apple yo-yoed in his throat. He backed away, closing the door.

Father said: "Perhaps this isn't the best time. When we call again, I'd like to discuss this hope for the future with you. Have you got a Bible? If you do, have a look at some of those scriptures."

We went out of the garden and Father wrote down the details. He said: "I think we may have found a sheep there, Judith. I think we may very well have found a sheep."

It was now twenty to twelve. We might just do it, I thought. It wouldn't take much; two or three more calls where we talked for a while.

At the next house, a man in a vest and trousers held up with string came to the door. The vest ended a bit above his waist and his trousers ended a bit below it. In between, his flesh was the color of the lard Father saves from the lamb on Sundays and there were lots of pale hairs. Father said: "Hello, Clive, how are you? I expect you know I'm a Christian. My daughter and I have been sharing a hope for the future with your neighbors."

The man didn't look at Father at all. He grunted and looked down the road. His chin stuck out.

Father said: "I don't know about you, but this world seems to be in a pretty bad way to me."

Clive looked down the road one way, then he looked down the road the other. He seemed to be holding his breath, because every now and then a little bit of air escaped. He put his arm on the doorpost above my head and his flesh juddered. In his armpit, pale hairs clustered like two little forests pointing in different directions.

Father said: "But the Bible promises we are living at a time when God will sweep this world away. Would you like to live in a world where there is job security and poverty is a thing of the past?"

Clive nodded to someone walking on the other side of the road. He let a little bit more air escape. But still he didn't look at Father.

Father said: "Could I leave you with a leaflet that explains things a bit more?"

Clive didn't do anything for a minute. Then he shook his head, very slowly, from side to side.

Father said: "Well, never mind. Perhaps we can talk again another time."

Clive grunted, lifted his arm off the doorpost, and closed the door.

"Satan has blinded their minds," Father said as we walked away.

We reached the end of one side of the street and began on the other. It was ten minutes to twelve. I really felt like we might just do it. All we needed was one more conversation.

We came to a house with a car engine and a child's pram in the garden. The front door was boarded up at the bottom, and the glass was taped across at the top. When Father knocked, a girl came to the door, holding a baby. She looked about fifteen. She also looked half asleep. She had black hairs growing on her arms and black hairs growing above her lip and black hairs growing between her eyebrows. I could see her nipples through her T-shirt. She had bare feet. The baby was fussing and chewing his fist and had no nappy on.

Father said: "Good morning. We've been asking your neighbors a very important question: Do you believe God will do anything about the world?"

The girl's eyelids seemed too heavy to lift. She said: "What?"

Father repeated the question.

She swayed a little. "Are you the Mormons?"

"No," said Father. "We're sharing with your neighbors a hope from the Bible." He handed the girl a leaflet.

She screwed up her eyes. "D'you want money?"

"No." Father smiled. "It's yours to read if you want to. But I'd really like to tell you about the hope for the future, which—"

The girl opened the door. She said: "I can't stand here with 'im, I's too cold."

Father said: "Oh. Well. That's kind of you," and we followed her into the house.

The house smelled of frying and gerbils' cages and damp and something else, a sickly smell that made my stomach curl, that reminded me of someone. The girl led the way into a room at the back of the house.

I had never seen anything like that room. The floor and walls halfway up were covered in lino. There was no furniture except kitchen cabinets with no doors and a plastic table and molded benches that were fixed to the floor. A washing machine was going and had a broom jammed between it and the table.

We sat at the table. I put my hand on it and it was slippery and sticky. I took my hand off again and put it on my lap and hoped the girl hadn't noticed. She raised her T-shirt and began to breast-feed the baby. Around the girl's nipple there were little black hairs. I felt hot and looked at her feet. Between the girl's toes there were little red marks. They looked like they had been bleeding.

Father read part of Matthew, Chapter 24, about the signs of the end. He said: "It's not hard to see Jesus is talking about our day, is it?" He pointed to the verses but the girl seemed to be having trouble focusing. Father said: "Have you got a Bible? If you have, look up the scriptures in this magazine. I think you'll find it very interesting."

Then we heard what sounded like a truck pull up in front of the house and a door swing to. A rush of cold air came in from the hall as the front door slammed. Father stood up and smiled. He said: "Perhaps next time we call, we can discuss any questions you might have."

We went to the kitchen door and Father put his hand out to open it, but as he did, it opened inward and standing there was Doug Lewis.

Doug looked at Father. He looked at me. He looked at the girl, and she rushed out of the room. I heard the baby begin to cry as Doug's eyes slid back to Father.

Father said: "Hello, Doug. I didn't know you lived here. We were just talking to your daughter about . . ."

Doug seemed to be as surprised as we were. Then he said, in a voice that was more like a growl: "She's not my daughter."

Father took my hand. "Well, I'm sorry if we've inconvenienced you. We didn't know you lived here. We'll be going now."

We went through the kitchen door and my heart was beating so slowly it was hard to breathe. We walked through the hall and it was like being underwater.

Then Doug shouted: "Damn right you'll go!" He seemed to have suddenly woken up. *"Get out! Get out of my house!* Don't ever come back! Don't ever step through the gate! *Don't set foot on the fucking pavement!"* He kept shouting as we went through the front door and down the path. It was difficult to think and walk at the same time, though it was what I wanted to do more than anything, because my head felt like it was being battered from side to side and I was afraid I might faint.

"We don't want any of your satanic mumbo jumbo, McPherson! You come here spouting about goodwill and scab off and leave the rest

of us to take the fucking flak!" There were people staring from windows now and from the other side of the road and from the next-door garden. *"Oh, and McPherson! Keep that little witch away from my son! Getting him into trouble all the time! Tell her to put the finger on someone else, d'you hear me? STAY AWAY FROM MY SON!"*

We kept walking but I was in a dream, I had fallen through ice and I was sinking. The spot of light above my head was getting fainter and fainter. As long as I keep walking, I thought. As long as my legs keep moving. And then my legs felt like bits of string, because suddenly I saw Neil ahead of us, standing astride his bike with Gareth and some other boys. He must have come home with Doug in the truck.

Doug was still shouting as the boys began riding. They rode closer and closer. They stood up on the bikes and leaned from side to side. As they passed us, showers of stones spewed up from the wheels and the wheels made a tearing sound. The boys rode, in circles; the stones flew faster.

Father kept walking. He didn't stop and he didn't turn round and he didn't let go of my hand. He walked right down the middle of the road. I didn't see how the bikes kept missing us but they did. It seemed to me we were walking through the Red Sea and there were currents of electricity passing back and forth between Father and me and crackling in the air all around us.

We turned out of Moorland Road. The boys shouted. They threw a stone or two. Then they dropped back and it was just Father and me, the wind whipping around us and banks of cloud moving over the valley below.

Father held my hand for a few more moments and then he dropped it.

A Lie

FATHER DIDN'T SAY anything all the way home. I ran alongside him. Every so often I glanced up at his face, but it was set in a mask and I couldn't read it. When we got home he went straight into the kitchen. He put his bag on the table, then turned round. He said: "What's this about you and Neil Lewis?"

"I haven't done anything," I said.

Then he shouted: *"Don't lie to me, Judith!"* and it was like being winded.

"All right!" I said. "I wanted to punish him! I wanted to punish him for what he does to me every day. *I hate him!*"

Father's face was dark. "What do you mean, 'punish' him?"

I tried to breathe slowly. "I made things," I said. "In the Land of Decoration. I wanted bad things to happen to him. And they did."

Father said: "I have *told* you, Judith, about this *NONSENSE!* I *warned* you no good would come of it!"

"It's not nonsense!" I said. "I *did* make things happen!"

Father came close to me. "Do you have any idea what I'm dealing with?"

I tried to keep looking at him but couldn't, so I looked at the floor.

"Doug Lewis and I have never got on, but now things are a hundred times worse. Here I am trying to keep things together, trying to keep food on the table, trying to keep a roof over our heads—and you go around stirring things up with his son!"

"I haven't stirred anything up."

"You told him you could perform miracles!"

"I didn't!" I said.

"Then what was Doug talking about?"

I looked at my shoes. "I wrote about the miracles in my news book; Neil read it out in class."

Father banged the table hard with his hand. "But *damn it*, Judith—you *can't* perform miracles!"

My body was full of shaking blood. *"I CAN!"* I shouted. "I've got special powers! Everything I've wanted has happened. Every single thing. But I didn't mean to tell anyone—I wanted to tell *you*, but you *didn't believe me!"*

Then Father shouted: *"YOU DO NOT HAVE, NOR HAVE YOU EVER HAD, SPECIAL POWERS!"* and I stumbled backward and covered my face.

When I looked again, Father's hands had dropped to his sides and his face was white. He said: "What do I have to say to get through to you? What do I have to do to make you *grow up?"* He shook his head. "For the last time, Judith, have you threatened Neil Lewis or aggravated him in any way? *Look at me!"*

I looked at him, and I said: "No."

Giving It Back

I SAT IN my room and I looked at my knees. "You told a lie," God said.

"Father would have been more upset if I hadn't."

"Another lie," said God.

"Oh, be quiet!" I said. "I should never have listened to You in the first place! I wish I had never found out about the miracles. If I'd listened to Father, none of this would have happened.

"Well?" I said after a moment. "Haven't You got anything to say?"

I stood up. "You know what I hate about You? The way You just disappear when You feel like it. I wish *I* could disappear!" I sat down and put my head in my hands. "It's like talking to myself."

"God," I said after a while, "I don't want to be Your Instrument anymore."

He couldn't let that go. "What do you mean?" He said.

"I don't want the power," I said. "I'm giving it back."

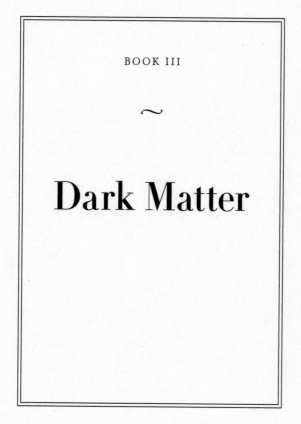

BOOK III

~

Dark Matter

Through My Window

IT GOT DARK in the room. Shadows spilled over the floor and slipped down the walls. They skimmed the ceiling and the hot-air balloon light shade and traveled like clouds over the Land of Decoration. They appeared and reappeared and went elsewhere.

I watched the streetlights go on and the moon come up. The moon was so bright that it had a halo. It looked like chalk dust and the moon like chalk and the sky looked like a blackboard and all over the blackboard there were pinpricks of stars. I remembered it was written that the sun would be darkened and the moon wouldn't give its light, and I wondered if when the end of the world came it would be like a giant eraser had wiped the moon and stars out and rolled up the sky like a blackboard, with a snap. I thought how nice that would be.

I heard the hall clock strike eight. I heard it strike nine. I heard it strike ten. Then I must have closed my eyes, because when I looked out the window again, I had slipped down on the pillow and there was a wet patch where my mouth had been.

It was very still and very cold. I had the feeling it was quite late and I felt uncomfortable, as if I had dreamed something bad and it was still dragging behind me. I felt confused too, as you do when you wake and aren't sure if it's morning or evening or can't remember where you are, which was strange, because I was in my own bedroom. I suddenly thought that I might not be real, or I was real and everything else was make-believe: Either way it was a pretty lonely feeling.

A sound made me look down. Six boys were standing astride bikes under the streetlight. Neil Lewis was there and his brother and some other boys, older than I had seen before, about fifteen or sixteen. I edged closer to the window and sat so that only my face was in the light. I didn't think they could see me, because the light was shining on the window.

They were doing wheelies and playing piggybacks and laughing and drinking from bottles and cans. Neil was sitting on top of another boy's shoulders. He threw a can into our garden and it fell into the golden cane. Neil's brother was drinking from a bottle. When he finished, he went right up to our garden wall.

What I saw next didn't make sense. The boy pulled down his trousers and crouched down. There were cheers and whoops, but the noises made no sense to me now and sounded like the horns of cars or the honking of ships or some kind of animal. Another boy came forward and went to the wall, and he undid his trousers and there were cheers again. I let the curtain fall back, and for a minute I didn't think anything at all.

I don't know how long I sat there or if the noises went on below, because I didn't hear a thing, but when I looked again, the street was empty.

After a minute I stood up. I wasn't sure what I was going to do but I went to the door. I opened it and went along the landing. At the top of the stairs I stopped because my heart was beating so hard I felt ill. But it was as if my brain had switched off.

I could hear Father sleeping in the back bedroom. He was breathing hoarsely. I could hear the indrawn breaths. The spaces between the breaths were so long I thought he might stop breathing altogether, but the breath always came back again. It rose and rose, and stopped right at the top, and for a moment it was nowhere. Then it began all over again.

I wondered how people didn't die every night, how their heart kept bringing them round without being asked to, perhaps without them even wanting it to, and I thought how amazing it was. I suddenly felt sorry for my heart. It was gripping me and letting me go and gripping me all over again, like a little man clutching his hands and saying: "Oh, oh, oh." I said to my heart: "It's all right." But the little man went on clutching his hands, and I felt sadder than I ever had in my life and didn't know why. After a minute I went on down the stairs.

I turned the key in the front door, and opened it and moonlight spilled across the hall. The street was silent. Cold was like smoke in my nostrils.

I went through the gate and looked at the pavement. I don't know how long I looked at it. I didn't even know it was a pavement anymore, there were blank spaces where there should have been words. After a while I went back into the garden and picked some leaves. Then I went through the gate, picked up what was on the pavement, and carried it and put it behind the golden cane.

I did it again and again. I wasn't thinking about what I was doing. I was thinking about other things, and all the time my heart, my heart, was beating, beating.

I said: "What am I?"

"Dust," said a voice.

"Is that all?" I said.

"Yes," said the voice.

"What about my heart?"

"Dust," said the voice.

"What about my mind?"

"Dust," said the voice.

"My lungs?"

"Dust."

"My legs?"

"Dust."

"My arms?"

"Dust."

"My eyes?"

"Dust."

"I see," I said.

"Dust you are," said the voice, "and to dust you will return."

The more the voice talked, the heavier my arms became and the heavier my legs became and finally even breathing was difficult.

Then I looked down and saw that the pavement was clear, and I went back with water from the watering can and washed it. I scrubbed it with leaves and with grass. I scrubbed so that little white curls of skin appeared on my knuckles.

"Dust," said the voice, and I nodded.

I closed the gate and put the watering can back and washed my hands under the tap. The stars were so bright now that they seemed to be pulsing.

"But stars are made of dust," I said suddenly.

"Everything is," said the voice.

There was a glimmer for a moment, something I wanted to catch hold of. But it disappeared too quickly. I went inside, locked the front door, and went upstairs to bed.

Dust and Stars

ONE OF MY good thoughts is that there are no big things in this world, only lots of little things joined together, that there are other worlds in which we are as small as the smallest person in the Land of Decoration, that the band of the Milky Way people thought was everything is itself just one of billions of other galaxies and beyond that a cosmos at least a billion, billion, billion times larger than even the farthest part of the universe scientists can see with the biggest telescopes, and beyond that other cosmos that reach into infinity.

I like to think about how it could all go on still farther, that we only know about things like space and time because of light, so there is no way we can know what happens where it is dark, that other worlds could be out there, other dimensions, other Big Bangs, which is only another way of saying God. I like to think that all that has happened is the universe has taken a breath and bounced up and we have appeared for a moment before the ball falls back and the breath is withdrawn again. I like to think that from a certain point all things are the same, and the whole of our story is no more than the paint on the knob on the top of the Eiffel Tower, and we are the layer of pigeon poop on top of the paint on top of the knob.

I tell myself that small things are big and big things are small, that veins run like rivers and hairs grow like grass and a hummock of moss to a beetle looks like a forest, and the shapes of the countries and clouds of the earth look like the colors in marbles from space. I think how the shell of a nebula of oxygen and hydrogen looks like the splash made by a droplet of milk, when the sides rise up in a crown. I think about the pictures of rocks and of dust and of galaxies in space and they look no more than snowflakes in a blizzard, and black holes look like pearls in deep cases, superclusters like bath bubbles—like honeycombs, like cells in a leaf, the grid of a bumblebee's nose. That the whorls of a nebula and the caverns of a fire glow with the same light and your eyes get warm and filled up looking at both.

I tell myself that wildebeest scurry like ants, the earth is a blue bubble floating in darkness, a cell is a spaceship. The pieces of comet-shaped rock, which are light-years across and thrust out of a nebula when it explodes, are heads of corn in a blue sky, if you are lying in a field in summer when the sky is cornflower blue, and the corn is reaching into it. I say to myself there are palaces in clouds, mountains in rock pools, highways in the dust at my feet, and cities on the underside of leaves; there is a face in the moon and a galaxy in my eye and a whirlpool at the crown of my head.

And then I know that I am enormous and I am small, I go on forever and am gone in a moment, I am as young as a baby mouse and as old as the Himalayas. I am still and I am spinning. And if I am dust, then I am also the dust of stars.

A Cornfield

I LEARNED YOU can do things you didn't know you could the night I went down to the street to clean up the mess the boys had left. I learned that nothing is impossible and the only reason it seems to be is that it just hasn't happened yet. These are useful things to know.

On Monday, Neil didn't say anything about us coming to his house. Perhaps it was because his father had told him not to have anything to do with me, but it could have been because Mrs. Pierce didn't take her eyes off him. She picked on his spelling, on his grammar, on the dirt beneath his fingernails, and on how far behind he was. He didn't say anything, but more than once I caught him watching me. I wanted to shout: "I'm not doing anything to you! I'm never going to do anything to you again!" but I just had to sit there.

That evening I said to God: "I'm not doing anything to him, but Neil is still angry."

"There's nothing you can do," God said. "You set the wheel in motion. It's easy to do things, not as easy to undo them."

"Well, I'm not making anything else happen," I said. "I'll never make anything happen again!"

"We'll see," said God.

That week I didn't make anything new in the Land of Decoration; I just told stories. I told a story about a red balloon that wanted to go higher and kept on going until it reached outer space but after a while couldn't be sure which way was up anymore, or which way was in or out, or which way was the future and which way was the past and in the end it couldn't be sure it was going anywhere at all.

I told a story about an Eskimo who caught an enormous fish and they became friends and the fish didn't want to go back to sea. But it couldn't live on land with the Eskimo, because it kept breaking the ice the Eskimo was standing on, so they made a boat from a whalebone and the fish towed the Eskimo away with him and neither was seen again.

I told a story of a fiddler who played so beautifully that even the birds in the trees began singing his songs back to him night and day. The only time they would be quiet was when he played to them, but he couldn't play at night, and he couldn't sleep, and he couldn't eat, and finally he broke up the fiddle and ran away.

I told a story about a cornfield. The corn was green and called out to the sun to warm it. The sun warmed the corn and the corn became yellow. The corn thrust itself into the sky. It blossomed, it jostled, it fingered the blue. "Warm us some more," it said. The sun licked the corn heads. The corn became darker. It chattered and rustled. A little smoke appeared at the edge of the field. A little flame too. "Warm us some more," said the corn. The flames were made of a sports drink wrapper. They spread as the wind carried them. The corn began to crackle. Someone rode to the nearest town and rang the bell in the square. People came from all around with buckets and hoses and kettles and tanks full of water. But though they worked all afternoon and though the corn cried out to the sun that it was burning, the sun did not stop; soon there was nothing left but a space where a field used to be.

THE LAND OF Decoration seemed to me to be getting uglier. I couldn't remember why I ever began making it. The streets looked jumbled, the fields brown, the rivers dull, the sun just a bulb, the mirror sea a stupid idea. Perhaps it was always like this, I thought. I wondered what other things I had not been seeing clearly.

It occurred to me that I had been worrying about Neil Lewis when all along I should have been worrying about Father. On Wednesday I went to the corner shop after school to buy sweets, and a newspaper said: VIOLENT CLASH BETWEEN PICKETERS AND WORKERS LEADS TO THREE ARRESTS. It had a picture in it of a man lying in front of a lorry, which was driving through the gates at the factory, and there were police with shields and helmets and horses fighting men with baseball bats and dustbin lids. A man with blood coming down his face was being held by the back of his sweater. I was so surprised I just stood there. Father hadn't told me about any of that.

I went to the top of the road and looked down the hill to the factory and I saw how strange it was really, like a sleeping beast, a black thing with funnels and towers and ladders and pipes and above it these huge clouds of smoke like clouds of breath. And somewhere inside it was Father.

THE BOYS KNOCKED every night, but Father no longer went outside. There were more boys than I had seen before, the big boys, about four or five of them, and there was Neil in the midst of them, spitting and swearing and riding on the others' backs. Father phoned the police, but by the time they arrived the boys had ridden away. It became a game with them to scarper down the backstreets as soon as they heard the cars. The police found nobody, we went to bed, the boys came back, and it all began again.

On Thursday night something different happened. There wasn't any knocking, just a flip of the letter box. Father waited a minute, then went into the hall. He was standing by the door with a piece of paper in his hands.

"What's that?" I said.

Father's face was blank. "Nothing," he said. "Nothing."

"Is it a note from the boys?" I said.

Then Father said: "Judith. Please." As if he was hurt, as if I was hurting him. He had never spoken to me like that before, and I went back to the kitchen.

"I'd like you to send up a car," I heard him say. "They are still here. . . . Yes . . . I can't say over the phone." He was silent for a minute. When he spoke again it was quieter. He said: "Let me tell you, you are making a big mistake. . . . Yes . . . I certainly will. I'll bring it down first thing."

"You're taking that note to the police station?" I said when he came back into the kitchen.

"Judith, I would prefer it if you didn't listen when I'm talking on the phone." He threw some more coal in the Rayburn, then shut the door firmly and said: "From now on I don't want you walking to school the back way anymore; go along the main road, all right? And don't go out of the playground at lunchtime."

"OK," I said.

"And keep out of that boy's way. He's not a nice individual. I'm going to speak to the school tomorrow; if the police can't do anything, maybe they can."

"Really?" I said. I began to feel sick.

"Yes," he said. "This has to stop."

We were sitting by the Rayburn a few minutes later when something hit the front door hard. There were shouts. The voices sounded older than Neil and Lee's, and there was laughter. There was another blow to the door and we heard the bushes crash in the front garden. Father cleared his throat once, sharply, and it sounded to me as if he couldn't get his breath.

We were both very still as the noises went on and the air around us seemed to be getting thinner and more difficult to breathe. It went on, and on. And on. I didn't understand how noises could paralyze you, but that's what they were doing. I wanted to move more than I've ever wanted anything in my life, but I couldn't. Father's skin looked as if someone was tightening it at the sides of his head. Suddenly he jumped up and went to the dresser. He took down the Bible, opened it, and handed it to me. "Read it," he said.

"What?"

"Read."

"Where from?"

"Anywhere."

When I still looked at him, he said: "Go on!"

"Therefore thus saith the Lord concerning the king of Assyria: He shall not come into this city, nor shoot an arrow there, nor bare a shield before it, nor erect a rampart against it. By the way that he came, the same way he shall return, he shall not come into this city, saith the Lord."

"Louder," Father said.

"For I will defend this city, and save it, for my sake, and for the sake of my servant David. And it came to pass that night that the angel of the Lord went out and smote in the Assyrian camp a hundred and fourscore and five thousand: and when they arose early in the morning, look, there was not one living."

"Louder!"

But my throat ached as if it was in a vice. Father snatched the Bible and began reading himself. He held the book away from him and read in a clear voice with his chin raised. He read till the hall clock chimed nine, through the laughter and voices outside, and I kept my head bowed.

A police car arrived again just after nine, but Father hadn't called it this time. I wondered who had and thought perhaps it was Mrs. Pew or Mr. Neasdon.

Father told me to sleep in the middle bedroom and I didn't ask why. He took a long time coming up, and when he did I heard him slide the bolt home on the front door and drag something heavy across it.

The Sixth Miracle

I DON'T KNOW if Father phoned the school or not, but in the middle of our math lesson on Friday Mr. Williams came to talk to Mrs. Pierce and they went out of the classroom; after a minute they came back in and Mrs. Pierce said: "Neil, Mr. Williams wants to talk to you." Neil flushed dark red, and followed Mr. Williams out of the room. After ten minutes Gareth and Lee were called out too. Neil didn't come back to class, but Gareth and Lee did, and they were pale and quiet.

I asked Mrs. Pierce if I could go to the toilet, and she looked at me sharply and said: "Are you all right?" I nodded. In the toilet I thought I was going to be sick, but in the end I wasn't. I just sat on the floor by the bowl, leaning my head against the tiles.

I could feel Mrs. Pierce watching me for the rest of the day, and at home time she said: "I know things are difficult right now, Judith. We are going to support you and your father. I want you to know that. We are going to see that this sort of thing stops."

LATE THAT NIGHT a voice woke me. Father was pulling back the blankets and saying: "Get up quickly, Judith."

"Is it Armageddon?" I said.

"No, it's a fire."

"The Land of Decoration!" I said. And though a few days ago I had thought it was stupid, I realized I wanted it very much indeed.

"Just put your dressing gown on."

Father took my hand and we ran along the landing and down the stairs. "The Land of Decoration!" I said again. "Let me get it! Please! Let me put part of it in a bag!" I was afraid I was going to cry, though I knew how much Father hated it.

He said: "The fire won't get to your room, Judith; the firemen are on their way."

We held our sleeves over our faces at the bottom of the stairs, because smoke was coming from underneath the front-room door, then went through the hall into the kitchen and the back garden.

Mrs. Pew was standing by her back door in dressing gown and hairnet. She didn't have her lipstick on or the white stuff on her face, and she looked almost normal except for the wobbling. She was fiddling with her hearing aid calling: "Are you all right?"

Father said: "We're fine. But could Judith stay with you for the time being?"

Mrs. Pew said: "Of course!" and held out her hand, and he told me to go with her.

Mrs. Pew made me hot chocolate and I sat at her breakfast bar and tried to see through the window into our back garden while Oscar sat on the windowsill, grumpy at being woken and flicking his tail. "A dreadful business," Mrs. Pew said. "Truly dreadful. I'm always worried that a fire will start in this house. So far, thank the Lord, I haven't had one."

I heard a big engine pull up out front and doors slam. In the sky there were blue flashing lights. I heard men's voices in our house. The back door was open and I heard shouting and a steady sound and every now and then a heavy noise as though they were dragging something heavy.

Not long after I had finished my second hot chocolate, Father came back and said it was all over. The damage was mainly by the front-room window.

Mrs. Pew said: "How on earth did it start?"

Father said a brick had been put through the living-room window. He said there was a rag tied around a brick. The rag was soaked with petrol. A match had probably been thrown in afterward. He said it all very calmly.

Mrs. Pew blinked and blinked and touched her throat. I thought she was going to faint. She said: "You must stay here tonight! You can't go back."

Father said: "I think Judith had better, but I want to keep an eye on the house, so I'm going to sleep in the front room."

"But the window is smashed!" said Mrs. Pew.

"The firemen are going to board it up," said Father. "I'll come and get Judith in the morning."

I went to the door with him. "*Can't* I come home with you?"

"No. You're better off with Mrs. Pew tonight."

"*Please,*" I said.

"It's one night, Judith."

I SLEPT IN a room at the back of Mrs. Pew's house in a soft feather bed that smelled of potpourri. The smell made me feel sick. The softness of the bed made me feel I was falling. I wanted to race back to my room, where there were floorboards and blankets and it didn't smell of anything at all. I began to rock back and forth.

"God," I said, "how could You let this happen?"

"If I were you, I would be asking Myself the same question."

"What?" I said. "What do You mean, I should—Hello? *Hello?*" But there was no answer.

That night I dreamed of a house made from a shoe box. A Lego brick had been pushed through the window. There were flames of orange paper, and when they moved, they crackled. The flames reminded me of something, but I couldn't think what. The fabric doll was asleep in the front bedroom and I shouted to her to wake up. The doll ran along the landing and woke the pipe-cleaner doll. Flames were climbing the stairs. They beat at them, but they faded then glowed into new life again.

When I woke, it was like coming up through water, the opposite of drowning, though it felt just as bad. And then I remembered what the flames reminded me of: the cellophane wrapper from a bottle of sports drink.

THE NEXT MORNING, while it was still early, Father came to take me home. I looked at him as we went through Mrs. Pew's gate into our back garden, but his face didn't tell me anything; there was no expression on it at all.

Inside the house, everything smelled of smoke. The front-room tiles were black and the walls were black around the window and there were pools of black water on the floor. The armchairs were black and eaten down to the stuffing. The paint on Mother's sewing machine was bubbly and flaking. Where the window used to be there was now a board.

The front garden was like one of the pictures in the leaflet showing what it would be like after Armageddon. The golden cane around the front-room window was burned to the ground and so were the Christmas roses. The cherry tree was charred and the ground full of cinders. A rug, armchair, and table were piled up by the gate, and they were black too.

My room was as I left it: the bedclothes thrown back, the Land of Decoration just the same, the two little dolls I dreamed about safe and sound.

I got down on my knees. I said: "Thank you!" over and over, and clasped my hands. Then I opened my eyes. And I stared.

Because in the middle of the Land of Decoration was the cornfield, the one that caught fire, and one half of it was covered with the wrapper from a bottle of sports drink.

Master and Servant

I SAT ON the side of the bath and said: "I don't understand, I don't understand, I don't understand." I wiped my mouth and flushed the toilet.

Then I went back to my room and I screwed up the drink wrapper and rolled up the field. I stamped on the earth and threw away the grass heads. I put the people and the containers of water back where they were. I said: "I don't understand. I didn't want to make a fire. I was playing."

"Didn't you realize that whatever you make can become real?" said the voice.

"No!" I said. "I thought I had to make something on purpose."

"When you made the field, you were frightened," God said. "Fear can make things happen. It's like praying for disaster."

"But that would mean something could happen at any time," I said, "that things come from nothing—out of thin air!"

God said: "It's worth considering that that model world has got a life of its own."

"Then I'll throw it away!" I said. "I won't keep it! Anyway it isn't me! It's You! It's not *me* who makes things happen! *You* made the fire! I said I wouldn't make anything else happen and I meant it. I don't *want* the power! I don't want anything to do with it!"

"Power can be a difficult creature to tame," God said. "Sometimes it's not certain who the master is and who the servant. Anyway, I'm afraid you can't just hand it back."

"Why not?" I said. "No one said anything about having to keep it."

"Well you're becoming very useful to me. And anyway, you can't switch the power on and off, you know."

"Then it's simple," I said. "I won't do a thing—ever again."

"Easier said than done."

"Watch me!"

"The power won't leave," said God.

"Please take it," I said and I bit down hard on my lip so that I wouldn't cry. "Nothing happens the way I think it will. Something always goes wrong."

"That's because Something and Nothing are more closely related than people think," God said.

Dark Matter

FATHER TOLD ME that there is a lot of Something in the universe and we can see it and measure it and it takes up space and things bounce off it and go on their way again. But for all of the Something there is just as much Nothing which can't be seen and can't be measured and people only stumble upon it by accident.

I have wondered if God made the Nothing or it came about by itself. Perhaps there could be no Something without Nothing. Just because the Nothing is invisible doesn't mean it isn't strong. It's more dangerous than Something, because you can't see where it is and it makes things disappear. In some places the Nothing is so strong that everything we know vanishes altogether. This is called Dark Matter.

Father said Dark Matter was what God used to create the universe. It drew things into itself, and those things were never seen again or came out the other end so misshapen they didn't look like themselves anymore. He explained Dark Matter as the outside surface of a box and matter as the inside surface. We are inside the box so we see only the Something. But if you took the same piece of cardboard and unfolded it, you would see that both are simply different sides of the same thing. In fact, if you folded the box back up again the wrong way, you wouldn't know the difference. This shows how close Something and Nothing really are.

How can you tell if you are dealing with Nothing or Something? How can you be sure if you're inside the box or outside it? You can't. And this is the problem: The inside and the outside, depending on where you're standing, look just the same.

A Fence

I WAS WRITING in my journal when I looked up and saw Father standing in the doorway. I pushed the journal away and said: "Are we going preaching?"

"No." His eyes were dark. "Put on some rough clothes and come downstairs." I didn't have time to ask any more, because he was gone. A minute later I heard the back door slam and some clattering. I put my journal underneath the floorboard and pulled on my dungarees and sweater and went downstairs. Father was hauling planks round to the front of the house. He thrust a bucket of nails into my hand and said: "Take these out the front," so I went into the garden and waited.

The world was blue and yellow and glittering like diamonds, and the air was so cold it burned the inside of my nose. The outline of the mountain looked like it had been drawn with a pin. A robin perched in the branches of the cherry tree and began to sing, and the notes cooled like drops of lead as they fell around me.

Father appeared after a minute with a saw and planks and two milk crates. He set up the milk crates and laid the first plank across them. "Hold it tight," he said to me and I held the end of the plank. Then he started sawing. His body shuddered with each stroke and the sound tore the air. His face was red. A plank fell to the ground and he reached for another. It was horrible holding the planks.

When the saw's teeth stuck, the plank brought me up with it. When the saw bent, my own teeth jumped.

Father began ramming the cut planks against the garden wall. I didn't know where he would put them, because there was already a wall around our garden and above the wall railings, like in all the front gardens, but I began handing him nails. He put the planks on either side of the railings and smashed the nails so far into the wood that it splintered, so far in that the heads disappeared. He hammered nails all over the place, at all sorts of angles; once he hammered his finger, and blood ran down his hand.

The planks were different sizes and different thicknesses. They began and ended in different places. If they weren't long enough, Father hammered on another one. If there was a gap, he threw cement into it, and stones, or pieces of brick. I thought he would throw himself in too if he could.

He didn't look at me and he didn't speak to me. Around about ten o'clock he started making noises like an animal. The noises made me sick in my chest and my arms feel like liquid. He said: "What are you staring at?" and I turned my head so he couldn't see that I was crying.

He worked all morning, not stopping to eat or drink, his breath filling the air in great clouds. I kept passing him things as fast as he shouted. He threw off his sweater; his shirt was wet with sweat.

A small group of people gathered on the opposite pavement. Mrs. Andrews was there and Mr. Evans and Mr. Andrews. I don't think they had ever seen a fence go up so quickly. At half past eleven Mr. Neasdon came out of next door and stood on the pavement. He had his hands on his hips and was blinking fast.

Father either didn't see him or pretended not to. "McPherson!" Mr. Neasdon shouted. "What's going on?"

"Fence!" said Father.

Mr. Neasdon said: "Did it occur to you to let us know before you started?"

"Hammer!" Father shouted. I handed it to him.

Mr. Neasdon looked up the street and back again. He shook his head, then he looked the other way. He threw his hands in the air. Then he finally looked back at Father and said: "How high is it going to go?"

"Don't know!" Father said. He swung the plank into place. "Nails!"

Mrs. Pew poked her head over the railings at the other side of the garden wall and said: "John, would you like a cup of tea?"

"No tea, thank you, Mrs. Pew!" Father said.

She fiddled with her hearing aid. "I have Tetley if you like."

"No tea! Thank you, Mrs. Pew!" Father said.

Mr. Neasdon said: "Whoa, whoa! Just a minute! I want to know how high this fence is going! It's already blocking out the light at our front and it looks bloody awful! You just don't do this without asking us."

Father continued to hammer.

Mr. Neasdon's chest began to go up and down. "You know, we've just about had it up to here with you! What with your proselytizing and your End of the World this and Armageddon that and you're not striking—but this is the limit! I'm not going to stand for it!"

Father shouted: "Nails!"

Mrs. Pew reappeared and said: "What about herbal?"

Mr. Neasdon's eyes bulged. He went inside, slamming the door.

Mrs. Pew came back later, but by that time we could only hear a voice saying: "John! John! I've peppermint if you'd like!"

IT BEGAN TO get dark at five o'clock. The group of people on the other side of the street went indoors. I expect they wondered if Father was going to go on all night, but no one came to ask him to be quiet.

Father told me to go inside, but I was feeling sick and wanted to see him in front of me, so I carried on handing him wood. I was cold though. "Isn't it high enough now?" I said at last.

"*High* enough?"

"We can't see the street anymore."

"Not high enough by half!" he said, and hurled the cement at the board as if he was teaching it a lesson.

Not long after that, I was handing Father a plank when a splinter went into my hand. Father didn't see. I tried to pull it out but it broke off, and after that it hurt whenever I passed him anything. It was quite dark then and Father rigged up the Tilley lantern on top of the planks and carried on working, tottering on top of another two milk crates. He asked me to go and fetch the carrier bags of glass for the bottle bank, and when I did, he jumped on them and stuck the broken pieces in the cement along the top of the wall and in the gaps between the wood where the cement was fresh along the outside. At nine o'clock, we went inside. Father's face was red, and around his eyes there were two white rings. He poured tea in the kitchen and his hand shook. He said the only thing left to do now was make a new gate and he would do that tomorrow.

We ate dinner in silence. It hurt to hold the fork. I didn't feel like eating anyway. Suddenly I said: "You forgot to say thanks."

Father stopped eating. Then he swallowed with a gulp and reached for his cup of tea. "Well, it's too late now," he said.

I stared at him. He cleared the last of his plate with a clatter, pushed back his chair, and said: "Is this finished?" I didn't answer, but he took my plate anyway and went to the sink.

"What's the matter with you?" he said as we were washing up.

"Nothing."

"Yes there is. Come on, out with it." Then he stopped rinsing the dishes and said sharply: "What's the matter with your hand?"

"Nothing."

He took the plate I was drying and opened my palm. The skin around the splinter was red and raised. When he touched it, I jumped.

"Why didn't you tell me?" he said, in a different voice altogether, and I shrugged and looked away.

Father turned off the tap. He told me to sit down and went out of the room. When he came back in he had antiseptic, cotton, a tin of Band-Aids, and a needle. He pulled up a chair and sat opposite me and took my hand and began stroking the splinter with the needle.

Father's face seemed to be completely empty now. I could feel his breath on my hand. He was gentle so it didn't hurt, but my eyes got full anyway and I couldn't look up.

He took a bandage and peeled off the back and pressed it down around the cut. "By there," I said, and he pressed it. "And there." He pressed the Band-Aid some more. All around us, the room had become very still.

Then he stood up as if he'd suddenly remembered something and said: "That should do it."

I said: "Do you think I need it wrapped?"

The darkness came back into his face. He said: "It's a splinter, Judith."

I put my hand over the Band-Aid and watched him go.

A Gate

WE DIDN'T GO to the meeting the next day, so I didn't have to decide whether to wear Josie's poncho or not. We didn't go preaching or read the Bible or eat roast lamb and bitter greens. Instead, Father made a gate.

I have never seen a gate like it, and I don't think anyone else had either judging from their faces as they walked by. Father worked on it all day in the front garden. There was ice on the ground and it didn't melt, because there was no sun. I took cups of tea out to him, but he told me to stay inside because it was so cold.

At ten to two Uncle Stan phoned to find out if we were all right. I thought it was strange Father hadn't phoned him or Alf before now to tell them about the fire, but I didn't like to ask why. I told Uncle Stan that Father was making a gate. He said: "Oh . . ." Then he said: "Well, as long as you're both all right . . . not ill or anything."

"No," I said. "Would you like me to get Father for you?"

"Is he busy?"

Father tottered past the window with the gate. "A bit," I said.

Stan said: "Well, don't bother him, pet." Then he said: "A gate?"

"Yes."

"Well, just let him know I phoned to say we missed you."

"All right."

I felt strange when I put the phone down. Uncle Stan's voice seemed to be coming from another world. I suddenly wished we had gone to the meeting. I wouldn't even have minded wearing the poncho.

When Father had finished the gate, it was taller than him and shaped like a church window. It was three planks thick, with metal studs in the front and right in the middle a brass knob that was as big as a hand and shaped like a spike. It took Father an hour to hang it, and the sweat ran down his face and he made a noise as if he were in agony. Afterward, he showed me how to unlock it and gave me a key. The key was longer than my hand and very heavy.

At dinner I said: "Uncle Stan phoned."

"Oh."

"He wondered if we were ill."

"What did you tell him?"

"That you were making a gate. He said to tell you they missed us." I took the plates to the sink and said: "Shall I get the Bibles?"

Father put his head in his hands. "In a minute."

I hadn't noticed his hands till now. They looked twice their normal size and were bright red, as if they'd been plunged into boiling water. There were cuts and dried blood and pieces of skin peeled back. His fingers looked like sausages about to burst out of their skins.

I washed and dried the dishes and fetched the Bibles. But when I came back, Father's head was on his arms and he was fast asleep.

A Ring of Stakes

On Monday, Neil Lewis wasn't in school and I was glad. Mrs. Pierce didn't seem to know about the fire and no one else did either, so if Lee and Gareth had been with Neil they hadn't told anyone.

When I went home, I saw Mr. and Mrs. Neasdon, Mrs. Andrews, and Mr. Evans standing on the corner of our road with bags of shopping. Mrs. Neasdon was saying: "We've got to live next door to that."

Mr. Evans said: "I can understand *why* he's done it, but you *don't* go and do that. I mean, look at that glass."

Mrs. Andrews said in a low voice: "If you ask me, I think he's losing it."

Mr. Neasdon shook his head. "He lost it long ago."

They stopped talking when they saw me, and Mrs. Neasdon smiled a wobbly smile. I didn't smile back. I heard her say when I had passed: "And God knows that child gets stranger every day."

I felt itchy as I walked to the house. I went through the gate and locked it behind me. I peered through a crack in the fence. The itching got worse. Then I picked up a small stone and climbed the cherry tree. I flung the stone as hard as I could over the top of the fence, then dropped to the ground. When I looked through the crack, they had all stopped talking and were looking at the house.

I waited till they began to talk again, then got another stone, climbed up the blackened cherry tree, and threw it as hard as I could. It caught Mr. Neasdon on the neck, and he saw me before I could jump clear. Through the fence I saw him stare at our house. Mrs. Neasdon put her hand on his arm. They went indoors.

I felt hot after they had gone and sat with my back against the fence, digging my shoes into the earth. I didn't go inside until the bus came with Father on it, though it was dark by then and I was shivering.

"What are you doing out here?" he said.

AT DINNER I said: "Mr. Neasdon said how much he liked the fence."

Father said: "I'm glad it meets with his approval."

After a few minutes I said: "Is it going to stay there?"

"For the foreseeable future."

"Good," I said. "I like it. It's the best fence in the world."

The Bible study that night was about Jerusalem. It turned out Jerusalem also became a Den of Iniquity after Jesus died, and yet it was the capital of the Land of Decoration. God let it be destroyed by the Romans in 70 A.D. Most of the people inside forgot to escape to the mountains, like Jesus told them to do, when the first troops came and went again. When the Romans came back, it was too late; they built a fence of pointed stakes around the city and the people starved and began eating their own children. "Only a few escaped," Father said. "Those who remembered what Jesus had told them. They went to the mountains and stayed there until the Romans went away. The Great Tribulation will be the same. We mustn't become complacent, because it will come like a thief in the night."

THAT WEEK, PEOPLE shouted if they wanted to speak to Father, and he stood on a milk crate and peered down at them. The postman had to throw our mail over the top of the fence because Father said a letter box was asking for trouble. I had told Father I liked the fence, but when I came home from school and someone was walking behind me, I didn't go in through the front but slipped down the lane and went in through the back gate.

I couldn't sit in my room anymore, because I didn't want to be near the Land of Decoration. I was trying to remember exactly where everything was and couldn't be sure if something had moved or not. I had a bad headache before bed and had to ask Father for some acetaminophen.

At night I slept with my back to the Land of Decoration, but then I felt frightened and turned back to face it again. Once I dreamed the little people were scaling the sides of the bed with ropes, and I woke as the little man I had made to look like Neil was nailing my hair to the mattress with toothpicks.

After school, I spent a lot of time walking around the garden, looking through the cracks in the fence. It was like being invisible, but we weren't invisible—we were the most visible house on the street. If our town had been Jericho, we wouldn't have had to tie a red cord to the window; God would have known which house to leave standing.

I had lied to Father about Mr. Neasdon liking the fence, but someone really did like it. On Tuesday Mrs. Pew was coming home with her shopping and said: "I wish I could have something like that. It would be ideal for hanging baskets." She asked me to ask Father if he could build her a fence, but I didn't. He was acting strangely.

He sat in the middle room every evening after the Bible study and went over bills—at least that's what he said he was going to do, but when I looked through the keyhole he was staring into space. He told me off for leaving the hall light on and for throwing a crust away because there was mold on it. He said: "It's only penicillin; you're lucky to have food at all!"

He went to bed earlier than usual and began sleeping on a mattress on the kitchen floor. Before bedtime he walked around the garden and checked that the back gate was locked. Then he came inside, turned the electricity off, and balanced an ax above the back door. I lay in bed looking out over the town and thought about those people in Jerusalem. I wondered who the Romans were this time, and if they came, would the mountains hide us?

A Vision

ON FRIDAY, NEIL Lewis came back to school. I felt him come into the room before I saw him though he didn't come in as he usually did. He sat down quietly. Then he did something strange. He glanced over his shoulder at me, as if to check I was there and in that moment I knew everything. I knew he had started the fire, he and his brother and his friends, and I began to feel sick. I wasn't sure if it was because I was angry or because I was afraid, but I knew I mustn't think about Neil Lewis anymore, not even for a second, because if I did I would do something bad.

On Monday I woke to a strange sound: a slap and a roar. The roar came a split second after the slap. I looked down to see Father standing on the pavement. He had a can of brown paint in one hand and a brush in the other. He was dunking the paintbrush into the can and splattering it against the fence. His face was screwed up as if he was crying.

I had never seen Father look like that, and it made me feel worse than I had ever felt in my life. I sat down on the bed for a minute. Then I went down. When I came through the gate, he shouted: "*Get back!* Your clothes'll be ruined!" But I had seen what was on the fence, the words sprayed in big looping letters, and this time I understood them all.

I went back to my room and curled up and shut my eyes. I put my fingers in my ears and pressed hard and kept pressing. I ground my teeth. But I could still hear the roaring and I could still see Father's face.

I began to think I would like to hurt Neil Lewis badly.

MY HEAD WAS hot and full in class that morning, like it had been the afternoon I made the first miracle. We were making snowflakes at school, folding and cutting and opening circles of paper. I would normally have enjoyed making things, seeing how the patterns suddenly sprang into life when you opened out the snowflakes, but my eyes kept wandering to Neil.

He was sitting with Kevin and Luke, his cheek on his hand. He looked bored, half asleep: The sunshine was catching his hair and making his eyelashes whiter than ever. I thought that you would not know to look at him what he was like. You would never know what he wrote on people's fences and did to their gardens. I began cutting my snowflake again, but my eyes were getting fuzzy and I couldn't make the scissors go where I wanted. I looked up again. Neil was putting his thumb inside the corner of his nose. He saw me looking at him. And when he did he smiled so that his eyes became slits and his lip curled.

I looked down and bit into my lips and kept pressing down until I tasted iron. I thought of Father and what he had said about forgiveness. I thought of everything good and everything right and everything hopeful, but it was all I could do to keep cutting. Something was rising inside me, millions of small things, scurrying down my arms to my fingertips, crawling up my spine into my hair.

Specks appeared in front of my eyes. There was roaring. The room was getting darker.

I don't know what made me look up, but when I did I saw that someone was standing behind Neil Lewis. I couldn't see the person's face because it was hazy. The rest of the classroom was empty. The person's hands took Neil's head, brought it back, then down onto the desk. I jumped. The head made a dull sound and the desk rocked.

The roaring was getting louder. The hands brought Neil's head back again. His skin was stretched and his eyes were staring. His mouth was an "O." The hands brought the head down on the desk and Neil yelled. When his head came up this time, there was blood coming from his nose.

He tried to get up but lost his balance. The hands brought his head down again. This time it hit the edge of the desk and I heard a softer sound, like a cabbage broken open.

I opened my mouth but nothing came out. I was being pressed into the seat. My eyes were closing, I was falling. The hands brought the head down again. The face didn't look like Neil anymore. The hands brought the head down again. Neil had stopped yelling now. His mouth was a hole and his eyes were two bags of flesh and his nose had spread sideways.

Then someone was saying: "Judith! Can you hear me?" But the roaring went on and the hands went on bringing the head down on the desk.

"Judith!" Someone was shaking me. The roaring was stopping, the light was coming back, the room was full of people again.

Mrs. Pierce's hands were on my shoulders and her face was white. Anna and Matthew and Luke were staring at me. Everyone was. I looked around. Neil, too. He looked normal. Nothing had happened to him.

My body was wet. I thought I was going to be sick. Mrs. Pierce opened my hands and took the scissors. My fingers were cut and the snowflake was in tatters.

What Have You Done?

"WHAT HAPPENED IN there?" said Mrs. Pierce. I was sitting on the seats beneath the coat rail.

"I don't know. My head got hot."

"Has this ever happened before?"

Her face was more serious than I had ever seen it. She said: "We have to talk about this. With your father. I'd like you to ask him to come and see me as soon as possible. Right now I have to get back to class. Would you like to go home?"

I nodded.

"All right," said Mrs. Pierce. "I'll get someone to walk with you."

"No," I said, "I'll be all right. It's not far."

"No," said Mrs. Pierce. "Wait here and I'll go and get Anna to walk with you."

When she had left, I got up and went out.

I don't remember walking home, but I must have. I don't remember if it was raining or sleeting or blowing a gale, but it must have been doing something or other. I don't remember Sue not being there and having to cross the road myself, but I suppose I must have done that too. I don't remember turning in to our street or coming through the gate or unlocking the door or coming upstairs or sitting beside the Land of Decoration, but I must have done all those things, because then I remember staring at the figure I had made of Neil Lewis, standing up, and bringing my foot down hard on it. I remember the feel of the figure beneath my shoe and the roaring in my head and hearing myself say things I had never heard before, like "I will drain the very gorge from his veins"—though I didn't know what "gorge" was and whether it came from veins or another place altogether. I didn't know if I was speaking, because it didn't feel like my mouth or my voice, and when I caught sight of myself in the sea I didn't recognize my face either. Then the roaring grew less and I don't remember anything after that. I lay down and went to sleep.

When I opened my eyes, my head felt as if I had hit it and my tongue felt too big for my mouth. Light from the streetlamp was falling on the fields and the hills and the towns of the Land of Decoration. A voice was saying: "What have you done?"

It said: "I think you really have done something this time."

"No I haven't," I said.

"Look," said the voice.

I picked up the figure of Neil Lewis and looked at it. The head dangled, one leg was longer than the other, an arm was missing. The face was in pieces.

I pushed the arm into the body, but it wouldn't stay. I pushed the head on again, but it fell off. There was nothing I could do about the face. I leaned against the wall and closed my eyes. "It doesn't mean anything," I said.

"Like the fire didn't mean anything?"

"I'll remake it."

"What have I said about remaking things?"

"I don't care!" I said. "I'll do it. I'll make it right."

I got out wire and wool and modeling clay. I remeasured the wire and remodeled the head, but my hands were shaking. I remade the hands and the feet and re-dressed him and re-wigged him and repainted his face, but the eyes were smaller and the nose was straighter and the checks fuller than they should have been. I didn't have any more Wite-Out left to do the white stripe down the trousers, and the new figure was a good half inch shorter.

I pushed the figure away. "It doesn't mean anything," I said. But I knew of all the things I had made, this meant the most.

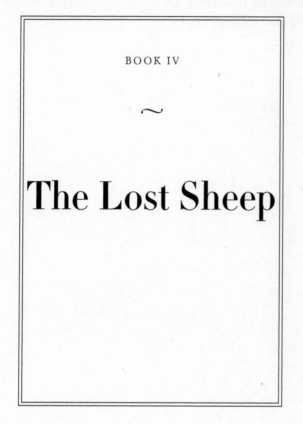

BOOK IV

~

The Lost Sheep

Waiting

UNTIL NEIL WALKED into the classroom on Tuesday, I felt sick. "There!" I said to God as Neil slouched to his seat. "Nothing! I told you so."

"Don't count your chickens," God said.

That night I wrote in my journal: Nothing has happened to Neil.

On Wednesday we finished our snowflakes and hung them around the room, got to the bit in *Charlotte's Web* where they are about to go to the fair, and wrote some more poetry. But this time my poem wasn't any good at all. I couldn't seem to do anything else either. I multiplied when I should have divided, confused nouns and verbs, pasted the wrong side of my graph to my math book, and colored my mercury red instead of silver.

Mrs. Pierce called me to her desk. She said: "Are you all right, Judith?"

"Yes, Mrs. Pierce."

"How's your hand?" she said. But my hands were fine, because the cuts had only been little.

Mrs. Pierce said: "Have you asked your father to come and see me?"

I flushed. "Yes," I said.

But it was important Father never did that, because Mrs. Pierce would let him know I was still talking about God and the miracles.

My book was open in front of her. Only two sums had ticks by them. She said: "It doesn't matter about the sums, Judith. You can do these standing on your head. I just wondered if you wanted to tell me what was worrying you."

I shrugged.

"Is everything all right at home?"

I nodded.

"How is your father coping with the strike?"

I thought about it. When he came in from work, Father's face was pale but his voice was calm. We ate dinner and studied the Bible. Then he went into the middle room to look at the bills on the metal spike and I went upstairs. He inspected the fence, came in, balanced an ax above the back door, and turned the electricity off. "I think he's OK," I said.

Mrs. Pierce said: "Remember, Judith: I'm here if you do need to talk to anyone. OK?"

"OK," I said.

ON THURSDAY WE got a letter from the civil court, asking Father to ring them as soon as possible. He said: "They didn't waste any time."

"Who?" I said, but he didn't answer. I had to look at the envelope. "What do they want you to do?"

"Take the fence down."

"Why?"

"It's *an antisocial gesture*"—he held the paper up—"*a safety hazard*, and *aesthetically incongruous*."

"Are you going to take it down?"

"In their dreams," he said, and dropped the letter into the grate. I took that as a "no."

That night I dreamed of the field in the Land of Decoration and the two little dolls I made first of all. The field wouldn't stay still, as if someone was shaking it, and the dolls clung to each other. The sun was bigger than before and seared their hands and faces. The grass was long and silken, but it was writhing as if it were alive and grasped at their ankles.

Something was coming, lolloping through the grass. It looked like a person, except there wasn't a head, only something bobbing like a balloon on a string. The fabric doll screamed and pulled at the pipe-cleaner doll's sleeve. It came off in her hands and she backed away.

The pipe-cleaner doll stared at his arm, then at the fabric doll. His face was blank. Suddenly his legs crumpled and he dropped to his knees. He continued to stare at her. She opened her mouth. Then the pipe-cleaner doll's eyes turned up, his head toppled backward, and his body fell at her feet.

ON SUNDAY IT was good to see everyone. It seemed ages since we had. They were shocked to hear about the fire. "Well, are the police *doing* something?" said Elsie.

"It's outrageous!" said May. She put her hands over my ears and mouthed to Father: "You could have been killed!"

Uncle Stan said: "Do you need anything? Do you want to stay with us for a while?"

Father said: "No, we're fine. It's all right now."

Then Uncle Stan said: "When did this happen, John?"

Father said: "Friday night."

Uncle Stan said: "You must be exhausted!"

"Yes," Father said. "Pretty much."

"Do you want us to come and give you a hand getting things straight?" said Margaret.

"No, no," said Father. "It's all taken care of."

I suddenly realized everyone thought the fire had happened two nights ago and that Father hadn't corrected them. No one knew about the fence either. Why didn't Father tell them? Perhaps he didn't want to worry them, I thought. But it was rather strange.

May shook her head. "Well, I hope the police find whoever did it," she said. "They should go to prison."

Father said: "You can't depend on the police."

"That's right," said Gordon, and everyone looked at him. If anyone knew about the police it was Gordon.

"Anyway, I know who did it," said Father. "But apparently there's not enough evidence." Then he laughed. "They want me to install a security camera."

Uncle Stan shook his head. "What's the world coming to?"

"The Tribulation!" Alf shook his head.

Elsie hugged me. She said: "At least you're safe."

May shook her head. "I can't bear to think of what might have happened."

"Do you think it's anything to do with the strike?" Stan said.

"Probably." Father nodded. "I'm not exactly flavor of the month at the moment."

I went out to the toilet and sat in a cubicle. It was cool there and quiet. I leaned my head against the plasterboard. I wondered what would happen if they knew I had done it all.

The Law

ON MONDAY EVENING a man with a briefcase and suit banged on the gate. I went and told Father, who I wasn't sure had heard, and he said to let the man in. I slid back the bolts and turned the key and pulled the gate open. The man stared at me. I think he expected to see someone taller. "Come in," I said. The gate crashed behind him and he jumped.

The man looked at the burned tree and the boarded-up window. He looked at the nailed-up door and the black earth and the broken bottles.

I led the way to the kitchen. Father was standing with his back to the Rayburn. The man touched his tie and said: "I expect you know why I've come, Mr. McPherson. You've received a letter from us expressing our concern about the existence of the fence and asking you to contact us as soon as possible."

Father said: "I don't see anything wrong with it."

The man said: "What's wrong was explained very clearly in the letter: It's an eyesore. It's also extremely dangerous. People could get hurt."

"That's the point," said Father.

The man looked at Father.

Father said: "Do you have any idea what we have been dealing with?"

"That's none of my business, Mr. McPherson. Take it up with the police."

Father said: "I've tried to take things up with the police. I've been trying for the last two months. There aren't many options left open to me."

"Well, I'm just doing my job." The man straightened his shoulders. "And I'm afraid your neighbors want the fence to go." He picked up his bag. "I'm going to go back to the office to make a report," he said. "If they deem the fence unsuitable to remain standing, you'll have to take it down; if that doesn't happen, we'll be issuing you a summons. Then it's up to the magistrate to decide whether it stays or not."

Father said: "Show the gentleman out, Judith."

Suddenly the man started. I followed his eyes to the ax above the back door. The man looked at the ax. Then he looked at Father. Perhaps it was strange to have an ax above a door. I now wondered if Father would have put it there a few months ago; I wondered if he would even have built a fence. Or whether he would just have said: "Judith, trials are stepping-stones bringing us closer to God."

The planning man and I went back through the hall, out the front door, and down the garden path. I undid the gate and watched him walk away.

The farther he went, the stranger I felt. "Wait!" I shouted, and ran after him.

He turned.

"Please let my father keep the fence!"

"I'm afraid that's not possible." He began walking again.

"Can't you make an exception?" I panted. "It's not really dangerous, because no one climbs up it. If it gets taken down, I don't know what Father will do!"

The man said: "I'm sorry, I can't discuss this any further." He began to walk faster.

"It's so much better with the fence! We don't get anyone knocking at the door anymore!" I said. "And no one starting fires! And no one vandalizing the cherry tree or putting things through the letter box. Can't you let it stay?"

The man repeated: "I'm sorry." He unlocked his car and swung into the seat. He slammed the door, looked over his shoulder, and pulled away from the curb.

"It's not *fair*!" I shouted.

The car disappeared round the corner. The man had forgotten to put on his seat belt.

The Seventh Miracle

I SAT IN my window. "How much longer, God?" I said. "How much longer till Armageddon? I want it to come and put an end to everything."

"It's close," God said. "Closer than you think."

"You always say that," I said. "They've been saying that for years."

"Well, this time it really is," God said. "If you could see the timetable I've got drawn up here, you'd see it truly is just round the corner."

"Imminent?" I said.

"Exactly," God said.

"But it's been imminent forever!" I drew my knees into my chest. "I want it right now, right now—today! I don't want to wake up in this world anymore."

"Well, you might have to be a little more patient than that," said God. "But I'm not joking: It really is very close."

I took a deep breath. "What will it be like, God?" I said. "I mean afterward?"

"Oh, wonderful," said God. "Everything you've always imagined."

"No more sickness or hunger or death?"

"That's right," said God.

"And you'll wipe the tears from people's eyes?"

"Yes."

"And Father and I will see Mother and everyone will live forever and it will be like it was in the beginning?"

"Yes."

"And will I have a dog and will there be fields and trees and a hot-air balloon?"

"Oh, all of that," said God.

"And will my mother like me?"

"I should think so."

"Tell me how long, God!" I said. "Give me a clue, just a little one."

"No one knows the day or the hour," said God.

"Except You."

"Yes . . . but it's variable. I really couldn't give you an answer on that at the moment."

"Well, I'm ready for it," I said. "Whenever it comes. It won't be a moment too soon."

WE WERE SITTING in the kitchen that night, reading about the end of Jerusalem, eating kippers and peas, when something thudded at the front of the house. Father's eyes stopped moving in the middle of the page. They stayed where they were for a moment. Then they began moving again.

A minute later there was another bang, only this time it sounded as though someone had driven a car into the fence. We heard laughter—high-pitched, husky, and broken. Something passed through Father's face and he pushed back his chair.

"Don't go!" I said, and jumped up. I don't know why I felt so afraid.

But he did. He went out of the back door. A few seconds later I heard the back gate swing to, a shout go up in the street, and running feet.

I sat for a while on the settee and then I began walking. I walked into the hall and around the front room. I walked into the middle room and back out again. I walked upstairs and along the landing and into each of the bedrooms and downstairs again.

When the hall clock chimed nine, I went upstairs and lay on Father's bed and breathed in the smell of him. I pulled his sheepskin over me. Perhaps I should have gone next door to Mrs. Pew and told her what had happened. Perhaps I should have phoned the police. But I didn't want to move. I watched the minutes go by on Father's little alarm clock in faint green numbers and thought how he must look at it every morning when he got up in the dark. Thought about him sleeping here, curled on his side, his head on this pillow where I could smell his skin, and there was a tugging in my stomach that wouldn't go away.

WHEN THE HALL clock chimed ten, I went downstairs and phoned Uncle Stan. "I don't know where Father is," I said when he picked up the receiver.

"Who's this?" said Uncle Stan's voice. It sounded sleepy.

"Uncle Stan?"

"Judith! Is that you?"

"Yes," I said, and I began to cry.

"What's happened? Where's your dad?"

"He went out chasing the boys. He told me to stay in the house. I don't know what's happened to him."

"How long ago?"

"Hours."

"OK. Now—stay where you are," said Uncle Stan. "Stay right there and I'll be with you in ten minutes, can you do that? I'm going to come right over and I'm going to phone the police. Don't worry, sweetheart, your dad can take care of himself. Just hang on and I'll be there." I heard him say something to Margaret. Then he said to me: "All right?"

"Yes."

"Right. Put the phone down, pet. I'm on my way."

As I hung up the phone, it began to ring again. "Judith." It was Father.

"*Where are you?*" I said.

"I'm at the police station."

"You're all right?"

"Yes, I'm fine."

My knees bent and I sat down on the floor.

Father said: "Judith, I'm sorry. There's been an accident. I just have to give a statement and then I'll be home."

Father said: "Judith? Are you there?"

"Yes," I said.

I wiped my face. "An accident?"

There was a pause.

"Neil Lewis got knocked down by a car. It happened as we were coming down the hill." Father's voice sounded strange. "He's going to be all right."

The receiver was in my hand and my hand was in my lap. A distant voice from the receiver said: "He hurt his back. He's going to be all right." It went on talking. Suddenly I heard it say: "Judith?"

I lifted up the receiver. "Yes."

"Look, just sit tight. I'll be home soon, all right?"

"OK."

"Are you all right?"

"Yes."

"I'm—I'm sorry. I shouldn't have gone out."

I heard voices in the background then, a man shouting and doors slamming. Father said: "I have to go now. I'll be home very soon."

When Father had gone, I phoned Uncle Stan back to tell him not to come, but Margaret said: "Oh, he's on his way, Judith. You say your dad's all right?"

"Yes."

"Well, thank goodness for that. Don't worry about Stan. Are you all right?"

Uncle Stan arrived a little later. I heard him knock on the gate and went out to undo it.

Stan said: "What on earth—"

"It's a fence," I said. "Father built it to keep the boys out."

"Boys?"

"Yes, the ones knocking on our door. Remember I told you?" Uncle Stan shook his head. "Uncle Stan," I said, "Father's called. He's all right."

His eyebrows shot upward. "He's all right?"

"Yes."

"Thank goodness! Where is he?"

"At the police station."

"The police station?"

I nodded.

"Yes," I said. "Sorry."

"It's all right, pet, I'm just glad he's safe." Stan's eyes were glassy. I saw his pajama trousers underneath his coat.

We went into the kitchen. Uncle Stan's hair was sticking up. He passed his hand over his face and said: "So why is your dad at the police station?"

I explained how he had been chasing the boys. "He said one of them ran across a road and got knocked down."

"Dear me!" said Uncle Stan. "And this is the boy who's been giving you trouble?"

"Yes."

I wondered if he remembered how I had told him about punishing Neil, but he didn't appear to, which was fortunate. He said: "How long has that fence been there?"

I debated whether to tell him. "Nearly three weeks."

"*Three weeks?*"

I wished I hadn't.

"Your dad didn't say anything."

I shrugged.

Uncle Stan looked around, at the dresser and the table, at the mattress Father was sleeping on propped up against the wall. Then he caught sight of the ax above the door. He flushed, and blinked quickly, as if he was trying to make something out. "Your dad been all right besides that?" he said.

"He's been worried about work. And the boys were getting to him."

Uncle Stan nodded. "It's terrible what they did to the garden. Your dad planted those things for your mother. That cherry tree was beautiful in the spring. And the window, and the front door . . ."

"But that's not all," I said. "They did things outside the house and put things through the letter box and rode around him and called him names in the street. They wrote stuff on the fence. And one night I went out and—Oh, it doesn't matter."

Uncle Stan shook his head. "Satan's certainly testing us for all he's worth."

"I thought only God tested us," I said.

He laughed quickly. "But that fence can't stay there, can it? Your dad's not going to leave it like that?"

"Father thinks it's all right. It's the man from the civil court who doesn't."

"Someone's been to the house?"

"Yes."

"Oh dear, oh dear." Uncle Stan rummaged in his pocket and brought out a packet of Rennie's. I was just going to offer him a cup of tea when we heard a car pull up. A minute later we heard voices coming up the back path. A man was saying: "I know, Mr. McPherson, but chasing them like that—what were you going to do if you caught up with them?"

Father's voice said: "I hadn't thought that far."

Then the back door opened and Father came in with a policeman and a policewoman, and first he said: "Judith," and then he said: "Stan."

I jumped up and then I stopped, because there was blood on his shirt and his sweater was rolled up in his hand.

Uncle Stan said: "John, what's going on?" and it sounded to me as though he was angry, and it was strange because he hadn't sounded angry till then.

Father came up to me and said: "It's all right. I carried Neil to the ambulance. He's going to be all right." He didn't say anything to Uncle Stan.

I sat down and looked at my hands.

"We'll leave you to sort yourself out," said the policeman. He looked suspiciously at Uncle Stan, then turned back to Father. "Keep yourself available, Mr. McPherson. We may need to take some more information in the near future."

The policewoman said: "And by the way, that fence is a complete safety hazard."

Father showed the police out. When he came back into the kitchen, he put his sweater in the washing machine. Uncle Stan said: "John, we need to talk."

Father said: "I know how this looks but, believe me, there's another side to the story."

Uncle Stan said: "What story? Have you seen out there"—he gestured to the front garden—"and that"—he pointed to the ax— "and this child, in a terrible state? And how on earth did this boy get hurt? What's happening, John? Why didn't we know about any of this?"

Father said: "Thanks for coming over, Stan, but I can't talk anymore tonight. We'll have to have this conversation another time."

They looked at each other. Then Uncle Stan breathed in suddenly, put his hand on my head, and said: "Well. Good night, sweetheart. Everything's all right now." He picked up his car keys and followed Father to the door. I heard him say again just before he went out: "We need to talk," and Father say: "Not now." Then I heard the gate shut, then the front door, and Father came back into the kitchen.

His eyes were very bright and very dark. He pulled up a chair and sat down in front of me and put his hands on his knees. He said: "I can see you're upset, and I'm sorry. I was chasing Neil Lewis and the other boys when Neil ran across a road. I didn't do anything. The police know that. Neil is being taken care of. He's going to be all right."

When I still didn't look at him, he breathed in and said: "I'm sorry, Judith. I really am. I shouldn't have gone out. But it's done now." He raised his hands and let them drop on his knees. Then he stood up. "Well, I think it's time for bed."

He made a hot-water bottle like he used to when I was little and said: "Come on." He went upstairs with me and put the bottle in my bed and I got in. Then he sat down on the side. I looked out the window and was glad it was dark so that Father couldn't see my eyes.

Beyond the windowpane there were millions of stars, light spilling out of them as if they were holes cut in fabric and something marvelous beyond. I wanted to speak, but I had to wait because my throat was so tight. I kept waiting. I almost gave up, but in the end my throat let me and I said: "Are we going to be all right?"

"Yes," Father said, and he, too, waited to speak. It occurred to me that he hadn't said: "Of course we are," or "That's a silly question."

Neither of us said any more for a minute, and my throat got tighter and my jaw began to ache. "Will you go to jail?" I said.

"No."

I said: "I was so worried about you," and my voice was not much more than a whisper.

Father looked down. He said: "I'm sorry, Judith. I shouldn't have gone."

I said: "What's going to happen now?" and my voice was just air.

"Nothing. Nothing is going to happen; what happened was unfortunate, but it's over now."

He sat with me a little while longer, then he said: "I have to get up for work tomorrow. Are you going to be all right?"

I nodded because I couldn't speak anymore.

I thought for a minute he was going to kiss me, but he just brought the blanket up to my chin and said good night.

The Best Day of My Life

THERE WAS ONE day when I thought Father loved me. On that day Father and I walked hand in hand for eleven miles.

We had been preaching and it was summertime and the evening was coming. We were a ways from here in a place called the Silent Valley, where there are not many houses and lots of trees. We hardly ever go, because not many people live there, so all the houses can be covered in an afternoon once or twice a year. The Silent Valley is full of fields. They lead down to a river. We walked down there, and sand martins were going into holes in the bank. There was grass long enough to wade through and a few flowers and some trees. It was one of those days when everything shimmers.

My hand was inside Father's and his hand was inside his trouser pocket. Father's skin was surprising. I could feel the veins in his hand and the hairs on his knuckles. I felt his leg muscles move. I remember thinking I must remember this moment, the weight of the sun, the feel of his hand. There was a quietness inside my head and between us, and I thought of the scriptures where it says the Men of Old walked with God and thought it must have felt like this.

Cars went by every now and then on the road, and the sound they made in the air, and the way the land seemed to wash around us, the cool grassy smell and the sounds of the earth breathing and the trees and green things swaying, did something to my stomach.

I don't know how we came to hold hands, but I know if I had spoken or if we had met someone or had to stop or cross over, or get something out of one of our shoes, we might have stopped.

Moths were in the air when we got home. We made tea and ate leftovers, sitting on the back steps and watching the stars appear one by one. There were more stars that night than I had ever seen before, and they were shooting through the sky in some sort of shower. The street was so quiet, I think everyone else must have been watching too, because there were no sounds of dustbins and dinners and people shouting and kids yelling.

Father told me that without stars we wouldn't be here and that everything in the universe came from them. He told me each star was a fire, and the fire burned out sooner or later and the star died, but before it did it made new ones. He said they collapse to form black holes, where the gravity is so strong that nothing can escape, not even light, so stars go from being the brightest things to the darkest of all. He said all these stars were ending and beginning all the time.

There was fire in me, and in Father, and heat all around us. We were traveling as fast as those stars, though we were sitting quite still. I was holding something enormous and my body was too small for it. I kept my eyes open so fiercely, they burned. I kept so still, my chest got too tight to breathe.

I sat still all the time those stars were flying, and we watched them cross the heavens and eventually they were gone, and after a while I could swallow again, and then I could blink, and then I could breathe.

Father and I sat on the steps a while longer and then we went inside. And that day was the best day of my life.

Dark

I HAVE NEVER liked the dark. I think if Mother were alive she would have sat with me or left a night-light on or something, but Father doesn't believe in things like that; he believes in Common Sense and Saving Electricity.

People say they are scared of the dark, but they're not actually scared of the dark itself; they're scared of the things in the dark, like monsters and ghosts. But I am afraid of the darkness itself, because in the dark there is Nothing.

The night of Neil's accident, after Father left, darkness pressed around me. It filled up my nose and my ears and my mouth. I struggled to breathe. I turned this way and that. I said to myself, I wouldn't talk to God. I was afraid of what I would say. But the dark kept pressing, and in the end I sat up and threw back the covers and said: "I undid it!"

There was silence. I started to cry. Then God said: "You can't undo things. I've told you before."

"*Why* did You let it happen, God?" I said. I wiped my face. "I should tell Father it was my fault," I said. "He should know."

"Don't," God said. "He'll hate you even more. Trust Me."

I thought for a bit. "Don't You ever get tired of it?" I said at last.
"What?"
"Being right."
"One thing I never get tired of," God said, "is being right."

The End of Judith McPherson

JUST BEFORE DAWN I dreamed I was in the Land of Decoration: It was dark and I was running for my life, and I could hear footsteps and every so often a shout: "Over here!"

I didn't understand how people knew where I was, because I wasn't leaving any footprints and I wasn't making a noise. Then I saw there was a trail of bright dust shining in the dark, and it was coming from my pocket, the one I had put the stone in that the old man had given me, but when I put my hand in the pocket there was only a hole and, trickling from the hole, glittering dust.

I tore off my jacket and threw it away and ran faster, but still the trail continued. I stumbled and fell and got up again, and then I was running at different speeds, fast one minute—and the hills and fields around me jumping this way and that, the way they do when you are thrown around on the back of a horse or in a very old film of cowboys and Indians—and slow the next, as if everything was flowing like treacle or honey, and that was worse because I couldn't make my legs go fast enough.

However I ran, the dust kept trickling, and I thought this stone must be enormous, bigger than the universe, and I hadn't known it. I ran and ran, trying to remember where the land gave way to the floorboards, but where the sand dunes should have ended there were more dunes and where the hills should have stopped there were more hills. The Land of Decoration went on and on, as I used to imagine it did, only now I wanted it to end and just come to the door or the radiator or the edge of the ring.

I had to stop to get my breath back and as I bent down I saw that the reason the dust wasn't stopping was that I was full of it, I was made of it, and there were holes in me everywhere. And as I began to run again, I knew that soon there would be nothing left of me except pipe cleaners, cotton, and a little bit of felt.

At Dead of Night

"NEIL LEWIS HAS had an accident and won't be at school for a while." Mrs. Pierce was standing in front of her desk.

"What happened, Miss? What happened?"

"He was involved in a car accident. Mr. Williams has told me they're taking good care of him in the hospital."

"When did it happen?" said Gemma.

"Last night," said Mrs. Pierce.

"When will he be back?" said Luke.

"We're not sure," said Mrs. Pierce. "It's just as well it's nearly Christmas; it will give him a chance to get better before school starts again."

For the rest of the day I tried to see if Mrs. Pierce was looking at me. I don't think she was, but I couldn't be sure.

There were Christmas lights on every one of the trees in the front-room windows as I turned in to our street that evening. The rooms looked warm. I was aching and pulled my scarf higher. I wasn't sure if it was because I had cried so much last night or because I was coming down with something.

"How was school?" Father asked when he got home.

"Fine."

"Oh."

"Yes. Mrs. Pierce said Neil had had a car accident. That he would be off till after Christmas."

"Right," he said.

"Was work all right?"

"Absolutely."

"Absolutely" is a word Father never uses.

We were reading the Bible later when a dustbin rattled in the back lane. Father jumped. Then he went to the window, looking first to the right and then to the left. When he came back to the table, he smiled and said: "Cat." He turned a page over, then turned back. "Where were we?"

I looked at him. "Here," I said.

"Oh yes."

He began to read. But before we had got ten verses further, he stopped mid-sentence, took off his glasses, and laid them on the table. He said: "I think we'll leave it there for tonight."

"We're halfway through the chapter."

"What better place to finish?" he said. "We can ponder what's going to happen next," and he got up from the table and didn't come back.

LATER THAT NIGHT I woke to voices. To begin with, I thought they were coming from the street, but then I realized they were coming from downstairs, and I crept onto the landing.

Halfway down the stairs I saw light coming from under the middle-room door. Inside the room I could hear Uncle Stan. He was saying: "Taking things into your own hands like this."

"What would you have had me do?" Father said. "If I hadn't heard that window smash, I don't know what would have happened. There was petrol—did you know that? I didn't know what to expect next."

"I understand," said Uncle Stan. "But—"

"No, you don't understand," Father said. "And you won't until you're in a similar situation. Yes, I know what it says here, but it's different when it comes down to it, I don't care what you quote me."

"A little boy has been seriously injured because of your actions," said Alf's voice.

"I've explained all that," said Father.

"Do you feel any remorse at all?" said Alf.

"That 'little boy,'" Father said, "is a complete hooligan. He has made my life hell for the past couple of months and—"

"I asked if you felt any remorse," said Alf.

There was silence for a minute, and I could hear the hall clock and the wind in the gutters and my heart. Then Father's voice said: "You know, Alf, I don't," and my stomach went up and down and I shut my eyes.

There were no sounds then, except for a rustle of paper and the fire crackling, until Uncle Stan said: "I'm very sorry to hear that, John," and he sounded sorry. "I just don't think you realize how extreme your reactions have been; you don't seem to be thinking clearly."

Alf said: "I think you should be marked, John. I mean, what sort of example are you giving?"

"Why shouldn't I protect my family?" Father said. "I've only done what was natural."

"But if you had faith, you'd leave things in God's hands," said Stan. "Faith means not doubting, not questioning, not asking why."

It was a minute before anyone spoke. Then Father said something in a low voice that was so quiet I couldn't hear and Stan said: "Oh, John. Why d'you bring that up?" and he sounded as though Father had hurt him.

Father said: "Well, she did, didn't she? She didn't doubt, she didn't grumble, she didn't ask why!"

There was another pause, then Alf said: "Sarah had great faith, John. No one's denying that." And I shut my eyes and leaned my head against the banister, because "Sarah" was Mother's name.

"Great *faith*—" Father's voice rose, then stopped short.

There was silence. Then Uncle Stan said: "Can't you see we're trying to help you, John, that we want the best for you?"

Father said: "D'you know, right now, Stan, right now, I'm not sure." A wave of hot and then cold washed over me. I needed the toilet.

There was another silence. Then Alf said: "We're going to pray for you."

Stan said: "You know the procedure. If we haven't heard from you in twenty days . . ." and Father said quietly: "Yes, I know."

The door opened suddenly and light fell across the hall, and I nearly fell over myself trying to get back up the stairs in time. I crouched on the landing and heard footsteps going to the front door. Father went out the door with them and I heard the bolts slide back on the gate, then Father locked it, came inside, locked the front door, and went into the kitchen.

I waited for him to come to bed for over an hour, but he didn't, so I went halfway down the stairs again. The hall light wasn't on anymore, but there was a light under the middle-room door. I went down the outside of the stairs where the steps made no sound, and when I got to the bottom I walked over the tiles until I could bend down and peep through the keyhole. Father was sitting in an armchair in front of the fire, holding the silver picture of Mother. He was looking at the fire, not making a noise, and tears were coming down his cheeks. He was letting them come and not wiping them away.

The Greatest Test of All

MY MOTHER AND father prepared a room for me before I was born. Mother decorated it and made curtains and a hot-air-balloon light shade, and Father made me a bed and a trunk. They wanted a baby more than anything and when they found out Mother was pregnant everything seemed perfect. But things went wrong.

When Mother was giving birth, she began to bleed. The doctors said she must have a blood transfusion or she would die, but she knew God didn't approve of them. She knew that it was written that we must not take blood into our body, because blood gives life and belongs to God. The doctors didn't understand and they wouldn't help her. Some got very angry. "Save the baby," she said. One doctor agreed to; the others walked out.

The greatest test of faith is to give your life for it. Mother gave her life for her faith. She saw me and was happy. She told Father she would see him in the new world. Then she died. She wasn't afraid, because God had promised to resurrect her. Father wasn't afraid, because he also knew God had promised. But I think he was angry, and I know he was sad.

He kept the house and garden as she had left it. He watered the Christmas roses, he pruned the cherry tree and golden cane. He dusted and polished her things and kept them safe. But he stopped smiling, he stopped laughing, and he stopped making plans.

I asked God if it was my fault Mother died, and He said that it was. I knew that already though. I knew it every time Father was angry with me. "What can I do?" I said to God.

"Nothing. I told you. You can do things, but undoing them—that's something else altogether."

Payback

IT WAS THE last day of the term. We took down our work from the walls, ripped the spare pages out of our exercise books, and put them in a pile to be used as scrap paper. When everyone went into the hall in the afternoon to sing carols, I crossed my arms, put my head down, and closed my eyes. For the first time in my life I felt better at school than at home.

A sound made me look up. Mrs. Pierce was closing the door. She said: "Nobody will miss me for five minutes." She sat down beside me.

"Judith, I hope you don't mind, but I wanted to have a word with you before the end of the day and I probably won't get a chance if I don't do it now. You don't say much, but I've been very worried about you lately and wanted to check up on you. What did your father say when you asked him to come and see me?"

I swallowed. "He said he would come up," I said, "but not for a while—because he's busy."

Mrs. Pierce said: "That's unfortunate. I'd hoped he would—" She sighed and said: "Judith, here is a letter. I'd like you to give it to your father. Tell him it's very important he reads this." She looked at me. "All right?"

I bit my lips and nodded.

Then she took a piece of paper out of her pocket and pushed it toward me. She said: "Judith, this is my phone number. I don't usually do this, but if you need to talk to anyone over Christmas, please call me."

"Thank you," I said.

"In fact," she said, "in the new year, regardless of whether I manage to speak to your father or not, I'm going to get you some help. I think there are a lot of things going on in that head of yours, a lot we could do to help you if we knew what we were dealing with."

"What do you mean?" I said, and I was frightened.

"It's nothing for you to worry about," she said, "just help from some professional people."

I didn't know what that meant, and I didn't want to know.

She got up from the table and said: "They'll be finishing in a minute. I'd better go back."

I looked at the paper, and suddenly my eyes were full and my heart was beating so fast. "Mrs. Pierce," I said.

"Yes, Judith?"

"There's something I do have to say, but I don't know if I can."

"Stop!" said God. But I had started.

Mrs. Pierce came back to the table. "Yes, Judith? I'm listening."

I felt dizzy. "If I told you I had done something bad . . ." I said.

"Yes?"

"If I told you I'd done something very bad . . . something unforgivable—"

"Judith—"

"No!" I said. "If this thing was very bad—"

Mrs. Pierce put her hand on my arm. She said softly: "Judith, I don't mean to make light of what you're telling me, but I'm sure you're not capable of doing anything very bad."

"I am!" I said. "It's worse than you can imagine!" and I began to cry.

She waited and handed me a tissue and then said: "And you can't tell me?"

I shook my head.

"Have you talked to your father about this?"

I shook my head. "He warned me about it—he told me it would lead to trouble, but I didn't believe him."

Mrs. Pierce was flushed. She shook her head and said: "Judith, I'm going to phone your father; the sooner I talk to him about this, the better."

When she said that, I began to breathe very fast, and she put her hand on my arm and said: "Judith, please try not to worry. I'm sure that whatever you did, you did it with the best intentions and your father will understand that; I really do think I should try to talk to him."

THAT AFTERNOON MRS. Pierce read the last chapter of *Charlotte's Web* to us, where Charlotte dies but is happy because she has done everything she could to save Wilbur and people think what she has done is a miracle. Of course the real miracle is that it was such a difficult thing for Charlotte to do because she was dying and yet she did it anyway. Mrs. Pierce stood by her desk as we trooped out and said: "Have a lovely holiday! Don't eat too many mince pies. I want you all in peak condition for next term." As I passed, she said: "Remember what we talked about, Judith." I nodded.

When I got home I burned Mrs. Pierce's letter in the Rayburn, and I was glad I had done it before I read it, because it made me more frightened than I could imagine thinking of Father reading it. But I stuck Mrs. Pierce's number in the back cover of my journal. Then I went upstairs to lie on my bed and ticked off the days till I could go back to school; I thought how strange it was to do that, to want to go back. Then I felt colder and got under the covers into bed.

A little later a car pulled up. I heard a door slam and then the gate swing open and a man's voice say: "Steady."

I got up and peered through the window, but whoever it was was now opening the front door, and I jumped because it banged against the wall. Someone said: "I'll get it," and it sounded like Mike.

I ran along the landing and down the stairs. And then I stopped halfway down, and so did my heart, because it *was* Mike. He had his arm around someone who looked like Father but I couldn't be sure: The person who looked like Father had his arm across Mike's shoulders, and his face looked like it had been pushed sideways, and there was blood on it, and his eye was puffed up and closed like a fetus.

Mike said: "Whoa!" when he saw me. Then he said: "It's all right, pet. Your dad's just fallen down some steps. He's going to be fine. Run and get some cold cloths, will you?"

I must have still been standing there, because Mike said: "Go on, there's a good girl." But I still couldn't move until the person who looked a bit like Father picked up his head and said: "I'm fine, Judith," and the voice sounded a bit like Father's too, except that the person's mouth sounded full of something.

I went back upstairs to the bathroom and began soaking a flannel under the tap. Halfway through soaking it my legs sat down on the side of the bath, because I knew Father hadn't fallen down steps and I knew it was something to do with what had happened to Neil, and I was pretty sure that a person had done this to Father and that person was Doug Lewis.

I got up and turned the tap off and took the flannel downstairs. Father was sitting at the table and the washing-up bowl was beside him. Mike was touching his eye with some cotton and Father's head was going back whenever Mike touched him. I put the flannel on the table and Mike said: "Good kid. Your dad's going to be as right as rain. Go and make us a cuppa, will you do that?"

I went to the sink and heard Mike say in a low voice: "You should have let me take you to the hospital." Father said something back and spat into the bowl.

I brought two cups of tea in and put them on the table, but Mike seemed to have forgotten he wanted them. He finished bandaging Father's eye and said: "Lift your shirt," and when Father did,

I saw blood on his stomach and a red mark that looked like the sole of a shoe.

Father put his hand to his eye and touched it. He took it away then touched it again, as if he had forgotten he had done it the moment before. When Mike had finished bandaging him, Father lay on the sofa. His face was white and his arms and legs lay any old how like a rag doll. Mike said: "I'll call on you tomorrow after work with some groceries." Father raised his hand but Mike said: "John, I'm telling you, not asking," and Father let his arm fall again. Mike said: "For once you've got to give in and let someone else take over." Then he put his arm round my shoulder and squeezed. Then he said: "See that he doesn't get into any more trouble, will you, Fred?"

Then he said in a different voice: "He's going to be all right, Judith; your dad's a toughie." But Father didn't look tough. He looked dead.

THERE WAS NO sound in the room. Beyond the window, street light spilled over the black garden and the broken cherry tree. My jaw was too tight to speak. I said in my head: "It's because of Neil, isn't it? It's because of what I made happen to him."

"An eye for an eye," the voice said. "A tooth for a tooth. A life for a life."

I began to cry. "But Father isn't dead," I said. I began to shake, my whole body. "*Why* didn't You protect him?"

God said: "My ways are unsearchable."

I said: "It's convenient being unsearchable, isn't it?"

Fish and Chips

WHEN I CAME downstairs the next morning Father was in front of the Rayburn. That day he got up to get dinner and that was all. I asked: "Shall I call May or Elsie to help?" but he shook his head.

The next day he sat in front of the Rayburn again. He hadn't shaved and he hadn't changed his clothes and he didn't seem to have slept much, because his eye—the one I could see—was blood-shot.

I couldn't ask him if he was going to phone Uncle Stan without letting him know I had heard the conversation, but when he unplugged the phone I felt shaky and said: "What if we need to call anyone?"

"We plug it back in."

I was pleased because now Mrs. Pierce wouldn't be able to get through, but I was worried that Father wasn't going to phone Uncle Stan. "But he will," I said to myself. "Now that Neil isn't knocking anymore, he'll calm down. He'll make the phone call to Uncle Stan anytime now," and all that day I didn't go far from Father in case he made the call when I wasn't there.

Over the next few days, the rest of Father's body turned all shades of blue and yellow, and green. A doctor came and looked at his eye and said Father was lucky, that he wasn't going to lose it but that he should have gone to the hospital. Mike came by every day after work and sat with Father. On Thursday he left an envelope on the table, and Father saw it as Mike was going out the door and told me to run and give it back to him, but Mike wouldn't take it.

The days were long without school. I wrote in my journal. I fed my mustard seeds some Baby Bio that Mrs. Pew gave me. I didn't dare touch the Land of Decoration. One morning I was so tired of nothing happening with the mustard seeds that I dug them up and spread the soil out on a plate and tried to find them. The ones I did find looked exactly the same as when Brother Michaels gave them to me.

I went round to see Mrs. Pew a bit. She showed me photographs of her and Mr. Pew on a tandem and taught me how to play "Chopsticks" on the piano and I held Oscar in a blanket while she gave him his worming tablets, but all the time I had a pain in my stomach thinking about Father, and though I was glad to get out of our house, I was more glad to get back.

He slept or sat with his eyes closed—in front of the grill, I wasn't sure which. He didn't say: "Don't slam the door," and didn't say: "Are you playing with that food or eating it?" and didn't notice when I was loud, which I was on purpose, just to test him. His eyes passed over things as if he didn't recognize them. He went to bed at eight o'clock. When I came down in the mornings, he was still sleeping. All he did was get up to make tea or stare at the open mouth of the grill, with its black tongue and the black space crusted with char and the black elements, as if there was some great secret in there.

We ate potatoes and bacon or sausages every night. I cooked them, because Father said I could, and didn't get them right once, but he didn't notice. There was no more praying and no more reading the Bible and no more pondering, though I did enough pondering for both of us. On Sunday, Father took his eye patch off and began reading the newspaper, so after dinner I took away the plates, then fetched the Bibles. I said: "We've been forgetting."

Father looked at the Bible for a few minutes, then sucked in breath through his nose, as if he was waking. He said quietly: "I can't do this right now, Judith."

I felt a flash of heat as though I was falling. "But it's important!" I said. "It's Sunday and we didn't even go to the meeting! We haven't done the study for ages!"

Father raised his eyebrows and shook his head. "I can't get my head round it at the moment, Judith."

It made me feel terrified when he said that. I said: "What do you *mean?*"

"I just need . . . a bit of space."

"*Space?*"

He sighed. "Sometimes things are too complicated for children to understand."

"I can understand," I said. "Tell me!"

But he got up and sat with his back to me.

"Well, I'm going to read," I said. "I'll read for both of us."

Father said loudly: "I don't need anyone to read to me!" I thought for a minute he was going to get angry, but the look left his face as quickly as it had come and he said: "I just need some peace."

I did read, and it was all about the Nephilim and the flood and how God destroyed everything. Because it was such a long time since we'd done the reading I'd forgotten where we were and began reading wherever I opened the Bible, which happened to be Genesis, though the flood wasn't a very good subject at all, and I wished I'd never started halfway through. I was glad—though astonished—when Father interrupted and said: "Do you fancy fish and chips?"

"What?" I said.

"I said, would you like some fish and chips?"

I wondered if this was some sort of test, but he kept looking at me, and he didn't look like he was trying to trick me, he only looked incredibly tired.

"Yes," I said at last.

We put on coats and walked through the rain down the hill to

Corrini's. It was the first time Father had been out of the house, and he kept pulling his coat collar higher and shivering.

He blinked beneath the lights in Corrini's and people stared at him. He said: "Cod and chips please" and the woman dug into the metal tray, filled the cone, wrapped it, and said: "Three pounds." She had to wait to use the till and while she was waiting, the man using it looked up at Father, then back down again.

Father bought four cans of beer from the package store and then we went home. I held the fish and chips in my arms, and the rustling and the smell and the weight of them were almost too much to bear. When we got in, I ate them from the paper so quickly that a lump formed in my chest, and I had to wait for it to go before I began again. The chips were fluffy and squidgy, and the fish fell apart in little moist flakes. The batter crunched and then it oozed. It was so delicious that tears came to my eyes.

Father didn't tell me to slow down or get a plate or use a knife and fork. I was halfway through before I realized he wasn't eating. I said: "D'you want some?"

"No, they're for you," he said.

But I suddenly didn't feel like eating anymore. "Look at this," I said, and put two chips under my top lip and made an evil face. He took a sip from his can and smiled, then went back to looking at the grill. I wished he would tell me off for playing with my food.

I took the chips out of my mouth and looked down at the newspaper. I said: "Are you all right?"

"Why shouldn't I be?"

There were lots of reasons why he might not be but none that seemed possible to talk about. "I don't know," I said. I looked at the clock. It was past ten o'clock; he hadn't even realized it was bedtime.

"Look at the time!" I said.

"Oh yes."

I stood up. "Thank you for the fish and chips."

Still he didn't look at me. "You're welcome."

I said: "I'd better go to bed, hadn't I?"

"Good idea."

"Good night, then."

"Good night."

I went to the door, but when I got there I laughed and turned round. "You are all right, aren't you?"

Something flickered in his face. He said: "Of course I'm all right!" and looked almost like himself again.

"Oh, good," I said, and I felt better than I had done all day.

Visitors

TWO DAYS BEFORE Christmas, Elsie and May came and tapped on the fence. I wouldn't have heard them unless I had been in the garden, but it was sunny and I didn't want to be inside.

"Cooeee!" May called.

"Hellooo!" called Elsie.

"Hey!" I shouted.

"*Judith!*" they cried. "Are you all right, my lovely?" They sounded a bit unsure; I forgot they hadn't seen the fence.

"Yeah!" I said. "Hang on, I'll get the key."

"We missed you!" said Elsie.

"Hang on!" I said. "I'll be back in a minute."

"Can I have the key?" I said to Father when I got into the kitchen. "Elsie and May are out the front."

"Oh." Father touched his eyes. Then he shook his head and said: "I can't handle that at the moment."

I stared at him. "It's Elsie and May," I said.

"I know who it is, and I said I can't handle it. Just say I'm not well."

I looked at him. "But you are," I said suddenly. A white-hot light flashed on in my head. "You're *fine*."

Father said in a low voice: "I'm not going to argue with you: Tell them it's very kind of them, but I don't want to see anyone at the moment."

I was breathing fast. "But we haven't seen anybody for ages!" I said. My voice was shaking and it was getting too loud. "What if *I* want to see them? *I* live here too!"

Father jumped up from the chair. "I don't want to see anyone at the moment, Judith, all right? *I don't want to see anyone!*"

I stood there, then ran out of the room. In the hall I got my breath and wiped my face. Then I opened the front door and went to the fence and called to May and Elsie and said Father wasn't feeling well.

"Oh dear . . . But are you all right, sweetheart?" they cooed.

"Yes." I leaned my head against the fence.

"Oh, well . . ."

There was silence for a minute or two. "Can we get you anything?"

"No. Thank you." I closed my eyes.

"Well, all right . . . we'll be off then—we'll see you soon, though, at the meeting."

"Yes."

"Give your dad our love."

"Tell him we're thinking of him."

"Goodbye, sweetheart."

I heard them go down the road, and then I slipped down the fence and sat on the soil.

I DIDN'T SPEAK to Father for the rest of the day, but he didn't notice because he wasn't speaking much either. Late that night he came up to my room and sat on the bed. He didn't seem to care whether I was asleep or not, but I pretended to be; he smelled of beer and I was afraid.

"We'll win in the end," he said. "They think they've beaten us, but they haven't!" He put his hand on my head and it was heavy and clammy, like being touched by a dead thing. I felt him sway on the edge of the bed, then he farted.

He said: "What have I—"

Then he made a noise that sounded like: "Gah!" and put his head in his hands and rubbed his hands back and forth over his hair and groaned. Then he began to laugh, and all the while he laughed he rubbed his head.

When he had gone, I didn't move for the longest time. I didn't want to breathe, but I had to. I suppose I had thought that once Father's body began to get better he would be himself again, but he wasn't, so something else must be wrong, and I didn't want to think what that was. I thought for the first time that perhaps Father had the Depression. Depression was a sin, because it meant someone despaired of God.

And I decided knocking on doors and smashed windows and heads down toilets and fires and even getting beaten up were nothing to this, because whatever this was couldn't be seen and couldn't be got at and couldn't be mended. It couldn't be fixed like a door, or an eye, or a tooth, or a house.

Christmas

THE NEXT DAY, we got a Christmas card from Auntie Jo. She had made the card herself, as usual, and stuck a photo on the front. In the photo she had her hair cut very short and was wearing enormous double-clef earrings and grinning, with a party hat on her head. She had her arms around two other women, and it looked like they were in someone's back garden at night. She looked as though she had been in the sun.

The card said: *Happy Christmas. Thinking of you both. Would love to see you. Come and visit. Love, Jo.* There was a long line of kisses. I sniffed the card but it didn't smell of anything. But I thought how Auntie Jo's fingers had been all over it. I imagined Auntie Jo smiling at me as she was on the front of the card. I asked Father if I could keep this card and he said that I could, so I stuck it on the wall above my bed. It made the whole room seem different, as if a window had been opened and fresh air had come in.

The Saturday after Christmas, Uncle Stan came to see Father. He came straight after dinner. Father offered him a cup of tea, but Uncle Stan didn't want one. They went into the front room and closed the door. I couldn't hear anything, so I went to my room and sat on the floor and took out my journal, but I just sat and looked at the page.

Then I heard the door downstairs. Uncle Stan said: "The announcement will be made tomorrow," and Father said: "Thank you."

About half an hour later Father knocked at my door. I scrambled up and put the journal under the floorboard and said: "Come in!"

He perched on the edge of the chair by my desk and said: "Judith, I've got something to tell you; I'm sorry about it but there it is. Uncle Stan has just been here and we've had a long talk: At the meeting tomorrow there'll be an announcement made saying I've been Removed. I want you to know I'm in agreement with it."

"Oh," I said. I didn't look up.

"I know this will come as a shock to you, but I can't in full conscience do anything else right now. What I came to say is this: It doesn't mean you have to stop going to meetings: I'm more than happy to take you and drop you off. I want you to do whatever you want to do."

I don't know how long he went on talking, I heard him say: "Judith?"

I swallowed. "Is it because you chased the boys?" I said. But it didn't really matter why now.

"That—and other things," said Father. He sighed. "I suppose I've been doing things my own way for quite a while."

I was feeling hot and thought I might faint. I said: "But you still believe in God, don't you?"

Father gave a very small laugh. "I don't know what I believe," he said. He stood up. "But if you want to go tomorrow, I'll drop you off."

I shook my head.

"You don't want to go?"

I shook my head.

"OK." He went to the door. Then he stopped and said: "Oh." He rummaged in his pocket. "Stan said to give this to you." I opened the piece of paper. On it was written:

D. S. Michaels
The Flat
The Old Fire Station
Milton Keynes
MK2 3PB

Dear Brother Michaels,

This is Judith McPherson, the one you talked to after giving your talk about the mustard seed. You gave some to me, do you remember? I hope you are well.

I am writing to thank you for coming to our congregation. Your talk changed my life. When I came home I made a miracle happen, and lots after that, but the first one was that night after you told us about faith. I made it snow by making snow for my model world. There is a world in my room made of rubbish. I made snow for it and then it really did snow, do you remember?

After that I made it snow again and then I made it stop snowing. Then I brought back our neighbor's cat and then I punished a boy at school. But now he is knocking at our house all the time and yesterday his dad threatened Father in the Co-op and called him a "scab."

The police are not helping. Nobody believes I have done any miracles. The thing is, now I don't know whether to try to make more miracles or not. Having power is not as easy as it looks.

You said that all we needed to do was take the first step, but now it doesn't look like I can go back to where I began. I think that it would have been better for me never to have discovered my power in the first place. I am confused about lots of things now, and so is Father.

Brother Michaels, something terrible has happened. I made the boys come to the house, and Father has got into trouble with the elders because he got angry. I should have seen that he would, but I didn't and as God says, it is easier doing things than undoing them. Father is not himself. I think he may have the Depression.

Brother Michaels, tomorrow Father will be Removed from the congregation.

I know Father will come back to the fold, but I am sure if you came and talked to him, it would help. You could say prayers for us. Would you mind praying right away, because the End is very close?

So many days now I haven't felt like myself, and I think I am sickening for something. I hope it is not the Depression, as I have heard it is contagious. Brother Michaels, when you came through the hall doors that morning, I thought you must have been an angel or something, and that was why no one could hear where you were from. I am sure if anyone can help us it is you.

By the way, the mustard seeds never grew. If you could tell me where to get some more, I would be most grateful. I hope you didn't get them in the Bible lands, because if you did it will take a long time to get some more.

Your Sister,

Judith McPherson

The Last Day of the Year

IT WAS THE last day of the year. It was a Sunday but not like any Sunday I had ever known. There wasn't any lamb and there weren't any bitter greens and there wasn't any meeting or preaching. The house was so cold, things felt wet to touch, and it seemed to get dark right after lunchtime. I sat by the kitchen window and thought that I had hated Sunday before but this was a thousand times worse. The one good thing was that I didn't have to wear Josie's poncho, but the more I thought about it, even that didn't seem a bad thing now.

"What can I do about Father?" I said to God.

"He's lost faith," said God. "There's nothing you can do."

"He hasn't lost faith," I said. "He's just confused." But I looked at Father, at his neck jutting forward, at his hands flat on the arms of the chair, at the mug of cold tea, at the mattress on the floor and the curtains half drawn, and I wasn't so sure.

I went up to my room and sat in the window and drew up my knees and watched the sky change from indigo to black and thought how not that long ago I had watched it turn white and fill with snow. The streets and gutters were running with yellow light. There was music coming from somewhere, and every so often I saw people going by; some were arm in arm, some were laughing, some were swaying and singing. After a while there were fireworks, and in the bursts of light I could see for miles. The fireworks stayed still for a second before they fell. I tried opening and closing my eyes so I would see only that flash of light, but most often I missed it.

At midnight, people began singing somewhere, the song about old acquaintances and cups of kindness that they always sang at the end of the year, and then I couldn't sit there anymore and got up.

"I chose the stone," I said out loud. I took a deep breath. "I chose to be powerful." I swallowed. "If I think hard enough for long enough, I will be able to think of something to make things better. But I am not making anything because that always goes wrong." I couldn't think of anything to make anyway. I pressed my head really hard with my hands and screwed my eyes up. But I couldn't think of anything at all.

I said: "Go back to the beginning," and I asked myself when things had begun to get bad and thought it was actually around the time of the strike.

I had made a factory in the Land of Decoration a long time ago. It wasn't the sort of thing I usually made, but I had seen the chimneys at the factory in town and thought how much they looked like toilet rolls, so I made them and put ladders from a toy fire engine going up the sides. I made the factory from a shoe box, with clay chimneys and cellophane windows and straws for the pipes. There was a Lego fire escape and a car park and a wire-mesh fence made out of a net that oranges had been in. I went over to the factory now and turned it round in my hands. The chimneys wobbled, but there was no sound inside, because it was empty. I'd taken the people out because I needed them for other things. And then I wondered what would happen if I filled it, if I made an inside.

"It might work," I thought—and it was such an enormous thought I didn't dare say it out loud.

Then I said: "But I said I wouldn't make anything else."

Then I said: "But what's the worst that could happen?" This wasn't like making a person. The situation at the factory couldn't get any worse. But then I thought I might be fooling myself. I walked round and round the room, thinking maybe I shouldn't and maybe I should and trying to think what else I could do instead, but I couldn't think of anything. I felt very excited and then I felt very scared, and then I felt tired of being excited and scared and just wanted everything to be over. "God," I said, "is this possible?"

"Most of the time, everything is possible," said God.

"But can I really make things better?"

"Yes," God said, "you can."

"All right," I said. And for the last time I went to the trunk and lifted the lid.

I had never seen inside the factory, so I knew this was going to be the hardest thing I had made yet. All I could do was imagine how things looked and hope for the best.

I worked all night, until I saw the light coming over the top of the mountain. Then I felt more tired than I have ever felt, and hollow, like a stalk, and I turned off the lamp and got into bed. "Please, God," I said, "make this turn out right."

The Field Again

AND AS I slept I had my favorite dream, the one about the two little people I made first of all, the fabric doll with the dungarees and flowers and the pipe-cleaner man with the green sweater, and they were Father and me.

Father was holding my hand and we were walking through a field, leaving a trail in the grass. Sometimes we went to the right and sometimes to the left. Sometimes I would be ahead and sometimes Father would be. I was asking him about the Land of Decoration, about what it would be like, and then he said: "We're here, Judith; you don't have to ask me anymore," and I looked around and saw he was right. For the first time it wasn't the pretend world but the real one, with real grass and real sky and real trees, and then I looked down and saw we weren't dolls but ourselves, and it was wonderful.

The sun was pink on our faces and our shadows grew long. I was talking and Father was listening; he was looking at me, and that was wonderful too. But after a while he began to talk before I had finished and his answers weren't making sense, and I realized he wasn't talking to me after all. Then I looked closer and saw that it wasn't me, and I wondered who I was, and where I was if I wasn't there, because I could still see and hear everything perfectly clearly.

I watched the two little people go through the long grass. They got smaller and smaller, then joined hands and began to run. I called to them, but I couldn't make them hear, I was big, and they were small and were running away from me. I wanted to be small more than anything then but saw that I wasn't and never would be.

They went down by the river where the sun was low and the sand martins were darting, and among the water and low light I lost them.

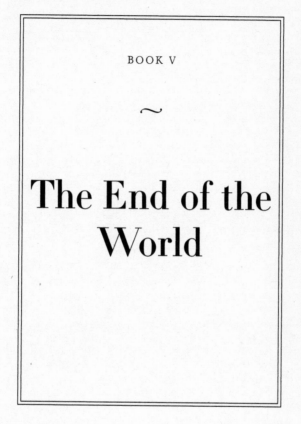

BOOK V

~

The End of the World

The Last but One Miracle

ON THE EIGHTH of January, Father came upstairs to my room. His face looked different so I knew immediately something had happened. He said: "The strike's over. Mike just telephoned."

I was so astonished I couldn't think of anything to say. He went away again and I looked at the place where he'd stood. Then I took up the loose floorboard and got out my journal. I wrote: *The final miracle has happened.* Then I wrote: HERE IS AN END TO MIRACLES.

SCHOOL STARTED. THE factory opened. When I came down to breakfast on the first Monday back to school, Father was frying sausages.

"Sausages!" I said.

He said: "I'm celebrating the return to the shed."

I laid two places at the table. A little watery sun came through the kitchen window and fell on our hands. Father ate three sausages and I ate two.

IN THE CLASSROOM, Mrs. Pierce was putting snowdrops in a vase. She said: "Judith! How are you?"

"I'm fine, Mrs. Pierce," I said.

She said: "You look better!"

"I am," I said. "Did you have a nice holiday?"

"Lovely. And the strike is over! Your father must be so relieved. I think everyone is; the town was quite a different place while it lasted."

Neither of us said anything for a minute, and we could hear the drips in the bucket. Mrs. Pierce laughed. "Now if we could just sort out this roof!"

That was when I said: "Do you know if Neil is coming back?"

"He is," said Mrs. Pierce. "He's a lot better."

"Oh, good," I said.

A little while later, everyone came into class. My stomach dipped when I saw Neil. He was on crutches. He looked very pale, even paler than usual, and he was watching where he was putting his feet so I couldn't see his face. And then I did. And a scar ran from his eye in a long line.

He saw me looking, but his face was different from how it was before. It was blank; not sad; empty. I couldn't even tell if he recognized me. It was as if he looked through me.

Mrs. Pierce said: "Class eight, I have some news for you. Mr. Davies has written to us to check we are all behaving ourselves. His daughter has just had a baby and he is helping to look after her."

Gemma said: "Is he coming back?" and Mrs. Pierce said: "No, he's decided to take early retirement." And I was very happy because it meant Mrs. Pierce would stay for good.

WHEN I CAME home that evening, I spread a tablecloth and put a bottle in the middle of the table. Then I went out to the garden. It was black and dripping and the air was raw. Through the empty branches of the cherry tree, I could see the mountain and the last bit of light glowing like embers. I picked snowdrops like Mrs. Pierce had done, then went back inside and put them in the bottle in the middle of the table.

The light didn't want to go that evening. I could hear the little kids playing on their bikes in the back lane as if it was spring already. When Father came in, he was white, but he smiled, and it was a proper smile. I asked him how work was and he said everything had gone smoothly. He said he was glad he never had to get on that bus again.

While we were having tea, I said: "Was Doug Lewis there?"

Father said: "No, he wasn't. I don't know where he is."

We didn't say anything for a minute. Then I said: "How are the potatoes?"

"Perfect," Father said.

AFTER TEA, FATHER said: "Come here." He took a leaflet out of his pocket. It was red and white and blue and had a picture of a hot-air balloon on it and said: *The Ride of Your Life! See the world as you have never seen it before!* He said: "Would you like to go?"

"Yes!"

"Right," he said. "That's that."

He lit the fire in the front room, and I sat by his feet while he sipped his beer and the flames played over everything. I thought things hadn't been this good for a long time—Father had never offered to take me on a hot-air-balloon ride and if he could just start going back to the meetings, things would be just about perfect.

Things went on being good: The next night I cooked macaroni and cheese. Father liked it, even though it was from a packet, and afterward he lit the front-room fire again. The day after that it was sunny. When Gemma and Rhian and Keri were skipping rope in the playground, Neil came up, and Gemma pretended she didn't see him, but they let me skip a bit with the rope.

And that evening, Father and I walked around the garden and Father said it would look better soon, the cherry tree would grow back and the golden cane and the Christmas roses. He said that in fact the fire had been good for the soil.

On Thursday I made myself go and speak to Neil, though my heart slowed so much I thought it was going to stop. (But I needn't have worried because, after I had finished speaking, it went twice as fast). I went to his table and stood there until he looked up, then I said: "I'm glad you're OK," and though it wasn't a great thing to say, I couldn't think of a better one.

Anyway I don't think he even heard me. He looked through me, then went back to his book. I stood there for a minute, then walked to my seat.

That evening Father did something he'd been putting off too: He began taking the fence apart. He did it with a crowbar, bending the bar backward and forward, and Mike helped him. The wood screamed and splintered, and the garden was soon full of glass and concrete and broken planks. Father saved the brass knob and put it on the mantelpiece, where it glinted gloomily. It seemed to know it wouldn't be needed again.

That night I cooked spaghetti Bolognese for dinner and fried the onions and mince and boiled the spaghetti, and all Father did was stir it. I asked if we could pretend the sauce wasn't from a jar, and we did, and while we were eating, Mike said: "Can I borrow the chef?" and Father said he would have to think about it, and I couldn't remember feeling so happy for a long time.

LATER, WHEN MIKE had gone and we were washing up, I said: "Can we invite May and Elsie and Gordon over?"

"Not now," Father said.

I waited a minute, then said: "Are you going to go to the meetings again?"

And he said: "Judith, I don't want to talk about this." So we didn't.

But later, when I was in my room, I said to God: "Please help Father."

God said: "I can't help him. He has to help himself."

"He's trying."

"Then tell him to try harder."

I took my journal into bed with me and turned over three

pages and wrote: *Is Father better yet?* Then I turned over another three and wrote: *What about now?* I kept turning over and writing and I fell asleep with it beside me.

The last day I marked was a Wednesday. But, as it turned out, we didn't get that far because the very next night something happened that ended all of that. It ended pretty much everything, and I didn't even see it coming.

Where to Find Mustard Seeds

D. S. Michaels
The Flat
The Old Fire Station
Milton Keynes
MK2 3PB

Dear Judith,

How nice to hear from you. Of course I remember you: and our conversation that Sunday and am very sorry to hear that recently things have been so difficult for you and your father. As this world nears its end, we must expect Satan to try our integrity. I'm sure that whatever happens, God won't forget the love your father showed for His name and will accept him back into the fold with open arms when he is ready to return. I am sure your own faithful example is an encouragement to your father. I am afraid I'm pretty busy and won't be coming to your congregation for some time, but I will pray for both of you.

As for the mustard seeds, I didn't know you wanted to grow them. I'm not sure how you'd go about it. I think most people just grind them up. If you want to try with some more, I got them in

Tesco. Failing that, you could try a health-food shop or a gardening store.

I look forward to seeing you again when I am next visiting your congregation.

Christian love,

Your Brother,

Derek Michaels

A Discovery

I CAME HOME on Friday, and turned my key in the front door but it didn't click. I thought I must have forgotten to lock it when I left for school that morning and was very glad Father was still at work and didn't know. I went into the kitchen and made a sandwich and a drink and then went upstairs.

I turned along the landing and was concentrating so hard on balancing the sandwich and my drink and thinking about the balloon ride Father and I were going on so I didn't see that my door was ajar. When I did, my stomach dipped. I pushed it open and I saw two things.

The first thing was Father sitting on the bed. He didn't look up and his face was red and crumpled as if he had been sleeping and he smelled of beer. The second thing was that he was holding my journal. Then the room shot backward and Father and the journal shot forward. I heard myself say: "Why aren't you at work?"

"There isn't any," he said, and when he looked up I saw that his eyes were glassy and half closed. "Two thousand laid off."

"What?"

"It's shut down," he said.

I blinked. "But you only just started back."

"The strike finished us. We've lost half our customers."

"It'll open again."

"I don't know," Father said. "You tell me. After all, you're the one with the magic powers, aren't you?"

I felt dizzy.

He laughed. "I expect you knew anyway! Perhaps *you* closed the factory! That's what you do, isn't it? You make things happen. *And then write about them in your bloody diary!*" As he said the last words he stood up, hitting his head on the hot-air balloon, and the room swung to and fro.

"*And there was me thinking Doug had it in for me because I was working!*" he shouted. "*That the trouble we had at the house was because of the strike! That it was boys being boys! You told me you would drop this miracle business, Judith! YOU GAVE ME YOUR WORD!*"

He came close and I saw the veins in his eyes.

I put down my plate and cup and I couldn't look at him, just kept looking down at my sandwich.

He said: "I *told* you, Judith! I *told you and told you* to drop it—" Then his voice broke, and he sat on the bed and his shoulders shook.

I said: "All I did was have faith," and my voice was just air. "God did the rest."

"*DAMN GOD!*" he shouted.

"I was trying to help," I said.

He stood up. He looked like a madman. He said: "This is what I think of your help." He picked up my journal and tore the cover away. He tried to tear it down the middle, but the spine was too strong and it bent this way and that. It made him even madder. He began tearing out handfuls of pages, and his hands were juddering and shaking. When there were just a few pages left, he threw the journal on the floor and looked around him.

I saw what was going to happen a second before it did but I was still too slow. I screamed and ran at him, but he had grabbed a field in the Land of Decoration, and houses and trees and cattle rained down on us. I clawed at his arms, but he pushed me back and began sweeping rivers and castles and palaces and cities up into the air. He uprooted trees, he flattened mountains, he crushed houses under his shoes.

I hung on to his arms, I hung on to his legs, we fell over, he got up again, he hurled the stars down, he broke up the moon, he toppled the planets. He tore at the sun, and the cage broke apart. The sea cracked with a sound like a plate, and the boats were cast up. The sky fell to earth and the earth broke apart. Beds and chairs, teapots and bushes, rose trees and washing lines, windmills, pitchforks, plum pies, and candlesticks came raining around us. Felt dogs howled, beaded fish flopped up and down, zebras whinnied, lions roared, fire-breathing dragons had their fire put out, scorpions ran in circles. I tried to save them but as many as I held I dropped again and all around us, the air was full of feathers and clay and wires and beads and heads and arms and legs and hair and fur and stones and sand and wings. And pretty soon there was nothing left but a heap of old rubbish.

Father stood panting and swaying. He was panting a little. He looked around, then lurched toward the door. It crashed behind him and I heard him stumble on the stairs. Then I fell down too, but I don't know where because there were no more places, and I don't know how long I fell because there was no more time. Dark filled my eyes because there was no more light, and there was no point in ever getting up again because what had been done could never be put right.

The End of the World

I WAS IN the dark when I heard a voice. The voice was saying: "Wake up."

"Leave me alone," I said.

"Wake up," said the voice.

"Go away," I said.

"You have to wake up," said the voice.

"Why should I?"

"You have to wake up," said the voice. "Because the world is ending."

I OPENED ONE eye.

In front of me was what looked like a forest. There were fibers sticking up and the fibers were green.

I opened both eyes.

My cheek was pressed against a piece of green carpet. The carpet had been part of the Land of Decoration.

I sat up.

A blanket covering me fell away. Moonlight was coming through the window.

I looked around. Then I leaned my head against the wall and didn't want to look anymore.

"Get up!" said the voice.

"Go away," I whispered.

"There's not a second to lose!"

"Go away."

"Don't you know what this means?"

"*Please* go away," I said.

But the voice wouldn't. "What do you see?" it said.

"Everything's broken," I said at last and closed my eyes.

God said: "Exactly!" He sighed. "Judith, I'm trying to help you here, but time is running out."

"Running out for what?" I said.

"Think about it."

I opened my eyes, and this time I said: "No."

"Yes," said God.

"No. You don't mean—"

"I do."

I shook my head. "That's impossible."

"What was that word again?"

"Impossible," I said.

"Have all the other things happened?"

"Yes, but . . . that would mean—"

"Armageddon," said God. He laughed. "You wanted the world to end. You asked Me about it often enough."

I needed to go to the toilet. I got onto my knees. "When?" I said.

"Imminently."

"How long have I got?"

"About two hours," said God.

"Oh my goodness," I said. I held on to the wall. Then I said: "I've got to tell people."

"You have told people," said God. "You've been telling them for years."

"They might listen if they knew it was coming tonight."

God laughed. "Do you think so?"

"They would if they knew it was really going to happen."

"Then it would be for the wrong reason," said God. "Anyway, how would you convince them?"

"I don't know," I said. "I've got to try."

"Judith," God said, "it's half past four in the morning. What are you going to do—shout from the rooftops?"

Everything was spinning. I thought how happy the Brothers and Sisters would be: May's chilblains would be better; so would Elsie's joints. Nel would walk again. Alf would grow hair. Uncle Stan's ulcer would vanish. And Gordon would never be depressed again. Josie would be able to make clothes for people for all eternity. And Father—Father would see Mother. And so would I!

"But," I said, "what about the other people?"

God didn't answer for a minute. Then he said: "You know what happens to the other people."

And he was right; I had always known, but now that it was about to happen it was different. "Isn't there anything You can do?" I said. "Perhaps the world isn't ready to be destroyed just yet! Perhaps there are still good things in it."

"Such as?" God said.

I tried to think. "Mrs. Pew!" I said suddenly.

"*Mrs. Pew?*" said God. He didn't seem to think much of my suggestion.

"Yes!" I said. "And Oscar! . . . And *Auntie Jo!* . . . And Mike! And Joe and Watson, and Sue Lollipop—and *Mrs. Pierce!*"

"They don't believe in Me," said God.

"But You can't just kill them!" I said.

"You knew this would happen."

"What about the children . . . the people who haven't heard about You . . . the people who didn't listen when we went to the door, because they were on the phone, or the baby was ill, or they'd heard bad things about us, or it was raining?"

"I'm sorry," God said, "that can't be helped. I can't hang around forever. There'll always be those who don't know or don't listen or are too busy. It's not My fault."

"It's not theirs either!" I said. I was beginning to feel as though I would like to be sick as well as go to the toilet. "Can't You just *forgive* them?" I said.

God laughed. "You're a fine one to talk about forgiveness! Look, I've waited since the Garden of Eden to do this. You don't expect Me to put it off a few more weeks?"

"So Father hasn't made the end of the world come after all?" I said.

"Well, yes and no. This is all besides the point. It's happened; I would have made sure it did one way or the other."

"And now it's gone," I said, and I looked around again. "If only I could put it back together! But I can't. It would take too long."

But I wasn't really thinking about the Land of Decoration anymore. I was thinking about Mrs. Pew and Oscar, about Sue Lollipop and her trip to the Bahamas, about Mrs. Pierce and Mike. I was thinking about so many other things too that it seemed they were crowding into my mind because it might be the last time they would be remembered—thinking of the way the world was in the snow and how it would be in the spring, how the cherry tree would come back to life, and Mother's Christmas roses, how in the summer the mountain would become green, and how Father and I would go up in the hot-air balloon and see the whole valley. I was trying to imagine it all gone, and it was really difficult.

"So I can't save them?"

"No."

I sat down on the floor with a bump and pressed my hands together to try and stop them from shaking. I said: "What will it be like?"

"The biggest thing the world has ever seen."

"And then," I said, "the new world."

God said: "That's what you want, isn't it?"

And I didn't say anything, because it was what I had wanted for as long as I could remember.

I closed my eyes. "No more sickness, no more death?" I said.

"That's right."

"And You'll wipe the tears from people's eyes?"

"Yes."

"And Father and I will live there, and we will see Mother, and it will be like it was in the beginning?"

God said: "What was that?"

"And we'll see Mother again."

"Not that bit," said God. "The other bit."

"And it will be like it was in the beginning."

"No, no, the first bit," said God.

"And—Father and I will live there . . ." I said.

"That's it," said God. "You see, that's the bit I'm not sure about."

"*What?*" I said.

"Well," said God, "your father—I mean, can you really call him a believer? His attitude hasn't been right for some time now."

I blinked. "Father believes in You!" I said. I laughed. "You know he does! He's just been tired lately; things got on top of him—"

But God was saying: "No. I'm not sure he believes in Me at all."

"Are you *listening* to me?" I said. I jumped up. "You have to save Father!"

"It doesn't change the fact that he's lost faith in Me."

"No!" I shouted. "He hasn't! Can't You do anything?"

And then God looked at me. I felt Him look, and everything went still and my skin prickled. He said: "If I were you, I'd be asking myself that question."

"*Me?*" I said. "What can *I* do?"

God laughed. "Judith, look at what you've done already!"

I blinked. Then I put my head in my hands. When I took it out I said: "I've done quite a lot, haven't I?" And then, in a smaller voice, a voice so small that no one but God could have heard it, I said: "If anyone dies it should be me."

"Clever girl," God said softly.

"*What?*" I said.

"Well," said God. "You're right, of course; if it hadn't been for you, none of this would have happened. You are the only one who can save your father. He's sinned, Judith; he's lost faith—the greatest sin of all. He deserves to die; he *will* die; unless someone saves him. . . ."

"Who?" I said. "How?"

God sighed. "Don't you remember? An eye for an eye, a tooth for a tooth—"

"A life for a life," I said.

"If someone were to give Me their life instead . . ."

"Oh," I said, and my voice was quiet, like a breeze on its way somewhere else.

"It's the only way," said God. "The Fundamental Law. Remember?"

I felt wind buffet my face, as if I was standing at the edge of a cliff, and I felt the ground shift under me.

"You love him, don't you?" said God.

"Yes." But I wasn't thinking about Father anymore. I wasn't thinking about anything just then.

God said: "Now, are you going to save him? Hurry up and decide or you may as well not bother."

"Yes," I said, because there wasn't really any decision to be made; there had been a moment when I wondered if I would get to see the Land of Decoration after all, then that, too, stopped mattering.

But I had to be sure of something. "If I do this," I said suddenly, "You have to promise me—You have to *promise* me—Father won't die."

"Where's your faith?" said God.

"*I need You to promise!*" I shouted.

"All right!" said God. "Dear me! You have My word."

I swallowed and looked at my shoes. I said: "Then can I see him?"

"If you're quick."

I went to the door. I meant to go quickly, but my body was moving as if its battery had run down.

At the door, I put my hand on the handle. "God," I said, "can I really save him?"

"Yes," God said, "you can."

The Biggest Miracle of All

I CLOSED THE bedroom door and went along the landing and none of it was real. I went down the stairs step by step, holding on to the banister, and they weren't very real either. At the bottom, light was coming through the panels in the kitchen door. I went along the hall and turned the handle.

Father was sitting with his back to me at the table. He was the only thing that looked real. I closed the door.

I could see his shirt rise and fall. I could see the hairs on his head catch the light. I could smell him and hear him breathing. I stood there for ever so long, just looking and listening to him.

Suddenly he turned. He put his hand on his chest and said: "You frightened the life out of me."

"Sorry."

"I thought you were asleep."

His voice wasn't thick anymore and his eyes weren't glassy, and his face was gray now instead of red. He said: "I came back up and put a blanket over you to keep you warm. I didn't want to wake you. . . ." He looked very sad.

He stopped talking and I was glad, because I had a lot to say to him and not much time to say it in. I took a deep breath and said:

"Father, I'm sorry I got you into trouble with the elders and I'm sorry I didn't listen to you about the miracles."

He shook his head and passed his hand over it. "Oh, Judith, it's not your fault. You really didn't help things, but there would have been trouble anyway, what with the strike and everything."

"No!" I said, and my heart beat hard. "It was me! If you knew half the things I've done!"

Father said: "All right; let's not get into that now."

I hung my head and said: "I did it all."

Then Father said: "Judith!" so I was quiet.

He put his finger and thumb in the corners of his eyes as if they hurt him. When he took them away, his face looked grayer than before and his eyes were red and more tired than I had ever seen them. He said: "I'm sorry about your room."

"It's all right."

He put his head in his hands. "It's not all right, but it's done now. I was drunk." Then he took his head out of his hands and said: "You know I love you very much, don't you?"

The words were so strange. They rolled into the middle of the room and rocked there between us, and we listened till they settled, and afterward there was such silence.

I was trying to think quickly, I was trying to think what to say, but there was a pain in my heart and breathing was difficult. Father turned back to the table. He said: "I love you more than you know."

Then my heart hurt more than it had ever hurt before in my life, and I thought it might have broken, but I knew what to say. I said: "I do know." And suddenly I did.

I remembered how he had looked after me all this time even though I had made Mother die, how he had taken me to the doctor when I was little and read the Bible to me to help me talk, how he had warned me about the miracles only to protect me, hadn't told me about the strike so it wouldn't worry me, had chased the boys away to protect me, taken my hand so I wouldn't be afraid when we walked through the bikes, forgiven me for lying, built the fence to keep me safe, pretended the note through the door wasn't about me, sat on my bed after the accident and told me everything was going to be all right, offered to take me to the meeting though he couldn't come in, bought me fish and chips and walked hand in hand with me that day for eleven miles, and was going to take me on a hot-air balloon.

He was saying: "I haven't been much of a father to you, but I tried. There are things I've never been able to say to you, things about the time after your mum died, how you were suddenly there, asking for attention, asking to be taken care of, asking so much, and I had nothing—heck, I could hardly take care of myself; sometimes I couldn't even look at you because you reminded me so much of her." He sighed. "This probably isn't making much sense. . . ."

He was saying other things as well, but he was going too fast and I was still thinking of the first thing he had said, the thing about loving me. What he said after that didn't matter much. He stopped talking in the end and didn't look at me again, and I was glad because he didn't like seeing people cry. He said: "Well. We have to look to the future now," and I said: "Yes," but I couldn't think properly.

Then he said softly: "It's almost tomorrow. You'd better go up." And I remembered that it was late, later than he or anyone else realized, that I had only come to say goodbye, but I still couldn't make myself go.

He said: "We can talk some more tomorrow."

"OK."

"Good night, Judith."

"Good night."

When I made no move, he turned back around, and I went to the door. "Father?"

"Yes."

"Don't worry about anything! Everything is going to be fine. It's going to be better than you think."

He laughed, a dry sound that broke off too soon, and nodded, but he didn't turn round again.

He said: "Go to bed now, Judith."

I couldn't think of anything else to say then so I looked at him for the first and last time, then I opened the door. I closed it behind me and wiped my face. Then I went upstairs step by step, holding on to the banister.

The Space Where Miracles Happen

AND THIS IS how I learned that everything is possible, at all times and all places and for all sorts of people. If you think it's not, it's because you can't see how close you are, how you only need to do a small thing and everything will come to you. Faith is a leap; you're here, the thing you want is there; there's a space between you. You just have to jump. Walking on water and moving mountains and making the dead come to life aren't difficult; you take the first step and the worst is over, you take another and you're halfway there.

Miracles don't have to be big things, and they can happen in the unlikeliest places. They can happen in the sky or on a battlefield or in a kitchen in the middle of the night. You don't even have to believe miracles are possible for one to happen, but you will know when it does, because something very ordinary you never thought would amount to much has amounted in the end to quite a lot. That's because miracles work best with ordinary things, the more ordinary the better; the greater the odds, the bigger the miracle.

A Life for a Life

MY ROOM WAS in darkness. I said: "Are You there?" but no one answered. I went to the window and drew back the curtains and the moon came in. It was silvering the factory and the electricity and making the train tracks gleam like glue left by a snail.

I looked out at the town at the television aerials and chimneys and rooftops, the telegraph wires going up and down the valley, and above it all the dark mountain, darker still against the white of the moon, and it was funny, but for the first time it all looked quite beautiful, like Brother Michaels had said, and in a few minutes it would be gone.

I turned back to the room. I pushed aside masts and forks and garden fences, branches and thatches, strands of rainbow, wires that birds used to sit on, white horses from the top of waves, wisps of cloud. The magic had gone now; the sun looked just like a wire cage, the sea a mirror, the fields like pieces of fabric, the hills papier mâché and bark.

I wondered what Father would do with the Land of Decoration. He would probably put it out in black bags for the garbagemen. The egg-carton hills would be paper, the toffee-barrel house a new toffee barrel or a tin can or cup, the milk-carton houses more milk cartons and other things when they were empty, the feathers and straws might become real birds' nests again, the wood and heather would become new trees and new heather, the stones would one day become mountains again, the shells become sand, the sand glass, and the glass perhaps a new mirror.

Nearly everything would be changed, but one or two things would remain what I had made them. Perhaps the barrel with the sail—perhaps it really would find its way to sea and the tiny fisherman see real birds overhead, taste real spray on his lips, and real breezes would make his cheeks pink. Perhaps some very small pieces of cloth, some of the glitter, or the smallest of beads, might stay right here in this room under the floorboards, in nooks and crannies with the spiders and mice.

Then I remembered that there wouldn't be a room, and Father wouldn't do anything with the Land of Decoration: and the Land of Decoration wouldn't be anywhere—or, rather, it would be everywhere, because it would be real.

I fetched a chair and put it in the space I had cleared. I got onto the chair. "Thirty-one minutes," said a voice.

"There You are," I said. Then I stopped. "It is You, isn't it?"

God said: "Who else would it be?"

"I don't know," I said. "You sounded strange for a minute."

"Strange how?"

"Different," I said. "Well—sort of like *me*."

"Don't be silly," God said. "You're you and I'm Me."

"Yes," I said. "Sorry. A lot has happened tonight."

I balanced on tiptoes and unscrewed the lightbulb.

"Twenty-nine and a half minutes," said God. "And counting."

I put the bulb on the chair and it rolled back and forth.

"Quietly!" said God. "We don't want interruptions."

I unscrewed the hot-air-balloon lamp shade and put it on the chair too, but it fell onto the floor.

"Great," said God. "That's just great."

I tested the light cord. I got down and fetched my school tie. I got back up and tied one end of the tie to the cord above the light fitting and tugged it. I tied a loop in the other end of my tie and loosened it. I put my head through the loop. The material felt soft next to my skin. I expect it wondered where my collar was.

The room looked strange from the ceiling: like a box, smaller than it had ever seemed before. I wondered if I had already stepped off the chair, because my arms and legs felt like they were falling, but they weren't, and I wasn't, I said to myself; there was a rushing in my ears, as if the tie was tightening. But it isn't, I said to myself. Not yet.

I looked at the Land of Decoration. "It was so good in the beginning," I said. "Now I think it would have been better if I'd never made it at all."

"We all make mistakes," said God.

"What did You say?"

"I said: We all make mistakes," God said.

"We?" I loosened the tie.

"You, Me—everyone."

I was beginning to feel sick. "Are You sure about this?" I said.

"Oh yes," said God. "One hundred percent. Twenty-three and a half minutes."

There was a sound in the room like a creature panting. "What's that noise?" I said.

"It's you," said God. "Can't you breathe more quietly?"

"No," I said.

My knees were behaving strangely now, as if they wanted to fall forward, though I was afraid of that more than anything, and my left leg wouldn't stop tapping the chair.

I took one foot off the chair and held on to the tie. I closed my eyes and lifted the other foot off too. Darkness throbbed and jumped in front of me. Colored lights and whistling sounds filled my head. I put both feet back on the chair and hung on to the tie and my body was wet, as if I had been running, and my teeth were chattering.

"Nineteen minutes, nine seconds," said God.

My foot slipped. Something hot dribbled down my legs. I swallowed and was trying hard not to cry.

"Nineteen minutes and two seconds," said God.

Then I said: "You know what I wish?"

God laughed. "I'd think carefully before you make another wish. The last ones haven't turned out very well."

"I wish You would go away and never come back."

"What?" said God.

I hung on to the tie. "I would like," I said, "to never speak to You again."

God said: "You don't mean that."

"Yes," I said, "I do."

"Be careful what you say," said God.

"It doesn't matter," I said. "You can't do anything to me now."

God said: "You'll be sorry."

"No," I said, and took my hands away from the tie. "I already am."

One Good Thought

IT GOT QUIET in the room. I took a deep breath, but I couldn't kick away the chair.

I tried to think what Father would do if he were me and I knew he would try to think of a good thought. So I tried. I thought how good it was now that God had gone away, like it was in the beginning. But it wasn't like it was in the beginning, because now I knew nothing I had made was good after all.

I tried again. I thought how in a few minutes Armageddon really would be here and all the bad things would be washed away and the world would be how it was always intended to be. But then I remembered all the people God would destroy, and pretty soon I couldn't think about that either.

Then I looked down and caught sight of one of the little people I had made to begin with. An arm had come away from the body, but the face was still the same. And that is when I had the best thought I have ever had in my life. I thought of Father going into the Land of Decoration and meeting my mother again.

Father would see Mother standing a little way from him. Something about her would make him go toward her. Then she would turn round and he would not be able to believe it. But he would have to believe it, because it would be true. They would go walking together, leaving a trail in the grass, sometimes my mother's hand would be in Father's and sometimes his arm would be around her shoulders. And all the streets and all the rivers and all the names and places of this world, all the people that were and are and will be, would be nothing to this moment.

I knew it was possible, I knew they really could be together if I could just step forward. But I still couldn't do it. And then I realized it wasn't that Father didn't love me but that I didn't love Father enough. And when I thought that, the world split apart.

I undid the tie and fell off the chair and began to cry, though it wasn't much like crying and more like being sick, like turning myself inside out. I don't know how long I'd been crying when I heard someone say: "Judith." Father was standing there.

His face was white. Then he was beside me on the floor pulling me to him roughly, holding me so tightly, saying over and over: "I'm sorry"—and it was all very strange, as if I was dreaming.

I don't know how long we stayed like that, but we were in no place and there was no more time. We were borne up high; we were burning. I never knew another person could do that to me, and perhaps I was doing it to him too.

And then something happened. The clock in the hall began to chime, and I stopped breathing and looked at him. I got to my feet and my chest was rising and falling.

He said: "What's the matter?" He said: "Judith! What on earth—?"

I listened to those strokes, and at each one a little part of me passed into nothingness, and as each new stroke came, a new piece of me took its place.

Then the strokes were over and I looked at him. I said: "We're still here."

He blinked. "Where d'you expect us to be?"

"I don't know."

"Judith, what are you talking about?"

I began to cry again. I said: "We're alive, aren't we?" I held on to his sleeve, his shoulder. My hands were hungry.

He said. "Judith," and then he was crying too.

I said: "I tried to save you. I thought the world was ending," and we didn't say anything more for a while. Then he laughed and sniffed and said: "Well, it looks like it's still here to me."

I shook my head. I stared at him. "What are we going to do now?" I said, because I really couldn't think of anything; I couldn't see how it would go.

Father wiped his eyes. He said: "Well, we could have breakfast."

"*Then* what?"

"I don't know—we could go for a walk."

"*Where?*"

He thought for a minute. "Up the mountain—the Silent Valley, maybe. We could watch the sunrise."

I wiped my eyes. I looked around. "What about the Land of Decoration?"

"We'll take care of it when we get back."

My eye caught the card of Auntie Jo and I took hold of Father's sleeve. "Let's visit her," I said suddenly.

He looked at me and then at the card. I kept hold of his sleeve. I gripped it tight. He said: "All right." He got to his feet, as if he was very tired, and then he helped me up.

We were going through the door when I stopped.

"What is it?" he said.

"I thought I heard something," I said.

He looked at me. "All right?"

"Yes," I said. "I must have imagined it."

How to Make a Hot-Air Balloon

AND NOW I will show you how to make a hot-air balloon, one that really does fly. It is not very difficult once you get the basic shape right.

You will need:

a wire helium balloon
all-purpose glue
string
scissors
acrylic paint
a small basket
a needle
burlap
cotton thread
tissue paper
a net bag oranges come in
cardboard (no thicker than a Weetabix box)
very sticky tape
a sharp pencil
rice

1. Take a helium balloon that is shaped like a pear. Not

the flattened kind, not the perfectly round kind, not the novelty kind. Trim the seam that runs around the edges.

2. Cut a rectangle of cardboard and curl it around the bottom of the balloon so that it is a little cylinder and hides the tail. Glue it together on the inside and tape it to the balloon.

3. Paint the cylinder and the balloon in wide, brightly colored stripes.

4. Take a net bag oranges come in and cut off the label. Drape it over the balloon and gather it so that it tapers to the bottom. Sew down each fold of net with the cotton thread. Turn it inside out and snip off the net folds. Turn it the right way out and place over the balloon fixing it to the bottom of the cylinder at several points.

5. Attach string to the cylinder by boring holes in it with a pencil. Take a small basket (the very light kind that comes with little soaps), and attach four strings to it—one at each corner.

6. Push the stem of the balloon through the center of the basket and cut the stem at the very bottom into four. Open out the end, folding them beneath the basket. Tape in place.

7. Shred yellow, orange, and red tissue paper and gather into a tongue of flame attaching it to a wire taped to the inside of the cylinder.

8. Wrap up tiny people and sit them in the basket.

9. Light the flames above their heads.

10. Make four little burlap sacks of rice and attach them to the insides of the basket with plenty of string. If you want the balloon to fly, put the sacks on the ground.

You can forget the sacks altogether, but I would leave one attached, otherwise the balloon will soar up to the ceiling and bump around for days and crash when you're not there to catch it, and lots of small people will die; it may fall on a town or a school or a marketplace and then even more will die. Or if you are not in a room but in the open air, it really will sail away and the little people will never be heard of again.

Of course, they will have the time of their lives because the view will be marvelous; it's coming down that is the difficult thing. So always leave something attached. If you want to go higher, just let out more string.

Acknowledgments

Thank you to Clare for discovering the book, and for her care and advice.

Thank you to Clara—a fellow lover of little things—and to Sarah, for such sensitive and transformational editorial advice.

Thank you to Anthony, Val, and Mike for taking time to read the first draft and for such helpful feedback.

Thank you to Mark, Sos, Richard, and Karen for believing I could do something long before I did.

Most importantly, thank you to my mother, an extraordinary human being, for never giving up.

About the Author

GRACE MCCLEEN is an author and singer-songwriter who lives in London.